The
THREADS
of MAGIC

D0182865

Other titles by this author

The Books of Pellinor:

The Bone Queen

The Gift

The Riddle

The Crow

The Singing

Black Spring

The River and the Book

The Threads of Magic was written with the assistance
of the Australian Government through the Australia
Council, its arts funding and advisory body.

Australian Government

**Australia
Council
for the Arts**

The THREADS of MAGIC

ALISON CROGGON

WALKER
BOOKS

First published in Great Britain 2020 by Walker Books Ltd
87 Vauxhall Walk, London SE11 5HJ

2 4 6 8 10 9 7 5 3 1

Text © 2020 Alison Croggon
Cover illustration © 2020 Matt Saunders
Calligraphy © 2020 Jan Bielecki

This book has been typeset in Palatino

Printed and bound by CPI Group (UK) Ltd, Croydon CR0 4YY

British Library Cataloguing in Publication Data:
a catalogue record for this book is available from the British Library

ISBN 978-1-4063-8474-1

www.walker.co.uk

For all the revolting witches

Royal Family of Clarel

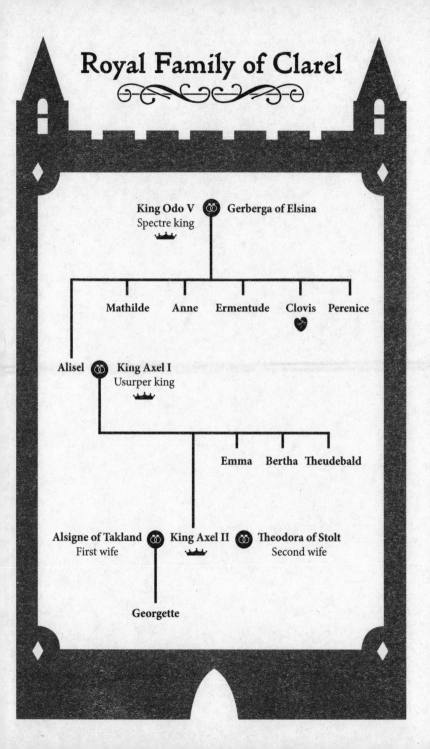

Chapter One

PIPISTREL WAS DEEP IN THE CHOKE ALLEYS. IT WAS black night, blacker than the inside of a cash box, so black you couldn't see your hand in front of your eyes.

This suited Pip. He didn't want to be seen, and when he didn't want to be seen even a witch's cat would have trouble spotting him. He scuttled through tiny alleys, some little wider than his own body, making his way unerringly with senses other than sight. Up and down broken and slimy steps, through courtyards the size of wardrobes where even in summer only a few shame-faced rays of sunlight ever visited, along streets that were no more than tunnels of blackened brick and stone, past windowless walls and doorways like carious mouths exhaling rottenness.

Pip knew the Choke Alleys like the back of his hand. Better, probably: it was so long since his hands had been washed that he might have had trouble recognizing them clean.

Tonight he was proceeding with rare caution. He'd slither into a passage only when he was sure beyond all doubt that it was empty. When the rubbish stirred and snored, some drunkard sleeping off his last flagon of gin, the boy started and ran as if a demon were at his heels. A cat fight that exploded by his ear made him jump out of his skin. If he saw any shadow that looked vaguely human, he retraced his steps and went another way.

When at last he reached his destination – a doorway that looked no different from any of the other doorways, its lintel cracked, its wood battered and discoloured – he studied it doubtfully from a distance, and decided to use the back way. He climbed a pipe and slipped in silently through a third-floor window, and stood in the tiny bedroom that belonged to him and his sister, breathing fast, his bony chest going up and down.

God's nails! he thought to himself. *By the Ghost of the Holy Mother, that was wild.*

There was no sign of El's sleeping form. She was waiting up for him, and he'd said he'd be late, he *said*.

When he recovered his breath, he stole down a short passage until he reached another door. A dim light wavered through the gap underneath it. He wiped his hand over his nose, squared his shoulders and entered.

In the main room stood a girl maybe a year or two older than he was – fourteen, fifteen, it was hard to tell. Even in the kind light of the oil lamp her face looked pinched and pale, and her mouth was drawn down in two deep lines.

"Where've you been, Pipistrel?"

Using his whole name meant she was angry.

Pip shrugged. He didn't feel like a fight tonight, after all he had been through. "None of your business."

"Don't you give me face like that. I've been sitting here eating out my heart for hours and hours. I thought you were dead."

"You always think I'm dead." Pip shrugged past her and into the room beyond, and flung himself on one of the two rough stools which, with an old chest that served as a table, were its sole furnishing. "I'm dead tired, is all."

The girl looked at him, her lips pressed together, her eyes blazing. Her face was eloquent with all the things she wanted to say, but instead she shut the door and sat down next to Pip.

"I don't want to fight," she said.

"Me neither," said Pip.

They sat in brooding silence for some seconds, while he pondered whether to tell El what had happened. The

11

problem was, he was bursting with it. He had to tell someone.

"I'm hungry," said El dolefully.

"Listen, I didn't get anything to eat. I got something else. Something precious."

"Gold?" said El in a whisper, her pale face lighting up. For El, gold conveyed a picture of impossible romance and adventure. One of her ambitions was to someday make her way to the Royal Plaza in Clarel, where nobles lived in airy palaces with carriages of gold and jewels in their hats.

"I don't know. It's something precious, something very precious." Pip was leaning forward, talking low. He didn't want anyone else to hear, and the walls here were thin as hessian. "I robbed the wrong person. He didn't look like a noble, but he was." For a moment his voice rose indignantly. "Nobles have got no call going around dressing like commoners. Anyway, I reckon that if we play our cards with what I've got, we might end up eating like kings every night off plates of gold."

El, her anger forgotten, looked at Pip with her eyes glowing with hope. It transformed her: suddenly she seemed like an angel, with her fair hair standing out all around her head like a halo.

Pip almost turned away. It broke his heart when his sister looked like that. She was older than he was, but he felt that he was more grown up. There was something too innocent about El. He often feared for her. Sometimes she was very like a small child, and it often took her longer than most people to understand things. But there was a light in El, the way her face would glow when she was happy or hopeful, that made your heart lift. She saw things that other people didn't, because they were in too much of a hurry. And her word was always true.

He reached into his shirt and pulled out a silver box. El's face filled with awe. The silver was tarnished and it was a little battered, but she had never been so close to anything so beautiful. The lid and sides were moulded with a relief design of dragons studded with amethysts, and in the middle of the lid was engraved a coat of arms featuring a bird with a woman's face and another dragon embellished with red gems.

"That's a coat of arms, the sign of the noble," said Pip. "As clear as clear."

Slowly, as if she hardly dared to touch it, El reached out and stroked the lid with the tip of her finger. The metal felt smooth and soft and cool.

"What's inside it, Pip?" she whispered at last. "It must be something very valuable, to have a box like that."

"I don't know," he said.

"Let's look."

They caught each other's eyes, suddenly frightened, although they didn't know why. They stared at the box a while longer. It didn't have a lock, just a little silver catch – shaped like a tiny claw – under the lid.

Very carefully, Pip tried to spring the catch with his grimy fingernail. It wouldn't budge.

"Let me have a go," said El. She was fascinated now, leaning so close her hair brushed Pip's cheek.

"No, it's mine." He held it possessively against his chest.

El pouted, but didn't argue. Pip examined the box more closely. Maybe it had rusted shut. But silver didn't rust… He took out his knife from his belt and slid the tip under the catch, but again it wouldn't move.

"Maybe it's soldered," he said.

"You'll have to break it."

Pip struggled with the catch a little more, breathing noisily through his nose, and then tried pushing the knife under the lid and prising it open. That didn't work either. At last he sat back, staring at the casket in frustration.

"I can't see why it won't open," he said, shaking it. There was definitely something inside. He held the casket up in front of his eyes and addressed it directly. "Why won't you let me in?"

Pip's hands prickled, like an attack of pins and needles, and he let out a soft curse. El looked at him enquiringly.

"Nothing," he said. "Just my hands went all funny. Probably just because I'm tired."

The pins and needles were getting worse, and he put the box down to shake out his fingers. This was frustrating. What was the point of a treasure if you couldn't see what it was?

"Maybe if you ask it more politely," El said.

"It's a *box*."

"It can't hurt. Being nice, I mean."

Pip shrugged and picked it up. The pins and needles got worse when he held the box, but he tried to ignore them. He stroked the lid gently, as if it were a frightened kitten. "All right then. Please, box, let me open you up."

There was a tiny *snick*, and Pip and El's eyes met.

"It heard you!" said El.

"I probably loosened something before," said Pip. His chest was tight with excitement. He eased the lid open slowly to prolong the moment of anticipation, and they peered inside.

For a few moments both of them were silent with bafflement. Nestled on a bed of red velvet was something that looked like a rough black stone, about the size of a small apple.

"It's nothing, really," said El, her voice thick with disappointment.

15

Pip was disappointed too, but he didn't want to believe that his find was of no worth. He took out the object and turned it around in his hands.

"It must be precious," he said. "Why would they put it in a box like this if it wasn't precious?"

He tested its weight in the palm of his hand. It wasn't heavy and felt like leather, he thought, but hard, like leather gets when it's dry and cracked, almost as hard as stone...

Suddenly he started, almost dropping the thing, and put it back in the box as if it burned his fingers. He slammed the lid down shut, breathing hard.

"What is it, Pip?" El looked into his face, which had gone as white as paper. "What's wrong?"

"I'm not sure."

He had thought he knew what the object was. It looked like a very old, very shrivelled-up heart, like the lambs' hearts he had seen at the butchers, only smaller, and black and hard with age. There were the thick veins at the top, chopped all roughly, and the shape of it, the different muscles smooth against each other … *a lamb's heart,* he thought, *or a child's.* And as those thoughts went through his head he had felt it squirm in his hands, as if the heart was beating. As if it had come alive.

Chapter Two

"YOU LOST THE STONE HEART."

The statement was said in a flat, unemotional voice, but in such a way that Sibelius d'Artan began to tremble. He licked his lips and looked around the room in a panic. It was illuminated by a single gold candelabra that cast more shadows than light. The richly decorated walls had several dark alcoves, each of which, Sibelius suddenly thought, might hold an assassin. He tried to speak, but his mouth was too dry.

"I said, you lost the Stone Heart."

Sibelius fell to his knees in terror. "Your Eminence," he gabbled. "Forgive me. It was no fault of ours. The most lamentable intersection of events conspired to—"

"Silence, you fool!"

Cardinal Lamir, the most powerful man in the Holy Church of Clarel, looked down thoughtfully at the

17

figure trembling before him. The price of incompetence was death. He would ensure that Sibelius's was most interesting.

"Let me reprise. Disguised as commoners, you and your companion were skulking through the poor quarters at twilight when you were surprised by a pair of thugs. Having fought them off, you found that the box was missing. It's possible that you dropped it, but it could be that someone picked your pocket."

Not daring to speak, Sibelius nodded. In dressing as commoners and eschewing an armed guard, Sibelius had followed the Cardinal's precise instructions. But Sibelius knew that reminding the Cardinal that the error was in fact his own would do nothing to deflect his wrath.

"Having searched the area, you return to me more than twelve hours later, by which time it is impossible to put any enquiries into motion with any guarantee of efficacy."

Sibelius didn't even dare to nod. There was a long, agonizing silence.

It was often said of the Cardinal that he was like a snake. This was a little defamatory against snakes who are, on the whole, timid, sun-loving creatures that would have to work hard to attain the Cardinal's air of

Arctic implacability. But at this moment the comparison seemed more apt than usual. His thin, reptilian face was pinched with fury and his eyes glittered venomously. His black robes, stiff with golden embroideries of fleur-de-lys, stood out from his shoulders, so that he looked like nothing so much as a huge cobra, poised to strike.

"I don't suppose that you actually *remember* the urchin you saw?" said the Cardinal emotionlessly.

"I – I got a very quick glimpse of— That is," said Sibelius, recollecting that his life hung by a thread, "I'm sure I'd recognize him if I saw him again."

The Cardinal let his cold eyes rest on Sibelius's back, which was shaking visibly. The man was probably lying, but he might yet be of some use and, after all, he needed his skills. It made little difference whether he had him killed now or later.

"You are dismissed."

Sibelius shuffled out backwards on his knees, scarcely able to believe that he was alive.

Taking up this work for the Office for Witchcraft Extermination had been the worst mistake of his life. The Cardinal had recruited him shortly after he arrived at the Palace of Kings to tutor the Princess. He had been a gentleman scholar with a modest but growing reputation when the Crown had summoned him. Back then he

19

certainly could not afford golden buckles for his shoes. Now he had two pairs, one studded with emeralds, plus four pairs of silver buckles for second best. Yet increasingly he wished he had been able to remain in his comfortable house in the country, where he had spent most of his time staring out of the window, pursuing his research into arcane scripts and writing execrable but terribly correct poetry.

Five years before, when Cardinal Lamir had first approached him, Sibelius had been flattered. He'd had a heady sense that he was entering a mysterious world of real power, that he would be privy to dark secrets only known to the initiated. But as time passed, doubts began to creep in.

Secretly Sibelius had begun to wonder if the people the Office arrested and tortured were witches at all. But now he was trapped: if he refused the work, it would be considered at best suspicious and at worst treacherous. And the Cardinal, an intimidating figure even at a distance, became much more frightening on closer acquaintance. He was incalculable and ruthless, with a seemingly uncanny ability to read the minds of his subordinates. While the rewards for those who did well were enormous, the punishments for displeasing the Cardinal were horrifying.

When the door shut behind Sibelius, the Cardinal tugged at a bell-pull. Shortly afterwards a man entered the room.

Like the Cardinal, he was dressed entirely in black, but unlike the Cardinal his clothes were not relieved by the dull sheen of gold. He looked as if he were cut out of sheerest night. All that was visible beneath the hood which covered his head was a cruel, sensual mouth.

His name, Milan Ariosto, was incongruously gentle, bestowed on him by his despairing mother in the few hours she lived after he was born. Since that moment, gentleness had not been a feature of Ariosto's life. Anyone who saw him knew instantly that his business was death. When he passed people in the street they crossed themselves, even if they did not know that Ariosto was the most senior and most feared of the Cardinal's assassins.

"Have Sibelius d'Artan watched," said the Cardinal. "And summon your spies from the Choke Alleys."

Chapter Three

THE PRINCESS WAS BORED. SHE WAS TOO WELL trained to fiddle; instead her mouth pursed in an attractive moue of discontent and her blue eyes misted with a hazy aura of inattention. Her tutor droned on in the background, his mustachios drooping disconsolately. Like the Princess, he was having trouble concentrating on his work.

Sibelius glanced mournfully out of the open window, through which he could hear the *clack* of croquet balls on the lawn and irregular puffs of laughter. "Marcus Candidus told us in his *Geographica* that the seas of Oceania swirl in a whirlpool around the Continentia, before plunging into the eternal void off the edges of the world," he said. "And as we well know, he calculated that the City of Clarel is at the centre of the Kingdom of Clarel, which is itself at the centre of Continentia, and thus constitutes the very fulcrum of the world. And the Palace of the Kings is at the centre of Clarel, and the Most Royal Family of the Avergons is at the Centre of the Palace. Which makes Your Royal Personage the fulcrum of all fulcrums, upon which turns the fate of the entire world."

The Princess nodded absently, and Sibelius suppressed an irritation that even his carefully turned compliments could not lift the fog which so charmingly veiled those aristocratically blue eyes.

"Hence the history of the Avergons is of supreme importance, not only to yourself, but to lesser mortals. Now, as we know, it was your grandfather, the Lion of Avergon, Axel the First, who established his line in the City of Clarel, famously also known as the City of Five Rivers..."

Why does he keep telling me things I already know? wondered Georgette. She thought vaguely of her grandfather, who had died when she was six. She hadn't liked him much: he hadn't been very keen on washing, and he had a fondness for garlic and beans. Her few memories of him were somewhat pungent.

Georgette had an inconvenient memory, because this did not accord with the stories, illuminated in gold and coloured inks, which she read in her books. They related heroic tales of the Kingdom of Clarel being saved by Brave King Axel, who had cut out the canker of corruption rampant in the former Royal Family and had consolidated his claim to the throne by marrying the daughter of the man he had expediently executed. Georgette believed there were other stories to tell that were both truer and more exciting, but she was clever enough to know that she should not say such things, and so she kept them locked up in her head.

Except, every now and then, when it would do no harm...

"There used to be magic," said Georgette reflectively, interrupting Sibelius's flow and catching him off guard. "There were witches who could change people into toads. Wouldn't you like to see that? I would."

Sibelius was momentarily speechless with horror. Why did the Princess mention witchcraft, today of all days? Did she know about his other, secret duties? Sometimes he suspected that she did...

Sibelius's mustachios, Georgette thought mischievously, looked even more despondent than was their wont.

He stared at the Princess, his eyes imploring, and spread out his hands in a gesture of appeal. "Princess..." he said, smiling weakly.

A bell tolled in the distance, and Sibelius jumped. The

Princess yawned delicately, covering her mouth with the back of her hand to cover her smile.

"Oh, lunchtime," she said. "The Chancellor said I have to charm the Ambassador from the Vorn today."

She stood, and Sibelius bowed deeply and backed out of the room, feeling little beads of sweat running down his brow.

Georgette watched him leave, a crease between her eyebrows. It was true that she would very much like to meet a witch, but her life was so well ordered she was unlikely to meet anything more exciting than rows and rows of drooping mustachios. And no doubt one of them would be attached to a husband.

She was to meet her latest suitor the next day. He was the King of Awemt, a neighbouring kingdom with which Clarel had been at war since long before Georgette was born. His queen had died the previous year and Georgette's father now intended to make peace with Awemt, sealing the deal with his daughter.

Georgette didn't know how she was going to get out of this one. If she was reading the situation right, her father was plotting to get rid of his own wife, Queen Theoroda, so he could marry again. If he made peace with Awemt, he didn't need the alliance with Stolt, the mountain kingdom on their southern border, which came with his queen.

And after seven years of marriage, Queen Theoroda had failed to present the King with a son. King Axel wanted a lawful male heir more than anything else, but as yet the Princess was his only legitimate child.

Georgette didn't see why she couldn't be Queen of Clarel, but she kept that to herself. Kings always wanted sons.

I don't want to be married, she thought. *I'd be bored to death.*

She stood up and gave her chair a bad-tempered kick with her rose silk slipper, and briefly hopped about holding her foot in a most unroyal fashion. There was a peremptory knock on the door and, without waiting for her command, which annoyed her, Duchess Albria, her chief lady-in-waiting, entered the room to escort her to lunch.

Georgette didn't like the Duchess – her face was too like a hatchet and she had very thin lips – but she took pains to conceal her dislike. She was sure the Duchess spied on her for Queen Theoroda. So she smiled, laid her hand on the Duchess's arm and paced obediently to the Public Hall to meet the Ambassador from the Vorn.

Chapter Four

PIP WOKE SUDDENLY, HIS BLOOD POUNDING. HE HAD
thought that somebody was calling his name, that someone … needed him. Someone, somewhere, was asking
for his help. But it was only a dream.

He lay staring at the mottled ceiling of the room, listening to the rise and fall of his sister's breath. It was
already broad daylight: the city had woken up, millions
of voices melding into the daily song of the city. A knife
grinder had set up his station in the street outside and
was calling for trade. Pip listened idly as the man bar-
gained, and then to the shriek of the grinding stone.
Maybe that was what had woken him.

He turned restlessly, thinking over the events of
the night before. He had been hiding behind some old
wine casks in an alley by the Duck Alehouse, waiting
for his chance to pickpocket late drunkards, when he

saw two thieves he vaguely knew jumping two men. Pip had already decided not to try these two; although one of them looked like an easy pick, there was something about the way that the other moved, a certain alertness, that warned him off. But when the thieves sprang from the shadows he tensed: there might be something for him after, if he kept his head down.

One man, the easy pick, had stumbled in the muck of the street onto his hands and knees. In the dim light that spilt out from the Duck, Pip saw a flash of richly embroidered silk underneath his dark cloak. This was no ordinary commoner. Something fell to the ground and, quick as a rat, acting on reflex rather than with any conscious intention, he scooped it up in one fluid motion, diving back behind the wine casks before anybody saw him.

The four men were too busy brawling to notice him, but now Pip wondered if the fallen man might have spotted him. This made him feel very uneasy. Pip didn't like being seen and devoted a lot of ingenuity to avoiding it.

The other man had scrambled up and drawn a nasty-looking dagger, taking his assailant by surprise. These thieves were streetfighters, mean and dirty, but their speciality was jumping rustics who didn't know how to fight back. They fled.

Pip watched as the first man brushed himself off,

cursing, and patted his pocket with an almost automatic gesture. Then, with growing anxiety, he felt inside it and turned it inside out.

"It's gone," he said, turning to his companion. "The treasure's gone."

"Gone? Are you certain? He couldn't have taken it – he didn't have…"

"It's not here."

"Maybe you dropped it," said the second man.

Neither of them spoke like commoners. They had the slight lisp of nobles. They looked at each other, and Pip read their thoughts as clearly as if he had heard them. *We're dead men*, they were thinking. *Unless we find the treasure.*

With a panic they had not shown when they were attacked, the two men searched the ground around them. Pip waited for his moment and slipped sound-lessly out from behind the casks when both of them had their backs turned. He stole out of the alley and started running. He was long gone by the time the men gave up their search.

All that fuss over a black, ugly thing that looked like the leavings from a butcher? He had expected some mar-vellous jewel, at least: a diamond, a rare pearl. He felt cheated.

He folded his arms behind his head and stared at the ceiling, trying to remember a time when life hadn't felt like a cheat. He had been little more than a toddler when their parents had died of typhus and he and El had been sent to live with an aunt in a small village in the country. Their aunt had taken what little money they had, fed them grudgingly and given them only the barn to sleep in. They were used as servants and beaten if they didn't properly attend to their duties. In the end they ran away and were drawn into the inexorable gravity of the City of Clarel.

After nearly starving to death on the street, they were rescued by Amina, the mother of El's closest friend, who found them lodgings with Missus Pledge. Missus Pledge was old and cranky, but underneath she was kind. They cared for her in her final illness, and when she died she left them her few belongings, including freehold of her apartment, having no one else to leave it to. They kept the faded parchment document that proved it was theirs in a hole in the floor, under a loose plank. It was their most precious possession.

Pip knew too many worse stories to feel sorry for himself. He and El were lucky: they had somewhere to live, and mostly they had something to eat. And now they had a treasure. Only it didn't seem like a treasure at all.

All his instincts told him the box was trouble. Perhaps he ought to throw it in the river and pretend he had never seen it.

No.

The word was so clear that for a moment he thought someone else had spoken, and he sat up and looked around the room before he decided it was his own thought.

No, he decided. It was his and El's fortune. It was their chance, if only they could figure out why those men thought it was precious. They might never get such a chance again.

For a while he indulged in a daydream. He would buy a new jacket – green velvet probably – and a cocked hat, and boots with shiny buckles. And he and El would have a slap-up dinner at the Crosseyes.

"Your good *menu, my fine fellow. A leg of ham, with pickles, and a dish of lights, if you please, and your pig sausage. A jug of your finest, and to follow..."* – here Pip perused the imaginary menu again, although he could not, for the life of him, read a single word – *"...a selection of your best cheeses."*

He would lift his eyebrow at El. *"Will that do, my dear?"*

And El, in a new dress of yellow silk and muslin, in her new shoes with little bows on the toes, with ruby-red earrings dripping from her ears and a ruby necklace at her breast, would giggle and nod, glowing with the fun of it all. And together they would eat the best meal in the house, while the landlord fawned and cringed at their elbows.

It was an attractive dream, but underneath Pip's fantasies ran a thick vein of streetwise common sense. The problem was turning his find into money. Pip had no idea how to do this.

Still, the box troubled him. It was strange, the way it had just opened like that when he asked, and he still had a faint feeling of pins and needles in his fingers. Did that black, shrivelled heart have something to do with magic?

Even to breathe that word in Clarel could mean death by fire. He'd have to be careful.

Chapter Five

GEORGETTE NEVER ENJOYED PRIVATE MEALS IN THE
royal apartments, but this occasion was worse than
usual. Like most of his subjects, she kept her opinions
of her father to herself. Axel was loud, vain and touchy,
as perhaps was permissible in a king, but in Georgette's
opinion, he was also a fool. After five heavy courses
and countless goblets of wine, he was even louder than
usual, and his face was flushed and shiny with sweat.

She had no fondness for her father, who had never
shown his daughter a single sign of affection. At first,
optimistic that he would soon have a son, King Axel chose
to forget that he had a daughter. Georgette had spent her
early years running wild with the servant children in the
Old Palace, in what she realized now was delicious freedom. She had shared their lice and fleas and childhood
illnesses, their games and secrets and colourful folklore.

When she turned twelve, her father brought her to Clarel Palace to be educated as a proper princess. She had been heartbroken, but after initial rebellion she had bowed her head to the inevitable. She was never beaten, but transgressions resulted in her being locked in a totally dark room alone for hours on end or, worse, an interview with her father, of whom she was frankly terrified. It was said that King Axel II took after his father, only more so, which some brave souls translated as meaning that he had inherited all his father's bad traits and none of the good.

A less intelligent girl might have continued her rebellions despite all the punishments, and eventually been broken altogether. But Georgette was surrounded by broken women, and she took careful note. She smiled at the foppish courtiers who prinked to gain her attention, and performed her endless and dull royal duties with the appearance of goodwill and dutiful obedience. She was especially careful to gain the good opinion of such powerful figures as Cardinal Lamir. Like everyone else, although she seldom admitted it even to herself, she was afraid of him.

Georgette knew that Queen Theoroda hated her. The Princess's elevation to heir to the throne meant that the King no longer hoped for a son. It had taken a couple of years for Georgette to work out why the Queen loathed her so much, and it didn't make her like the Queen any more when she did. But at least it was understandable.

By her fifteenth year Princess Georgette had been transformed from a wild and rebellious tomboy to a poised and accomplished young beauty. She moved with perfect bearing and impeccable etiquette, and she had a good general understanding of the official histories, heraldries, poetry, arts and major languages of Continentia, as well as a smattering of knowledge of such things as mathematics, astronomy and alchemy. Her sophisticated conversation and charm astounded visiting dignitaries, who waxed eloquently on her accomplishments when they made their reports to their kings or doges or dukes or bishops.

The only freedom Georgette insisted upon – granted as a sentimental indulgence after stubborn application, because of her otherwise irreproachable behaviour – was to visit privately with her old nurse, Amina. If Georgette loved anyone, it was Amina.

Over the years, the King had revised his opinion of Georgette. He showed her off as the jewel of his kingdom and plotted her most advantageous marriage. Georgette was clever at heading off these alliances with diplomatically phrased observations on how they might dim the glory of Clarel and weaken its power. And the King, who was a jealous man, had so far been happy to accede to her arguments, especially as they were so artfully turned that they seemed to him to be his own ideas and not Georgette's.

This time, though, her usual anti-marriage tactics weren't working. When she persisted, her father had thrown one of his rages and told her, spittle flying everywhere, that if she didn't marry King Oswald he would have her beheaded as a traitor.

Georgette stole a furtive glance at King Oswald, who was sitting in the place of honour next to Axel. The two men were a study in contrast. Oswald was thin and dark-haired and, she guessed, about fifteen years older than she was. He dressed soberly for a king, preferring the chaste luxury of pearls and diamonds over the showy rubies and emeralds favoured by her father. He ate sparingly and said little, limiting himself to polite nods and murmured courtesies.

If that were all, Georgette might have resigned herself to the doom of marriage. If she really had to get married, a sober, reserved man was a better bet than the spoilt, vain princelings she had met so far. But that wasn't all.

When they had been formally introduced, King Oswald's hand had felt like parchment, as dry and cold as the kiss he had dropped on her fingers. Unable to contain her curiosity, she flicked up a glance and caught his eye, before her gaze dropped modestly to her feet.

In that moment, for no reason that she understood, her whole body flooded with terror. She was exactly as afraid as if he had drawn a knife and held it to her throat. She suddenly remembered her dream, her mother's icy hand grasping her arm. She could still feel where the Queen's fingers had gripped her, as if she were trying to save her daughter from drowning.

It took a long time for the trembling in her body to subside, and she was quiet enough during the meal for the Cardinal to remark on it.

"It's very unfortunate, but I have a migraine," she said, smiling wanly.

"Your royal admirer might think you have taken him in aversion," said the Cardinal.

"Oh no!" said Georgette lightly. "Why would I do that?"

She pretended to concentrate on her meal, trying to trace the origin of her fear of King Oswald. On the surface it seemed completely reasonless. All nobles, in Georgette's opinion, were cruel, and on the surface King Oswald seemed no worse than any other. Until you looked into his eyes. The word that popped into her head was … *empty*. What did that mean? Why should that be frightening?

Empty, without soul. As if he were the living dead.

She pushed away the thought and attempted to be more like her usual lively self, but every time she looked at King Oswald she felt a sick thrill of terror. The dozens of candelabra threw a bright glare across the over-decorated room, which became hotter and stuffier every moment, and a flea had got into her corset and was biting her. It took all her willpower not to scratch or wriggle.

Maybe, thought Georgette, as the ninth and final course was being laid on the table, *I don't want to be a princess any more.*

It wasn't a new notion. Often, when she had been locked in a dark cellar for rudeness to a palace noble or some other minor disobedience, she had wished passionately that she was unimportant enough to do anything she wanted, like the children she had played with in the Old Palace. The illegitimate sons of the King had more freedom and power than she did.

But deep inside Georgette hoped that, if she were clever enough, if she were discreet enough, if she were patient enough, one day she would be Queen of Clarel. So she stuck it out.

She stared down at her violet syllabub, which was curdling in the heat. She had the strangest feeling of vertigo, as if an abyss were opening beneath her. For the past few years she had studied the court and read histories voraciously, planning how she could take power in her own right and change everything for the better. But if she were forced into this marriage, she would never be a proper queen. She would be taken to a country she didn't know, to live with a man who terrified her. She didn't have a choice. She had never had any choice.

If Georgette weren't a princess, she wouldn't have silk sheets or fancy dresses, and nobody would bow to her. She wouldn't have to talk to simpering courtiers or listen to pointless gossip, or spend hours watching dull ceremonial processions with her wired lace collar sticking into her neck.

That didn't seem so bad.

By the end of the meal, she had gathered her fears together and locked them up deep inside. She curtsied good night with her usual grace, offering her hand to King Oswald, her eyes modestly downcast so she didn't have to meet his gaze. Her ladies-in-waiting escorted her to her chamber and undressed her. She lay in her silk nightgown between her silken sheets, scratching the itchy fleabites with blessed relief, and stared at the darkened ceiling.

No, she thought, *I really don't want to be a princess any more. And I definitely don't want to marry King Oswald.*

I'll have to become a proper queen.

Chapter Six

WHETHER YOU HAD TWO LEGS, OR FOUR LEGS, OR wings, you had to stay alert in the dark alleys of Clarel. If you didn't pay attention, someone else would, and attention here was almost always bad news.

As a rule of thumb, anything abnormal was a warning sign. A silence that was deeper than it should be, a shadow slipping past where no shadow should be, footsteps where feet had no business: those were the obvious things.

Harpin Shtum, scholar and gentleman scoundrel, was heading home from a profitable afternoon playing bezique at the Five Tuns, not far from the Old Palace. He was as intimate with the streets of Clarel as anyone who had survived thirty-five years' hard cheating, and thought he knew every variation of bad news that the alleys had to offer. But he had never seen anything like this before.

According to the laws he had survived by, it couldn't signify anything except trouble.

He squeezed his eyes shut and opened them again. Surely he hadn't drunk that much brandy? A tipple, no more… But there it was, an impossible thing. In front of him, in the murky twilight, the air seemed to have a hole in it. He couldn't think of any other way to describe it. Holes didn't glow, though, and this one glowed: a dim greenish glare that illuminated nothing. He could see into the hole – or at least, it had a sense of depth – but he couldn't see what was inside. Whatever it might be, it was moving, with a roiling motion that made him feel faintly queasy.

His feet told him to run, but Harpin's curiosity overrode his instincts of self-preservation. The hole didn't seem to be doing anything, and it gave an impression of complete soundlessness, as if it swallowed noise. He looked up and down the street. Nobody was about; otherwise he might have called them over to check that it wasn't some strange trick his eyes were playing on him. Cautiously, keeping his distance, he walked around the hole. It wasn't visible at all from behind, and from the side it was a mere flicker in his vision. He could only see it clearly from the front, just at the angle at which he had turned the corner.

He picked up a pebble and threw it at the hole, again keeping his distance. It didn't land on the ground, as he had expected; it disappeared into the green space completely, as if it were somehow sucked inside. He walked behind, where the hole was invisible, and tried his experiment again. This time the pebble fell to the ground. Then he returned to where he could see the hole, and tried throwing in another pebble. Yes, it definitely vanished.

By now Harpin was fascinated. Gingerly, ready to spring back if anything happened, he reached out and touched the edges. Aside from a slight coolness, he felt nothing. He regarded the hole cautiously and reached forwards again. Again, nothing. Perhaps it was humming slightly, just underneath the range of his hearing. It was almost as if, he thought, it were saying his name. No, that was silly. But he did have an intense desire to step inside the hole, a desire which was growing stronger with every moment.

"What in holy hell are you doing, Harp? I didn't think you were that cut."

The voice, ringing cheerily from behind him, made Harpin leap out of his skin. He had been so engrossed that he hadn't heard footsteps. As he turned, he twisted his ankle and tripped into the hole. It flared so brightly that it cast bewildering shadows over the alley, and then seemed to fold itself up until it completely disappeared.

Harpin's fellow card-sharp Erasmus Quinn staggered, temporarily blinded, and blinked at the after-images that hung in the darkness.

"Harp?" he said, suddenly much more sober. "Harp? Don't play tricks on a man, Harp."

Nobody answered. Erasmus peered around. It wasn't completely dark yet, and he could see clearly all the way to the end. There was no sign of Harpin anywhere.

As Erasmus told some friends later, Harpin didn't fall into the thing; it was like he was sucked in by some invisible force. "An irresistible force, gentlemen," Erasmus said over his third gin, still trembling a little. "And then – *pffft!* – he just disappeared. Before my eyes. He vanished, just like that."

"You was seeing things," said another man, swirling his mug. "Happens to me sometimes, when I get a fever. Or am in my cups."

"I don't have a fever," said Erasmus belligerently. "Believe me or not, that's what I saw, with these eyes. The point is that I was seeing things, and then I wasn't. There was this green light and Harp was kind of poking it, and then he was … sucked in … and then he wasn't there. It's uncanny, that's what it is." He liked the word. "Uncanny."

"Well, you do look all shook up, that's true. We'll have a good laugh when we see Harp tomorrow."

"*If* we see him tomorrow," said Erasmus. He was getting sulky now at his friends' open scepticism. "*If.* I don't mind telling you that would be a mortal relief, to see his ugly face. If he can do tricks like that, he's cleverer than any of us give him credit for. And I don't care if you believe me. I know what I saw."

"It's magic, that's what it is," said another man darkly. "Black magic, if you ask me."

All of them looked uneasy at that, and changed the conversation.

In a corner of the tavern, another man dressed in dusty black from head to foot had been listening intently. Nobody noticed when he stood up and left. But few people noticed assassins when they didn't want to be seen.

Chapter Seven

GEORGETTE LAY CURLED IN AN "S" SHAPE, WITH HER hands folded neatly beneath her cheek, and drooled a little on her pillow. Sometime after the midnight bell, she stirred and cried out, and one of her ladies-in-waiting – who, as custom decreed, spent each night propped on a chair in the corner of the room in order to protect her mistress from horrors which might fly in the window, such as moths or vampires – jumped in her sleep and muttered something about burning cakes, before subsiding back into an uncomfortable doze.

Georgette was having that dream again.

The first time she had had this dream was on the night of her mother's funeral, although it had returned dozens of times since. Georgette's mother, Queen Alsigne, had died when the Princess was six years old.

This had not affected her much, since she had barely known her. On state occasions or holy days she was stuffed into an uncomfortable dress stiff with pearls and brocade and taken to a gracious and pale woman she had been taught to call "Mother" or "Your Grace", who took her hand gravely and regarded her with sad and distant eyes.

Ever since then, the dream had always been exactly the same.

She was a little girl, kneeling before her mother. As she stooped to take her daughter's hand, Queen Alsigne was haloed with a rich golden light that seemed to be beating out of her skin. Everything around them was dark, and in the shadows moved horrible, shapeless things that Georgette didn't dare to look at. Behind the Queen was a massive stained-glass window, a window which did not exist in Georgette's waking life. It was a magnificent picture of a crimson dragon, the sign of the Old Royals before King Axel I, rampant, its mouth spouting golden gouts of flame.

As Georgette stood up, still holding her mother's hand, the dragon seemed to come alive, although it remained imprisoned in the window. The queen turned to look at it, unsurprised, and smiled sadly.

"Ah, my little Georgette," she said, turning back and

looking at her daughter with those immense grey eyes, always so sorrowful and so beautiful. *"My sweet daughter."* (She had never said anything so fond when she had been alive, and Georgette's heart quickened with an unfamiliar warmth.) *"Do not forget the cries in the night. Do not forget."*

Usually then the Queen vanished, and the dragon would turn and fix its fiery eyes on Georgette, making her quail. But tonight the dream was different. Her mother grasped her upper arm. Her fingers were like ice, so cold they burned Georgette's skin.

"Your fate is darkening, child," said the Queen. *"Beware! Soon even Death won't stop him."*

"Who?" asked Georgette.

"The one who comes for you now."

The dread of nightmare rose in Georgette's throat and she pulled away in a sudden panic. But her mother tightened her grip until Georgette cried out with pain. The Queen leaned close and bent her mouth to Georgette's ear. *"Run, daughter,"* she whispered. "Run."

The queen let go and stood up, and before Georgette's eyes her graceful beauty shrivelled into a skeleton, which collapsed into a dry pile of bones on the floor. The dragon in the window turned its terrible eyes on the Princess and began to laugh. It knew that she couldn't run away.

Georgette screamed and screamed, but no sound came out of her mouth.

At the same time she heard a little boy weeping inconsolably. It was the most lonely, the most unbearable sound in the world. She knew the boy was alone and terrified and in pain.

This child was always in the dream. Every time before, Georgette had woken up torn between fear of the waking dragon and pity for the child. But this time she broke free of sleep in simple, undiluted terror, her nightdress drenched with sweat, her whole body shaking.

It's only a nightmare, she told herself. *It isn't real.* Then she looked at her arm and saw red fingermarks already purpling to bruises, exactly where the Queen had held her in the nightmare.

She stared in disbelief, her heart hammering. Maybe she had clutched herself, in panic? She crept out of bed to the window, where the moonlight was brighter, and tried to fit her fingers to match the marks. They were on the front of her arm, as if someone had clasped her from behind. And yes, there was a thumbprint on the back of her upper arm. No matter how she twisted herself, she couldn't replicate the bruises.

Georgette looked suspiciously at the snoring lady-in-waiting, but Lady Agathe wasn't the kind to play cruel tricks. Even if she was, there hadn't been enough time for her to return to her chair and fall asleep.

The terror wasn't fading like it usually did. It was thickening, a heavy dread coiling inside her, threatening to choke her.

It wasn't a dream. This time, Georgette knew it was real.

Chapter Eight

OLIBRANDIS SNIFFED AS HE TURNED THE SILVER BOX over and over in his hands. He sniffed continuously, so it didn't mean much, but Pip was on the alert for every tiny sign. "So, you picked this up in the alleys?"

"A quick pocketing, like I said," said Pip.

Olibrandis, Purveyor of Antiquities and Curiosities, screwed a glass into his eye and closely inspected the jewels. "Amethysts and garnets, my boy, nothing to write home about. But some nice chasing and repoussage work there, on the lid." He indicated the coat of arms – a dragon embellished with in red stones – with a grimy forefinger. "That's craftsmanship, that is." He clicked open the lid and stroked the soft velvet interior. "Likely held some gentleman's buckles."

"A nobleman," said Pip. "That's a dragon, that is."

"It is indeed." Olibrandis put the box down on the table

and sat back. "That there, in fact, is the coat of arms of the previous Royal Family, what we don't name these days, because none of us is supposed to remember." He took out a large red handkerchief and blew his nose loudly.

"You mean it belonged to a king?"

"More likely his privy counsellor, or some other such minion." Seeing the uncomprehending expression on Pip's face, Olibrandis expanded: "The nobleman who is honoured to help the king onto his privy and wipe his arse."

"Really?" said Pip, his eyes wide.

"When you're King, even your turds smell like roses." Olibrandis laughed wheezily at his poor joke, and then collapsed into a fit of coughing. He drew out his handkerchief again and spat into it, examining the result carefully before he folded it up and put it back in his pocket. "I'll give you four marks for it."

"Four marks! For a box of solid silver and jewels from a king?"

"Take it or leave it, my boy. I'm being too generous; most wouldn't give you three. Its value is scarce more than silver. The extra mark is for the craftsmanship, but I'm not sure it's worth my while. The Old Royals aren't in fashion, but someone might be curious."

Pip frowned and stared at the box, plucking at his

lower lip. He had come to Olibrandis, with whom he had enjoyed a long and mutually profitable relationship, because the dealer was honest, or at least, not as dishonest as the other fences he knew. The box would likely be sold for twenty marks or more in less than an hour. But Pip was hungry.

"Make it six and it's a deal," he said.

"Five, then," said Olibrandis. "And not a farthing more, if you break my back."

Pip watched gloomily as Olibrandis counted out the coins. He and El had argued that morning over selling the box. Her attitude towards it had changed sharply. She now said the box was giving her chills and she didn't want it in the room.

"It's no use just going to old Ollie," said Pip. "It's a treasure, remember?"

"It's evil, that's what it is." El flicked a glance at the box, and shivered. "It's bad luck."

Pip picked it up and stroked the soft silver lid with his finger. He didn't want to sell it. He couldn't rid himself of the conviction that this box would change their fortunes. "I told you, it's precious. It's *important*, El."

"Sell the box and throw that horrible black thing inside away." El was speaking so passionately that she was breathless. "I feel like … like it's *watching* me."

"So the one chance we get to better ourselves, we throw it away? What about our fortune?"

"Oh, Pip." El took his hand and held it tight. "There's never going to be no fortune for us. Don't you understand? It's just a daydream, Pip. A lovely daydream. But you can't eat dreams. And I'm so hungry I feel dizzy."

So Pip had taken the Heart out of the box – he thought of it as the Heart, although he still wasn't really sure what it was – and wrapped it in a piece of old cloth. He'd hidden it inside his breeches, where no nimble fingers could find it.

Touching it made him feel a little sick, as if he were on top of a tall building. El was right: it felt like bad luck. He could feel it pushing into his hips as he sat in front of Olibrandis, even though it scarcely weighed anything at all.

He left Olibrandis's shop the same way he had come in, by the back entrance, shouldering past piles of oddments – rusting chains, buckets of nails, boxes of old bottles marked "poison" – into the tiny alley behind. Five marks was still a decent amount: it was a month's worth of dinners, and maybe a shawl for El and a jacket for him. Two days ago he would have been cock-a-hoop, but he couldn't get past his dragging disappointment.

He kicked at some rubbish, deciding to go to the

Mascule Bridge and throw the Heart into the river there. The Mascule Bridge was popular with suicides; it seemed like an appropriate place to drown the hope that had surged inside him so powerfully.

Shortly after Pip left his shop, Olibrandis put the newly polished box in his window, with a tag indicating that this appealing silver buckle casket could be purchased by any person who had the necessary twenty-five marks. An hour after that, a man dressed entirely in black paused thoughtfully outside the shop, his attention arrested, and peered through the grimy panes. He glanced up and down the street, and then, as silently as a rat wearing velvet slippers, he lifted the latch and went inside.

Chapter Nine

PIP DRAINED HIS CIDER AND FROWNED INTO HIS empty pewter mug. At least in the Crosseyes Alehouse there wasn't a cockroach at the bottom, which had happened more than once at the Duck, but this did nothing to cheer him. Even the weight of the coins hidden under his jacket didn't lift his mood.

He was killing time waiting for El, who had gone shopping. El had chosen the venue to meet, one of the more respectable public houses in the Choke Alleys, and Pip wasn't in the mood. Right now he wanted to go home. He didn't feel like talking to anyone.

Jack Ranciere, apothecarist to gentlefolk, scowled at him from across the room and muttered something. Pip didn't respond. If he started an argument with Jack it wouldn't stop. Jack had been accusing him for years of stealing from him, an accusation Pip hotly denied with all the fervour of someone who, for once, was actually innocent. He had stolen from quite a few people in this room, but never from Jack. He turned away, leaning his elbow on the wonky table – a plank balanced precariously on two barrels – and gave the other patrons a misanthropic survey.

"Want another jug?"

It was Oni, El's best friend. She had recently found work at the Crosseyes and now lived in a small apartment by herself, not far from the inn.

Pip looked up unsmilingly into her dark eyes. "Why not?"

Oni picked up the jug. "Is El coming on here?"

Pip shrugged instead of answering, and Oni flashed him a look. "No need to be rude. I just asked."

Pip relented. Oni never looked down her nose at him, not like some others. "She's at the market. She wanted to buy a new scarf for the Midsummer Festival, but she's taking ages."

"Oh, you know El. She can never make up her mind. You should have gone with her, to help her choose."

"But I hate trying to help her buy anything."

"You'll have to be patient, then. Want something to eat?"

"I said I'd wait." Oni turned to leave. "No, maybe some bread. Have you got any eggs?"

Oni nodded, already busy with another customer, and Pip returned to his brooding.

When he had given El the money from Olibrandis, she had just assumed he had thrown away the Heart. Why, after all, would he keep such a grisly object?

Pip felt a little guilty, because he hadn't disposed of it. He had walked to the Mascule Bridge and, gripped by a strange reluctance, leaned over the parapet and stared down at the blackish-brown water that flowed sluggishly beneath. He didn't reach inside his clothes to take out the Heart, but he could feel it there, warmed by his own body heat, as if it were a live thing. Why should he throw it away? Maybe he could still discover what the Heart was, and find a way to turn it to their advantage. He thought of the expression on the noble's face when he had realized that they'd lost the treasure. It was important. Really important. Nobles wouldn't call a mere silver box a treasure; they had rooms full of gold.

He knew that he'd regret it for the rest of his life if he threw the Heart away without even trying to find out why it mattered. He was sure it was magic. Perhaps it was some kind of spell for getting rich, if he could only work out how to use it. He had already noticed how it changed temperature: right now it felt cold, like he had a snowball in his breeches.

After El had left with her basket he'd mooched around the Choke Alleys, wondering who he could ask, discreetly of course, about magic objects. There weren't any witches left in Clarel. He and El had sometimes suspected that Missus Pledge, the old lady who had given them their apartment, had been a bit magic: there had been one or two strange incidents … but she never said so outright. And anyway, she was dead.

He was halfway through his hard-boiled egg when El arrived at last, flushed and slightly out of breath, her hood drawn low over her face. She slid in next to him on the bench.

"You took your time," said Pip.

"No need to splutter egg all over me." El lowered her voice. "I got news. Bad news, Pip."

"What kind of bad news?"

"You know you went to Olibrandis this morning?" He nodded. "Well, it's all around the market. He's dead."

"Dead? Olibrandis?"

"It must have happened after you went there. I reckon it's to do with that box. I told you it was bad luck."

"Probably just a coincidence," said Pip. "Or maybe it's just a rumour. He looked right as rain when I saw him."

"No, *listen*, Pip. They reckon that he was tied up in his chair and then someone cut his throat – *whisht* – just like that." She drew her finger across her neck. "But he wasn't robbed; stuff was thrown everywhere, but the cash box was still there, and all his jewels, and most everything else, so far as people can tell. Lindy went in to sell some bits and bobs and found him sitting in his chair, with blood all over the floor."

Pip didn't respond. He had to admit that didn't sound like a rumour. He felt a stab of sorrow for Olibrandis, whom he had always rather liked. "Did you talk to Lindy?"

"Yes, of *course* I did. What you think I been doing? But there's worse. Someone is looking for you. A man cloaked all in black, Lindy said, like an assassin. Asking around the place, looking for a thieving young man called Pip what lives in the Choke Alleys, black hair, short, scrawny, legs like sticks, weasel eyes."

"Weasel eyes!" Pip was offended.

"He knows your name, Pip. He must have got it from Ollie."

Pip shifted uncomfortably. "There's probably hundreds and hundreds of people who look just like that around here. And probably lots of Pips among them."

El stole a glance around the alehouse and leaned so close to Pip that he felt her breath on his cheek. "He's offering silver for information. He probably knows

60

everything he needs to know already. Maybe he knows where our house is. I mean, we keep it dark, but that doesn't mean that people don't talk." She bit her lip. "It's got to be the same man what cut poor old Olibrandis."

Pip thought that seemed likely, but he wasn't willing to admit it. "But why would he cut poor old Ollie's throat? If he wanted to know my name, Ollie would have told him without that. It's probably about something else, like I said – some deal that went sour."

"I told you I had a bad feeling." El brushed her hair back from her face. "What if he's waiting for us at home? He might already be there."

For a moment they both imagined an assassin, skeletal and sinister, his face concealed in the shadow of a hood, hiding behind the door as they entered, his lifted blade shining in the dim light...

Pip looked furtively around the taproom, which was beginning to empty out after the noon rush. He wouldn't trust anybody here as far as he could throw them. If silver was on offer, the Choke Alleys would be solid eyes, looking for him.

"But we've got nowhere else to go," he said at last. "Where could we go?"

"Oni's got somewhere."

"But she doesn't like me."

"She never said she didn't like you. She just thinks you're annoying. Which you are."

It was Oni who was annoying, Pip thought, but he didn't say so out loud. He pushed away the bread. His stomach seemed to have unaccountably gone missing, and he wasn't hungry any more.

Chapter Ten

"BUT WHY WOULD AN ASSASSIN BE AFTER *YOU*?" ONI crossed her arms and stared belligerently at Pip. "You're not important. Assassins only go after important people."

After lunch, at El's request, Oni had begged an hour off from the innkeeper. The three of them had repaired to Oni's place, an apartment in a crumbling building a few streets from the Crosseyes. It had once been a mansion but, like most of the people who now lived there, it had fallen on hard times. Oni's apartment was on the fifth floor, an airy attic room that looked over the roofs of the city.

She was being annoying again.

"It's because of this box I found," said Pip, trying to be patient. "A silver box. It was precious."

El cast Pip a speaking glance. Against El's objections, he had argued that they shouldn't mention the

Heart to Oni. Without being able to say why, Pip felt they shouldn't talk about it. Part of him worried, irrationally, that someone might hear.

"So you want to move into my place with no notice and maybe for ever because you think an assassin is out for your skin because you stole a worthless silver box?" said Oni. "Pull the other one. It's got bells and spangles."

Pip had been annoyed by Oni for about five years. He and El had met her shortly after they arrived in the City of Clarel, when he was seven years old. She was a dark-skinned Eradian, but she had never lived in the Weavers' Quarter where most Eradians lived. Her mother was the housekeeper at the Old Palace and she had been raised there. Oni's mother had found Pip and El sleeping under a bridge near the Old Palace, half dead from starvation, and had given them a meal and introduced them to Missus Pledge, who gave them a place to live.

Oni and El had become best friends almost straight away. Pip had many acquaintances, but he didn't have a friend like Oni, and he was secretly jealous. Oni knew this, of course. It was one of the reasons she was annoying.

"I think, if you're going to ask such a big favour of me, you should tell me the truth," said Oni.

"I think we should too, Pip," said El. "It's only fair."

Pip squirmed under their double gaze. "But what if the assassin decides to torture you, like he did poor old Ollie?" he said.

"Lindy said nothing about torture."

"You said he was tied up in his chair," said Pip. "Of course he was tortured."

For a moment the three of them were silent. They had all known Olibrandis, and had often made fun of his wonky gait and wheezy voice. In a city full of liars, thieves, murderers and frauds, Olibrandis passed as a decent person. That was quite rare. Old Ollie hadn't deserved what had happened to him.

"An assassin would probably torture me anyway," said Oni. "That's what they do."

El leaned forward and dropped her voice to a low whisper, even though there was no one else in the room. "It's about magic. This treasure box Pip found…" She shuddered. "It opened by itself and there was this nasty leathery thing inside. It's bad magic – I could tell as soon as I saw it."

A strange expression crossed Oni's face, a flicker of caution. "But there's no magic any more," she said. "Not since they burned all the witches. You know that."

"Maybe there is," said El. "Just because something's against the law doesn't mean it doesn't happen. I mean, thieving's against the law, and Pip happens all the time."

"If it's about magic I don't want anything to do with it." Oni spoke with sudden violence. "If it's magic, you have to find somewhere else."

El took Oni's hand. "Please, Oni. We need somewhere to hide. Just for a few days. Just until it all dies down."

Oni squeezed El's hand, let it go and sighed heavily. "Maybe. If you're straight with me."

Pip was frowning at the floor. "I feel like I shouldn't tell," he said.

"Well then, try your luck on the street."

At last, with deep reluctance, Pip told Oni about the Heart, how he had accidentally stolen it from men he had thought were out-of-towners but who turned out to be nobles. He didn't tell her that he thought it had moved when he picked it up, or of his conviction that it was somehow alive. As he spoke, Oni went very still.

"It's a bad thing," said El, shuddering again. "I could feel it. I couldn't sleep with it in the house. It gave me awful dreams. That's how I knew we had to get rid of it."

"And where is it now?" said Oni.

"The thing? I told Pip to throw it in the river. You did, didn't you?"

Pip didn't answer. He thought that El would likely punch him if he said he had kept it.

"Don't tell me you still have it? Pipistrel, I *told* you, it's evil, it's bad luck." El was almost crying, and her chest began to heave jerkily, as it did when she was agitated.

"Show me," said Oni.

"I can't," said Pip. "It would be wrong."

"Show me." Oni was staring at him, her eyes burning.

Slowly Pip reached under his clothes and took out the Heart. It was warm to his fingers, warmer even than his own skin. It fitted pleasingly in his palm, smooth and leathery. It was uncanny, that was certain, but he didn't feel the same revulsion towards it that El did. It was magic, he was sure, but he didn't think it was evil.

El flinched and turned away, but Oni breathed in sharply. She bit her lip and reached out and touched the Heart with the tip of her finger, stroking it gently.

"Oh my," she said. "Oh, the poor, poor thing."

Pip looked at her curiously, his annoyance forgotten. "You know what it is?"

Oni sat back, biting her lip. She looked shaken. "I think you're in trouble, Pip. If I'm right. I might be wrong, though."

"So what is it?" El stole a look at the Heart, and then

turned away. "It's horrible, I don't want anything to do with it."

Oni was silent for a long time, her face troubled.

"You might as well tell us," said Pip, putting the Heart away. "We ought to know."

"I don't know if I can trust you, Pip." Pip opened his mouth, about to protest indignantly, but she held up her finger. "No, I don't mean that I think you're a snitch or nothing like that. It's more…" She trailed off.

"More what?"

"We got to talk to Ma."

"Your ma? Why? Could she help?" El turned around.

"There's a lot you don't know about us. Stuff you shouldn't know. For your sake, as well as ours."

"What are you talking about?" El looked offended. "I'd never do you down. You know that. Don't you? All these years…"

"It's not just me, El. If it was just about me, I wouldn't worry – well, not much. But it isn't." Oni paused again, frowning. "I got to go back to work, but we should meet up later and go to see Ma. Maybe meet me at Linkpin Square at the sixth bell. Don't you poke your noses out of this door until then, not one inch, and leave out the back alley. I just hope to the gods that no one saw us coming here."

"We was careful," said Pip. "I'm as certain as I can be that no one followed us. You said I was being silly. You said—"

"Yes, I get it," said Oni crossly. "You were right."

Now Oni was annoyed.

Chapter Eleven

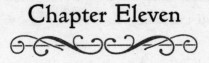

AS THE SUN DIPPED BEHIND THE CITY BUILDINGS, EL
and Pip headed by indirect ways for Linkpin Square.
"Square" was a grand name for a triangle where three
alleys met: it was a tiny patch of weedy ground over-
shadowed by dank tenements. It was twilight by the
time they arrived, but they felt hideously exposed as
they waited in the darkest doorway they could find,
their necks prickling as if unseen eyes were watching
them from the blank windows above.

Oni was late. El had begun to grow anxious, worrying that the assassin had tracked her friend down,
and maybe had already cut her throat, and her breath
came in little gasps. Pip hated it when El got like that,
and he was ready to punch Oni by the time she finally
arrived. Oni ignored his reproaches, saying shortly that
she couldn't help it, and that it would be better to keep

moving instead of wasting time arguing.

From Linkpin Square they made their way to the Old Palace. It took them longer than it normally would: they doubled back on their tracks and hid behind low walls, listening for stray footsteps, and once they made a short cut via an abandoned building, slipping in through a broken window. Pip was using all the tricks he knew but travelling with two others made him feel horribly visible. He was pretty sure, all the same, that nobody saw when they wriggled through a gap in the railings and dived into the overgrown park at the back of the Old Palace.

Once they were inside the grounds, Oni led them unerringly to her mother's kitchen garden where they climbed over the wall and knocked on the door.

Oni's mother wasn't pleased to see them, and told them to come back the next day.

"Ma, it's important," said Oni. "Else I wouldn't have come."

"It's Georgie's day."

Oni swore. "So what?"

"So you can't be here."

"I told you, Ma, it's important."

"How important?"

Oni looked over her shoulder, as if she thought the shadows might be listening, and lowered her voice to a whisper. "I can't say, Ma," she said. "Not out loud."

Her mother's jaw tightened. Oni met her eyes stubbornly, and at last she sighed and held open the door. "All right," she said. "But be quick."

She let them into her kitchen: a large, whitewashed room flagged with red clay tiles that stayed cool even in the fiercest heat of summer. At one end was a hearth with a roasting spit next to a covered oven, and at the other were rows of mullioned windows over a wooden workbench. The windows looked out onto the walled garden where Oni's mother grew all her vegetables and fruits. The eaves were heavy with dried herbs and bunches of garlic, and on the walls were shelves of bright preserves and relishes and pickles. In the middle was a long scrubbed table, with a bench against the wall and a miscellany of chairs.

Pip and El had visited this kitchen often over the years. They knew Oni's mother well enough to call her by her first name, Amina, although most people called her Missus Bemare. The Missus was a sign of respect more than anything else: no one seemed to know if she had ever been married. Oni's father was called Guilliame Tylova and lived in the Tailors' Quarter. Oni visited him now and then, to check how he was.

"Nobody knows what he does," said Oni once, when

El asked about him. "He always has plenty of money though. Ma says she doesn't quite know why she ended up with him, except that he was very handsome at the time. And then she got me, and who could regret that?"

Amina gestured for them to sit down. She wouldn't let them speak until she had lit several dark yellow candles with an unfamiliar, sharp scent and set them around the table, muttering under her breath. Pip raised his eyebrows at Oni.

"We don't want to be overheard," she said. "So shut up until she's ready."

El was watching with fascination, her eyes wide. "It's witchcraft, isn't it?" she whispered. "Is your ma a witch?"

"I said, shut up," said Oni.

"No need to be rude," said Pip.

"You don't know how rude *you're* being," said Oni. "So shut up."

After that Pip and El buttoned their mouths. Pip shifted uncomfortably. Something strange was happening with the Heart: he could feel it getting colder and colder in his pocket.

At last Amina seemed satisfied, and she sat down with them at the table, clasping her hands in front of her.

"So you'd better have a good story."

Pip then told Amina what he had told Oni: how he had

found the Heart, and how he was sure that an assassin had murdered Olibrandis. Amina listened in complete silence.

"There was a box?" she said, when he had finished.

"Yes, a silver box."

"Describe it to me."

He was beginning to get tired of talking about it. "Well, Ollie said it had excellent chasing and repoussage work, and it had amethysts and garnets that weren't worth much. It had a red dragon in the coat of arms; Ollie said it was the Old Royals."

"I wish you hadn't sold it."

"We was hungry," said El. "We didn't have nothing else."

"You had better show me the Heart."

When Pip touched the Heart, it was so cold he winced. As he put it on the table he noticed that it had a faint mist of condensation on its surface. Amina stared at it in silence, but she didn't touch it. She didn't look horrified or disgusted. Most of all, thought Pip, she looked *sorry* for it.

"Put it away," she said at last. "That is a terrible thing. I wish I had never had cause to see such a thing as that."

"I told you it was evil," said El.

"It's not evil in itself. Maybe it might do evil things. What caused it to be made is evil."

74

"So what is it?" said Pip, wrapping it up and putting it back in his pocket.

"I'm not sure that you should know."

Pip opened his mouth to argue, but was interrupted by the ringing of a bell several rooms away.

"Oh no," said Oni. "That's Georgie."

Chapter Twelve

THE OLD PALACE HAD BEEN CRUMBLING INTO GRAND decay for almost a century, ever since King Axel I built his new, showier palace in the centre of Clarel. Much of it was a maze of panelled corridors and rooms constructed inside faded ballrooms and reception rooms, where dusty scribes and officials scurried from office to office on their inscrutable duties. Even Amina, the Old Palace's housekeeper, wasn't quite sure what most of them did, although she thought it was something to do with tax.

Georgette breathed in the familiar smells of damp and stale cooking with relief. For the first time that day her feeling of panic subsided. She knew every corner of this place. It was the closest thing to a home she had ever known.

In the Old Palace, where the king put unimport-ant affairs like princesses he didn't want and obscure government departments, things ran on their own, mostly overlooked by the royal gaze.

Amina's door was always locked to keep out bewildered scribes, who sometimes got lost. It was a long time before she answered the bell this evening, long enough for Georgette to start wondering if she was out. How could Amina not be there?

She was just about to tug the bell-rope again when the door opened. Amina met her eyes unsmilingly, hurriedly let her in and turned the key behind her, and only then kissed her cheeks. Georgette wanted to hug her, but something made her hold back.

"What's wrong?" she asked.

It was unlike Georgette, who was a princess after all, to notice the feelings of others, and Amina gave her a narrow look. "Nothing, my dear," she said. "I've just got Oni here, with some friends who wanted advice."

Georgette's face brightened. "Oni!" she said. "I haven't seen her since, oh, for years…"

"No, that you haven't."

"It's not like I'm allowed," Georgette said, with sudden defensiveness.

Amina's face relaxed. "Yes, my dear, I know that. Anyway, it can't be helped. You might as well come to the kitchen."

Georgette wrinkled her nose as Amina showed her in. There were candles burning although it wasn't yet completely dark, and a strong smell of cassia and myrrh. Three people looked up as she entered. Georgette recognized Oni, but the others were strangers: a sharp-faced boy and a girl who looked a little younger than her. To her annoyance, she felt herself blushing under their gaze.

The fair girl was staring at Georgette in awe. "Is that real gold?" she said.

"*Ssshhh,*" said the boy next to her, in a perfectly audible whisper. "That's not how you talk to nobles."

"Hello, Georgie," said Oni. "You've changed."

Georgette heard a note of hostility in Oni's voice. For once she didn't know what to say. She hesitated by the doorway, feeling like an interloper.

"It's been a long time," she said to Oni. "I'm not allowed to see any…" She had been going to say "commoners", but caught herself. It was the condition on which she had been allowed to visit Amina, that she kept no other low company, and especially not the children who had been her friends when she ran wild in the Old Palace.

Amina was watching with a glint of amusement in her eyes. "These two here are Pip and El. And this is Georgie."

"Princess Georgette," said Oni. El gasped.

"We have an agreement that while she's in this house, she's not a princess," said Amina.

El was still staring at Georgette's outfit. It was richly dyed blue silk, with delicate lace beaded with tiny seed pearls at the cuffs and throat. Georgette's shawl, thrown over her bare shoulders, was embroidered with butterflies stitched with golden thread. Georgette had grown accustomed to such finery over the years, and her current dress, a costume for everyday occasions, was by no means the most impressive she owned. A large part of being a princess, after all, was looking like one.

Pip turned accusingly to Oni. "You never said you knew a princess."

"I said you don't know everything about me," said Oni. Now she looked as if she wanted to laugh. "Oh, do sit down, Georgie. Unless you've grown too fine for us. We promise not to make you dirty."

Georgette snapped out of her embarrassment and walked to the table, her skirts swishing. "I have to dress like this," she said. "And it might look nice, but it's tight and there are always bits sticking into me. And it's complicated to sit down." She drew out a chair and arranged herself into it. She had to sit two feet away from the table to accommodate her stiff skirts.

"Do you eat off golden plates?" asked El. Her eyes

were like saucers. "With jewels and everything?"

"Sometimes," said Georgette. "When I have to eat with my father."

"And do you really have someone to help you wipe your arse?" asked Pip.

"Now, you two, that's enough," said Amina.

"But Olibrandis said—"

"I said, be quiet."

"But—"

"I'll brew some tea," said Amina. "And meanwhile, you two, remember that you are to tell no one that you saw Georgie today. No one."

"I'm no snitch," said Pip indignantly.

"It's important."

Amina put a kettle on the hob and busied herself with crockery, while Onl studied Georgette with open curiosity.

"How is it, being royal?"

Georgette looked around the table, feeling that it was now or never. Why, this day of all days, were there strangers here? But this was her only chance. She took a deep breath.

"It's bad," she said. "You don't know how bad. I have to leave. I'm hoping that Amina can help me escape. Today. I have to run away today." As she spoke, her self-control wavered, and tears started in her eyes. Saying it out loud was different to thinking it in her head. It suddenly seemed real.

"You want to run away?" said El. She couldn't imagine why anyone who wore beautiful clothes and who never had to worry about meals would want to escape such a fine life.

"I have to," said Georgette fiercely. "Or I'll die." She turned towards Amina, who was standing by the fire, perfectly still, a cup forgotten in her hand. "You'll help me? You're the only one I can turn to…"

Amina slowly shook her head. "My dear, how could I possibly help you?"

Georgette's lip wobbled, but she forced herself not to cry. She didn't want to burst into tears, not in front of Oni and the others. Even if she didn't want to be a princess, she had her pride.

"Please," she said. "Please, Amina. My mother told me. I have to run."

Chapter Thirteen

JACK RANCIERE, APOTHECARIST TO GENTLEFOLK, HAD stern views about money. In particular, his view was that when money arrived in his pocket, it should stay there. He believed that Pip had swiped his purse several years before when he had been too drunk to really notice what was going on. He had never been able to prove it, but he had seen Pip eating a roast goose at the Crosseyes the day after his purse went missing and it didn't take a genius to put two and two together.

Pip had denied all knowledge and then appeared to forget all about it, but Ranciere never did. He nursed his resentment, biding his time. So when he heard that silver was going begging for any recent news of a young pick-pocket called Pipistrel Wastan, he asked around until he found the right person to talk to.

Yes, he knew this mongrel well. Yes, he had his

address. He lived with his sister, a straw-headed bit called Eleanor. He saw them often at the Crosseyes, plotting together, probably. "You reckon he murdered the old man? And him so young and all! Some is born with hearts as black as pitch. They was probably plotting with Oni, what works there. Thick as thieves, they are, Oni and that Eleanor. Well, they're all thieves, aren't they? Not respectable citizens, like us."

Ranciere sniffed and wiped his nose with his sleeve. The chief assassin, Ariosto, who was dealing with this informant himself, didn't bother to hide his expression of distaste. Bumping up rewards for information was a mistake, he reflected: it usually only resulted in a lot of wasted time chasing false trails. Jack Ranciere, who was smirking up at him from a chair he had not been invited to sit down in, seemed to offer as hopeless a lead as the last.

Ariosto studied his hands and noticed with irritation that his nails needed trimming. "So, who is this Oni?"

"She's a barmaid. Heard her mother is housekeeper up at the Old Palace, but who knows – that's hard to believe. Lives in the Cresy building, up at Ink Street."

The daughter of the Old Palace's housekeeper? Well, that was interesting, if it was true. "I thank you for your time," said Ariosto. He stood up.

"Well, where's my pay?"

"If it turns out that your information is useful, you will be paid."

In his indignation, Ranciere temporarily forgot that he was talking to an assassin. "No, hang on. I know your type. Winkle out valuable information and then go cheapskate. I was all upfront, told you what I know. I should be paid."

"If what you have told me is useful, you will be paid," Ariosto repeated coldly. "If it turns out that you have wasted my time, there will be another kind of payment."

The implied threat penetrated even the alcoholic fog of Ranciere's brain. He smiled obsequiously, bobbing his bald head up and down in a parody of a bow. "Of course, your honour," he said. "Of course."

Ariosto didn't deign to answer. He stared at Ranciere until the man shuffled out of his office, and then clapped his hands. A subordinate appeared instantly, as if he had materialized out of the murky air. Ariosto gave him Pip's address, and told him to search the apartment and to keep a watch.

"And also check the Crosseyes," he said. "Find out if a certain young person called Oni is there. If our information is correct, she lives in the Cresy building in Ink Street. Find her, arrest her and search her domicile."

Chapter Fourteen

"ALL OF YOU, TURNING UP AT THE SAME TIME..."
Amina said. "You came to me tonight, as if you were
called. That means something. Everything is connected."

"You're wise, Mama," said Oni, in a low voice. "That's
why people come to you."

"Maybe. I have to be wise now. But it's hard to be wise
when you're looking in corners and at shadows and the
right thing isn't clear. And I have to be wise for me and
for you. If Georgie disappeared while she was visiting
me, do you think the palace wouldn't think that I did it?
Do you think that the King wouldn't have me thrown
into his torture dungeons? And he wouldn't stop at me.
They'd arrest you too, Oni."

Georgette flushed and bit her lip. She hadn't thought
about that, although she knew how vengeful her father
could be. He was known for punishing whole families.

Once he had ordered an entire village to be burned down. It had been unfair to ask Amina to help her. But there was no one else...

"And then there's you two" – Amina looked at Pip and El – "running from assassins, which means that the Cardinal himself wants what you have."

"Lamir?" Georgette looked at Pip and El with surprise. "Why would the Cardinal be after *them*?"

Pip bridled. "Just because we don't have fancy clothes with fancy lace, it doesn't mean we're unimportant," he said. "I suppose you think—"

"Pip, stop it," said Oni. "The last thing we need is to squabble."

"But she said—"

"I know what she said. She can't help being a princess, any more than you can help being a pea-brain."

"I was only saying," muttered Pip.

"Cardinal Lamir hates people like me with a mortal hatred," said Amina. "And that makes helping Georgie dangerous."

There was a short silence, and then El, who had been gnawing her fingernails, looked up shyly. "People like you?" she repeated. "Does that mean you're a witch, Amina?"

"I craft magic, yes. I have the knowledge, yes. 'Witch'

is not my word. And I was taught other things than the witches in Clarel."

"So what should we do?" El's voice was pitched high and breathless. "I thought maybe you could take that … horrible thing and make it go away."

"I can't do that. It's something that can't be undone."

"But what *is* it?" said Pip. "I found it, and maybe some assassin is going to slit my throat because of it, like poor old Ollie, and I'd kind of like to know *why*."

"If any of you will be quiet long enough for me speak, I'll tell you." Amina paused, a shadow of sadness crossing her face. "El is right: it is a terrible thing. You call it 'the Heart', Pip, and you're right, it is a heart. Maybe you guessed, maybe it told you so itself. The heart of a little boy. A boy who died in such mortal terror that his soul has never found rest, beneath this green earth or above it."

El shuddered. "I knew it. I knew it was an evil thing."

"No child is evil," said Amina. "But evil was done to him." She paused, frowning. "There are many tales about this Heart. A lot of people think it's just a story. I never did, because my grandmother told me how it was made, and what for, and she knew the person who made it. But we all thought it had been lost."

"So it really is magic?" said Pip. "I was sure it was.

The nobles called it a treasure. I thought maybe it was a spell for making money."

Amina laughed out loud at that. "If only it was that simple! But yes, I suppose you could call it a spell. Or maybe a spell-breaker. It was made many years ago, when things in Clarel started turning from bad to worse. But the woman who made it never had the chance to use it."

Georgette was frowning. "I don't understand. What's this Heart, whatever it is, got to do with me?"

"Not everything is about you, Georgie," said Oni.

"I didn't mean it like that," Georgette said, flushing again. "It's just that Amina said before that everything is connected. And I don't see how…"

"Patience, Georgie," said Amina. She looked at Pip. "Show her the Heart, Pip."

Once again, Pip took out the Heart. For some reason he felt less reluctant this time. Maybe it was the candles, which seemed to hold them in a globe of light, keeping the shadows at bay… As he held it out, it pulsed under his hand and he almost dropped it. Georgette stared at it with fascination and then, like Oni, reached out and stroked it with a finger.

"Don't touch it," Amina said sharply, too late. "The fewer who touch it, the better."

Georgette drew back her hand, but she kept staring at it. The colour had ebbed from her cheeks. "It's the boy in my dreams, isn't it, Amina?" she whispered. "Remember, there's always that little boy, crying... He's so, so afraid..."

"What dreams?" said Pip, closing his hand possessively over the Heart and putting it back in his breeches. It didn't seem right that Georgette knew more about his Heart than he did.

Georgette looked up and Pip saw with surprise that her eyes were soft. "Dreams about my mother. There's always a child crying in the dark somewhere, and I can't help him..."

"So you dreamed that dream again?"

Pip thought that Amina was suddenly alert, like a mouse that had caught the scent of a cat and was trying to decide which way to run. He didn't like thinking that.

"Last night. Only this time it was different. This time my mother told me to run. She held my arm so hard she bruised it, and when I woke up..." She pulled back her sleeve to show the yellowing fingerprints on her forearm.

"Your mother is dead," Amina said quietly. "Or should be."

"She's dead in my dream," said Georgie, feeling defensive, although she didn't know why. "She shrivelled up into a pile of bones on the floor. It was horrible. That's never happened before either."

Amina held Georgie's gaze for a few moments, as if she were testing whether what she said were true, and then gave a tiny nod. "That's a good sign," she said cryptically. "We must hope for the best."

"I'm sure that she meant to warn me about King Oswald." Georgette stared at the bruises and then pulled her sleeve back down quickly, as if they shamed her.

"Who's King Oswald?" asked Oni.

"King Oswald of Awemt. I am to marry him. I can't talk my father out of it this time. He threatened to have my head cut off if I disobeyed him."

"Would he really do that?" said El, shocked.

"Probably not," said Georgette gloomily. "But he doesn't like having me as his heir, so if he can't marry me off, he might."

"Oh." El sat back in her chair. "I thought princesses didn't have to do anything they didn't want."

Georgette opened her mouth to explain that she spent her whole day doing things that she didn't want, but thought better of it.

"I met King Oswald last night," she said. "I knew then that I had to run. He frightened me more than anyone I've ever met in my life."

"Why?" said Amina.

"I don't know," said Georgette. "That's the thing. I don't know."

"Does he frighten you more than Cardinal Lamir?"

Georgette was surprised by the question, and thought it over before she answered. "I suppose I'm used to the Cardinal," she said slowly. "I mean, I meet him every week. But when I saw them last night, him and King Oswald. They did seem … alike somehow…" She trailed into silence, frowning.

"I'll tell you what you sensed," said Amina. "Something we have long suspected: that the Cardinal is a Spectre."

As she spoke, the candles guttered in a cold draught, their flames streaming behind them, almost going out. Pip's hair stood up on his neck and all down his spine: it was exactly as if someone had opened a door and the wind had come rushing in. But there were no draughts in Amina's kitchen.

Chapter Fifteen

PIP KNEW THAT THERE WERE THINGS YOU SHOULDN'T name, because naming them called misfortune to your door. He looked uneasily over his shoulder. Maybe there were unseen ears, listening as they spoke. Maybe there was a ghost, right there with them in the room.

Spectres. Maybe even thinking about them was perilous.

Amina put her finger to her lips. She stood up and circled the table, breathing gently on each candle. The flames bent before her breath and then sprang upwards, burning clear and straight, the fragrant smoke curling from each tip. She gazed intently at each candle flame, as if she were inspecting them for flaws, and then returned to her chair.

"Spectres," she said again. "That's what we're talking about."

"And that's to do with the Heart?" said Pip. He could feel a terrible dread opening up inside him, like a great big sinkhole in his middle.

"Oh yes. The Heart in your pocket was made because of Spectres. The boy it belonged to was the chosen vessel for the Spectre King of Clarel."

Pip didn't understand, but he didn't like the sound of any of this. El was right: he should have thrown the Heart away. Why hadn't he listened?

Maybe he had kept the Heart because, underneath everything, he felt a bit sorry for it. This Heart had belonged to a little boy. He tried to imagine what that really meant. He wondered who that child was, and what had happened to him.

El asked the question. "What's a ... Spectre?"

They all looked at Amina, even Oni. For long moments she didn't speak.

"I will tell you a story," she said at last. "But first, I must tell you a little about witches. You have all heard of witches. You know that magic is punishable by death, because the King and the Church say it is evil. And yes, sometimes magic is evil. There is nothing that people make that can't be turned into an instrument for harm. But the craft of magic is not evil. It was made so, in the hands of some who saw its power. They stole it and they broke its laws."

Georgette surreptitiously pulled out a small silver pocket watch and checked it. Amina closed her hand over the watch. "Patience, girl. There will be time." Georgette coloured and put away her timepiece, and Amina went on. "The third rule of magic is that it must never be used selfishly. And this is why."

"Never?" said Pip.

"Never," said Amina.

"So what's the point of having it?"

"See, you would be a bad witch," said El. "You never think about anyone except yourself."

"That's not true!" Pip said, the tips of his ears turning red.

"If you keep interrupting, you won't hear the story." Oni stared hard at Pip, and he had the strangest sensation that his lips had been glued together. He opened his mouth like a fish to check if that were true. Oni wore a mischievous look, and Pip had a sudden conviction that she was using magic on him, which would be typical of her, especially if she was a witch, too, which she almost certainly was. He decided to be quiet, just in case.

Amina sipped her tea. "So. Hundreds of years ago, in a country not far from here, there was a man called Rudolph of Awemt who was very gifted with magic. He rejected the laws because in his arrogance he believed

94

that rules didn't apply to him. He used his powers to serve his own ambition, and eventually he became king. At first he thought he had gained everything he wanted. But he realized that even with all his riches and power, there was something he didn't have. Nothing could prevent him from dying."

Amina was using her storytelling voice, which was hypnotic and comforting, like warm honey. It made Georgette feel that she was seven years old again, when her favourite thing in the world was Amina's stories.

"As he grew older, he became obsessed with death," said Amina. "He gathered astrologers and alchemists and scholars to his court and sent explorers to far lands to find the Fountain of Life. None of them discovered the secret to immortality. And he grew older still, and still he obsessed about his death."

She was silent for a while, her face serious and thoughtful, but this time no one said anything.

"King Rudolph had a son, his heir, and he envied him his youth. As time went by he began to hate him, because his son would take everything that he owned. And at some point, nobody really knows when, he began to practise blood magic. Blood magic is a witch art used in healing, but this king found a way to use it to put his soul inside his son's body."

"He *what*?" said Pip. "What happened to the son?"

"The Prince's soul was devoured by his father, and King Rudolph lived on in his son's body. To everybody else it seemed that the king died, like everyone else dies. But he didn't. After that he began to initiate others into his practice. Sometimes his subordinates, sometimes his allies."

There was a short silence. Pip glanced uneasily at the candles. They seemed to be burning faster.

"A Spectre hasn't escaped death," Amina said. "Like every living thing, a Spectre has died. But they exist beyond their death, not alive, but not dead either. And because their existence isn't life, they are jealous of everything that lives. They want everyone to be like they are, without joy, without love, without beauty. They are parasites who feast on the living and turn them into themselves. And because they refuse to be dead when it is their time, they bring only death."

"But that's awful!" said El.

"It takes a long time to form a Spectre, but because they don't die in the normal ways, they have all the time in the world. Every century there were more of them, always in the royal houses. The Spectres knew that only witches could recognize what they were, and so they began to persecute anyone who knew the craft. Before the Spectres, witches were welcome everywhere, but this changed fast. When King Odo the Fifth of Clarel became a Spectre himself, a hundred years ago, it happened in Clarel too."

Georgette gave a tiny gasp.

"Fifty years ago, a wise woman in Clarel began to wonder how to stop this wickedness. And then something unexpected happened. Axel Blanc, the son of a blacksmith, led a revolt against the Crown and took the throne. After he executed the King, he married the King's daughter, Alisel, to consolidate his claim to the throne, and he threw the King's wife and mistresses and most of his children into the dungeons of this palace. Among them was a prince called Clovis, who was seven years old. Clovis was your great-uncle, Georgie."

"So," said Pip, who was following the story closely, frowning in concentration, "they can be killed, after all?"

"They can be killed, but only with difficulty. Spectres can move through realms, from life to the In Between. That's why we use muffling candles, because if they choose they can eavesdrop from the In Between. Axel chopped off the King's head before he had time to send his soul to his next body; but that just a stroke of luck. And you can be sure that since then, Spectres are much more protective of their mortal bodies."

El looked bewildered and scared. "I don't like this story," she said, her voice wobbling.

"It is a bad story, I agree," said Amina, and smiled reassuringly. "But let me finish. The wise woman I mentioned knew that there were more Spectres in Clarel, even though the King had been killed. And she devised a spell that she said would break the chain of the Spectres. None of us know how she did it, but some people say that she worked out how to double the magic back on the Spectres themselves. What we do know is that to make her spell, she needed the blood of a child who was touched by the Spectres, but had not yet been consumed. Prince Clovis, as the King's chosen vessel, was such a child. So she took work in the prison where he was kept and waited her chance.

"Axel sentenced the Prince to death, because he was the rightful heir, and sent an executioner to the dungeon to carry out the sentence. The witch found him just in time, when his body was still warm. She cut out his heart, and with it, so the story goes, she made a spell that would destroy the Spectres. She put the Heart in a silver casket, bound with powerful spells, so she could use it at the proper time. But she died before she could release the spell, and for a long time we all thought the Heart had been lost."

"And now the Heart's been found," said Oni.

Amina nodded.

"Who was she, that witch?" asked El. "You said your granny knew her."

"She did. She was called Missus Pledge."

"Our Missus Pledge?" said El, her mouth open. "She must have been awful old."

"Old Missus Pledge was the mother of the Missus Pledge you knew."

Pip felt as if all his blood had turned to cold sludge. "Why don't you use the spell, now we've got the Heart?" he said, with sudden violence. "Just do it, and kill all the Spectres…"

"Nobody knows how," said Amina. "That knowledge died with Old Missus Pledge."

Georgette pictured her father. He was different from Cardinal Lamir. Obnoxious, violent, vain, petty, but not … cold. "I hate my father," she said. "But King Oswald is much worse. Is he a Spectre? I think that if he touches me, I will die."

"Rudolph was Oswald's ancestor. Or, to speak more accurately, Oswald is really Rudolph, in another body."

"Then why does he want to marry me?"

Amina considered Georgette, her head cocked to one side. "No doubt he wants the alliance with Clarel," she said. "But there will be other reasons. Spectres only use their own bloodline for their chosen vessels, and all the male children of his former wife are dead. You are the granddaughter of Alisel Livnel, the daughter of Odo Livnel, so your blood is noble. And because your great-grandfather was a Spectre, perhaps he thinks you will give him robust heirs."

There was a horrified silence, which was broken by Georgette. "Why did you never tell me this? Why didn't I know?"

"It wasn't my place to tell you."

"But this makes it all so much worse. I have to escape right away. Now. They're already talking about the wedding, and I know there will be no time for me to come here again because all my time will be dress appointments and lessons of protocol, and I can't…"

"Tonight you will return to the palace, as you always do," said Amina.

It had never occurred to Pip that he could feel sorry for a princess, but he did then. Georgette gasped, and for a moment she seemed to crumple with despair. But it was only a moment; then she straightened herself in her chair, expressionless, but very pale. "I understand," she said. "I didn't think about what it might cost you. I see now…"

"I didn't say that I wouldn't help," said Amina. "I think it's obvious that we can't let Oswald get his hands on you. For now, you will wait. You will behave as normally as you know how. You will do everything that you are told."

"And then?"

"And when it is time, we'll help you escape."

Chapter Sixteen

MOST PEOPLE IN CLAREL AGREED THAT THE CARDINAL was an unusual man. Although he was the highest cleric in the Holy Church of Clarel, and thus very rich, it was well known that he kept none of his wealth for himself.

Cardinal Lamir was personally responsible for the upkeep of at least a dozen orphanages in the city. Every urchin in the land feared being picked up by the watch and imprisoned in these places, which were notoriously cruel. He had also built five poor houses, where the homeless – and there were many of those – could find a bed and a meal, if they were prepared to endure a three-hour evening Mass.

The people of Clarel regarded their Cardinal with equal parts of fear and pride. They boasted to travellers of the generosity of their church, and sometimes even took them to see the nearest orphanages. These were clean, new buildings, if forbidding, and around them were impeccably neat lawns of chamomile and creeping mint that were trimmed by the children themselves. Sometimes the orphans could be seen in the city, walking through the streets in a long line.

There was no denying, all the same, that the Cardinal was as dangerous as he was charitable. The people of Clarel were well aware that it was better to speak well of him, and best to say nothing at all. Those who slighted the Cardinal had a way of turning up in one of the Five Rivers with bits missing.

He was even more unusual than most people realized. Tonight, in the privacy of his own library – a high, elaborately panelled room, which featured the largest collection of grimoires and other works on witchcraft in all Continentia – the Cardinal locked the door and turned around. His gaze flickered suspiciously at the beams of moonlight that thrust through the tall windows, as if they had no right to be there.

He paced across the room towards the long, gilt-framed mirror that hung at the far end of the room. The few guests permitted into this room always looked uneasily at this mirror out of the corner of their eyes. There was, the more sensitive thought, something disturbing about it, as if it were a doorway through which blew an unlucky wind.

The Cardinal smiled mirthlessly at his reflection, which winked back at him. Then he breathed on it and spoke some words in an ancient, forgotten language that no one spoke any more. The surface became opaque with mist, and when it cleared his face looked back at him as before. Only it wasn't quite his own face: its skin was blueish and a little mottled, as if it were on the edge of decay.

Lamir addressed his reflection, "Oracle of the Void, what am I not seeing?"

"It is hard to say," answered the reflection. "There are many shadows. Where there should be lines, there are fractures. Where there should be knowledge, there are holes."

"Has the woman Bemare taken the Stone Heart?"

"As you know, we have no knowledge where the thing is. And you are betraying your fear. Beware. Others will take note."

"We are so close," said the Cardinal. "So close. And the closer we are to the tipping point, the more delicate the affair." He paused, pulling his lip. He could only ask three questions of this apparition, and he only had one left. It was difficult to know which would be most useful.

"Is the woman Bemare a witch?"

"She hath a witchlike air."

"That's not an answer."

The mirror went misty for a few moments, and then the face swam back into focus. "We have not seen her in the ethereal realms," it said. "But she may have another face."

"What does that mean, beyond the ordinary diguises of witches?"

But his three questions were spent. The mirror's surface clouded over, and now he was addressing his everyday reflection.

The original plan had been for the Stone Heart to be retrieved with no fuss; but he had been forced to throw the weight of the assassins and now the Office for Witchcraft Extermination into the search for it. He was beginning to attract notice. Even Ariosto, his most faithful and unquestioning subordinate, was beginning to question why.

It was too early to reveal himself: that had led to their undoing before, when the last Spectre King of Clarel had met his death. The Cardinal shuddered at the thought. No Spectre should ever die. It was against nature.

So close. And yet so far...

Chapter Seventeen

"I DON'T LIKE IT, PIP," SAID EL. "I DON'T LIKE ANY OF this."

"Me neither," said Pip sleepily. "But it could be worse."

It was near midnight the same evening. Pip and El lay under warm woollen blankets on pallets stuffed with straw and lavender in Amina's tiny spare bedroom. Besides the pallets, there was only room for a carved wooden chest that smelt of camphor. A blue woven rug softened the clay tiles. It was the same room they had slept in years and years before, when Amina had brought them in from the street.

Despite everything, they were warm, sheltered and fed. Pip, who by disposition as well as necessity lived almost entirely in the present, was too drowsy to worry.

As on that first night, they were unusually clean.

After Georgette left the Old Palace, Amina had given them supper – a rich, delicious stew – and then looked Pip and El over with a critical eye.

"When did you two last have a bath?"

"I'm clean enough," said Pip. He didn't like bathing, and besides, the grime made him hard to see in shadows, which was useful.

"Face it, Pip," said Oni. "You stink."

Pip was incredulous. "We're being stalked by murderous assassins and supernatural parasites, and you're worried about how I smell?"

"I think a bath is a brilliant idea," said Oni. "Not even your own sister would recognize you without all that dirt."

"It's unhealthy, putting your whole self in water," argued Pip. He had unpleasant memories of his last bath at Amina's, many years ago now. "It's poison. The landlord at the Duck had an old aunt who *died* after she took a bath – just keeled over dead as a doorknob the next day."

"I'm not having vermin in my bedding," said Amina.

"If you give me a basin, I'll flannel myself," Pip said handsomely, as one willing to make a concession.

"A bath it is, then." And a bath it was, despite Pip's vehement protests. Water was boiled, a copper hip bath brought out into the kitchen and Amina arranged a screen, to save Pip's modesty.

El didn't mind washing nearly as much as Pip did. She went first, and after a lot of splashing came out wearing a clean linen nightshift and smelling like a bunch of flowers. Amina and Oni threw out the water and replaced it, and then it was Pip's turn. He disappeared behind the screen, and then poked out his head.

"Into that bath," said Amina.

"What should I do with the Heart?"

"Oh." Amina thought for a while, and then left the room, returning with a small linen pouch. "Put it in this. It has charms against being lost and for good fortune."

Pip took the pouch and vanished again. It was a long time before they heard him getting into the hip bath. He had to unpeel a lot of clothes.

While Pip unwillingly immersed himself in the hot water, Amina combed the nits from El's hair. El leaned against Amina's knee, her eyelids drooping. She remembered when she was little, when she still had a mother to brush her hair. She didn't think about that often because the memories hurt, and it wasn't worth thinking about the old days if they only made you sad. Tonight, she didn't feel sad.

Pip came out from behind the screen a few minutes later, clutching a towel around him, dripping and sulky. Amina looked up and inspected him.

"You're still dirty," she said. "There's a scrubbing brush in there, and soap. Use them. If you don't, I'll come in and scrub you myself."

Oni giggled. Pip threw her a filthy look and disappeared again. This time he took longer, brooding as he scrubbed himself. His pride was hurt by this humiliating and unnecessary ritual, but it would be even worse if Amina bathed him, so he was thorough.

When he finally passed Amina's critical eye, he tied the Heart around his waist and dragged on the nightgown. The linen was pleasantly rough against his skin, and the Heart felt warm again, like it was happy. The Heart belonged to him: he felt this very strongly. He hadn't liked putting it down on the floor where it would be all alone.

He watched Amina combing El's hair. It was spread out in a golden fan across Amina's lap.

"You got pretty hair, El," he said. "It's as pretty as Georgie's."

El opened her eyes and smiled. "You think so, Pip? Really?"

"If you had dozens of flunkeys like she has to make it into curls and things, it would be much prettier than hers."

"You'd never say that about my hair," said Oni.

Pip was going to retort hotly that he had never said it about El before, either, but after the meal Amina had given them earlier, he felt unusually generous. He studied Oni's close-cropped, curly head. "Your hair's really pretty too," he said. "I bet if you had lots of ladies putting gold in it and that it would look like you was a princess."

"I wish I could have dresses like Georgie's," said El dreamily. "And golden necklaces and everything."

"No, you don't," said Oni. "Remember she said that they all stick into her, like pins?"

"You kids," said Amina. "You're like a bunch of magpies. Anybody would think you were five years old."

Oni grinned. "That's just Pip," she said.

El turned to look at Oni. "You never said you knew Princess Georgette," she said, trying to keep accusation out of her voice, but not quite succeeding.

"You both knew Georgie. Don't you remember?"

Pip frowned. He did vaguely remember a blonde-headed girl, one of the many children Amina had helped over the years, who might have been a scruffy version of the Princess. They had never become friends.

He saw El's face shift from recognition to outrage. "But she was a princess. A real princess! I can't believe you never said. Why didn't you tell me, Oni?"

Oni was quiet for a while. "Georgie was just one of us," she said at last. "Mostly. She was around from when I was a baby; she was my milk sister, and then she went to be a princess and I didn't see her again until today. And anything to do with the royals... Well. It's better not to talk."

"Seems there's a lot you never talk about," said Pip.

"For good reason," said Amina. She ran the comb one last time through El's hair. "Your turn, Pip. And, Oni, get the clippers."

"I don't want my hair cut," said Pip quickly.

"All the Cardinal's spies are hunting someone who looks like you," said Amina. "So the less you look like you, the better."

Pip had to admit the sense of that, but he watched sadly as his pigtail fell to the floor. His neck felt chilly without its oily clump of hair.

"What happens now?" he said. "El and me can't go home. And that's all we got, those rooms. Everything we own. What if someone breaks in and steals all our stuff?"

"It's not like we got anything to steal," said El. "Why would they bother? Aside from Missus Pledge's will."

Amina's hands stopped moving. "A will?"

"Missus Pledge told us the will says the rooms are

ours, so nobody can take them away. She showed us the words and explained what they meant."

Amina started combing again. "I would like to see that will," she said.

"Missus Pledge said to keep those papers safe as safe," said Pip. "So we put them under the floor. There's a secret place. Nobody would find it."

"If the Cardinal's men have been through your room, I guarantee they have found it."

"No!" said El. "It's ours!"

"There's nothing to be done now. We'll think what to do tomorrow. Perhaps they haven't found it." She put the louse comb down on the table. "You can get up, Pip."

"What'll we do?" wailed El, wringing her hands. "If we've lost the deed, we got nothing. We got nowhere to go."

"Hush, child. We'll work it out. For now, as you're free of pests, you can sleep in this house. And we all need to sleep." She stood up, brushing off her knees. "You have the Heart safe, Pip?" He nodded. "I'll get on with burning those clothes, then."

Chapter Eighteen

GEORGETTE HAD BAD DREAMS THAT NIGHT. SHE didn't remember any of them when she woke, but they left her with a residue of dread. She was sitting in her nightgown staring at her reflection in the mirror, wondering when Amina would help her escape from the palace, when Duchess Albria, her senior lady-in-waiting, sailed into her chamber. She was holding a gown of stiff cloth of gold that was usually reserved for high festivals.

"Not that one," said Georgette impatiently.

"Oh no, Your Highness," said the Duchess. "This is the only dress in our wardrobe that suits for the betrothal."

"What betrothal?" For a moment Georgette couldn't breathe. "No one has mentioned any such thing."

"Your father informed me earlier that King Oswald offers for your hand today," said the Duchess. "Sadly, your suitor's haste means that we don't have time to have another dress made up, as is proper, but this one is perfectly adequate to this occasion. There are orders in hand for your wedding raiment, of course..."

All Georgette's ladies-in-waiting exclaimed out loud.

"He must be burning with love for you, dear Highness," said Lady Agathe, clasping her hands to her breast. "He saw your face, and he fell. I knew it that evening, when we sent you out. How could any man resist such beauty?"

Georgette rather liked Lady Agathe, despite her silliness. She was kind, which was rare in King Axel II's court, and would be hurt if Georgette snubbed her. All the same, it took all her self-control not to respond sharply.

"No doubt King Oswald has business that he must attend at home," said the Duchess, who never missed the smallest chance to depress Georgette's pretensions. "It isn't good for a ruler to be absent from his realm for long."

"Probably," said Georgette, as lightly as she could. "So when is this ceremony to take place? And how will I know what to say?"

"My understanding, Your Highness, is that you need say nothing." The Duchess picked up the bodice. "Allow me, Ma'am."

Automatically the Princess held out her arms to permit the Duchess to fit the bodice around her chest,

114

drawing it tight as she did up the tiny pearl buttons that ran down the back. Georgette hated this dress at the best of times. It was so stiff and tight that she could scarcely breathe inside it, and the gold thread woven through the silk was so heavy it was hard to move.

Georgette had often thought that when she became Queen, she would start new court fashions: light, comfortable dresses that were soft against your body, and that never made you sweat like a pig in summer. The way things were going, she would never be Queen now.

Be obedient, Amina had said. *Be good and dutiful.* Georgette reminded herself that a royal wedding, even a rushed royal wedding, couldn't happen in three days. It wasn't proper unless there was pomp, and pomp takes time. Georgette forced a smile, but couldn't bring herself to respond to the chatter and speculation. Her ladies-in-waiting put her silence down to anxiety, which was only natural, so handsome as her suitor was, and of course, having a new court far away in a strange city...

It was difficult to remain calm. Georgette had no idea how Amina planned to help her escape this marriage. She couldn't help wondering if Amina had deceived her, to make her go home without protesting. Hurtful though that thought was, Georgette could understand such an action. She might have done the same thing herself. The

Princess's rank would be some sort of shield if plans went awry, but Amina would have no protection at all.

On the other hand, Amina had never lied to her before. It was one of the reasons Georgette trusted her.

The betrothal was to take place in the throne room immediately after chapel that morning. The Princess had enough time to collect herself, and by the time she was escorted to the throne room, pacing slowly towards the royal dais past rows of solemn nobles, she had perfected an icy, expressionless exterior: the blank face suitable for a baby-making queen, that gave nothing away. After she curtsied before her father, she looked up and briefly caught Queen Theoroda's eye, and realized that her stepmother wore exactly the same expression.

Georgette's betrothal was likely a death sentence for the Queen: King Axel had no reason to be married to her, as he no longer needed the alliance she had brought with her. And the King, still desperate for a male heir, could only marry again if he were a widower. Even in the midst of her own distress, even though she heartily disliked the Queen, Georgette felt a pang of pity.

The Duchess had been correct: she needed to say nothing. King Axel, after making a short and pompous speech about the peace that would reign between two kingdoms and the union that would seal it in the bodies

116

of these two young royals, took her hand and placed it in King Oswald's. His hand was as cold as a pane of glass on a winter morning. The dread of her nightmare returned, thick in her throat: now the trap was closing, and she had nowhere to run.

King Oswald stepped out to the front of the dais and held their linked hands high. The courtiers and officials stood and applauded. And that was it. Now she was betrothed, there was no getting out of the wedding. She hadn't even been given the chance to refuse. She wasn't permitted to say anything at all.

Georgette numbly received the congratulations of the important nobles who were seated with the King. Cardinal Lamir smiled, if a mere curve of the mouth could be considered a smile. Queen Theoroda had turned pale to her very lips. Then the Duchess escorted the Princess back through the throne room. The lesser nobles all bowed as she passed, like a field of grass before a breath of wind.

Nobody watching would have thought that Georgette was in complete despair.

I'm nothing more than a cow for sale to the highest bidder, she thought bitterly. *I've never been anything else. Why did I ever think I was?*

For the first time, she understood why the other

suitors had failed in their petitions for her hand. It wasn't because of her cleverness at all. It was because the most powerful men in the kingdom had other plans.

Chapter Nineteen

"NO. AND THAT'S FINAL."

"But, Ma…"

"Oni, I swear if you don't listen to me on this, I will…"

Pip, watching from near the kitchen stove, thought that Amina was going to explode with rage. It was a bit frightening when Oni and Amina fought, and they'd been quarrelling for almost an hour now.

"Ma, you can't tell me what to do. I'm not five any more." Oni was at the door, already lifting the latch. "I have my own house. I make my own money."

"That's not the point. It's too dangerous."

"It *is* the point, Ma." Oni opened the door. She was about to pass over the threshold when she turned around and smiled mischievously. "I know how to hide, Ma. I know all the tricks. I know because I was taught by the best in the business: you." She blew a kiss, and then shut the door gently behind her.

For a few moments there was a charged silence while Pip and El sought uncomfortably for something to say.

To their surprise, Amina started laughing.

"She's my daughter, all right," she said. "Damn it."

Oni left the Old Palace the same way they had come, darting through the cover of the overgrown gardens. It was just after sunrise. Pools of mist gathered in the hollows, wisping up into nothing where beams of sunshine pierced the trees. When she reached the broken fence, she checked carefully before she crept out, then drew her hood over her head and walked briskly down the deserted street.

It took her an hour or so to make her way to Pip and El's building. By then people were out, hurrying to the bakeries for their morning bread or opening stalls in the marketplace. The sky was a clear, pale blue, letting fall its light like a blessing on the narrow lanes of the Choke Alleys. The tenements and peeling shops and taverns looked almost pretty, although it would take a lot more than sunshine to do anything about the smell in this quarter. It was going to be a perfect summer day.

Oni's pace slowed when she reached Omiker Lane. It was a tiny street the length of six buildings, all in varying states of decay, and the sun hadn't reached it yet. Oni wondered if it was just the coldness of the shadows that made her shiver as she sauntered along, pretending she was just another passer-by.

Pip and El lived in a building in the middle of the street. Most of the windows were shuttered and the doorways were empty, aside from a cat that studied Oni balefully as she passed. She might have felt less uneasy if she had spotted someone who looked like an assassin. If watchers weren't outside they were likely to be inside, and they would be more difficult to avoid.

She turned down Hangers Alley at the end of Omiker Lane and slid into a gap between two shops that was scarcely wide enough to admit even her slight body. The stench hit her like a wall: the buildings leaned in close together above her head so there was nowhere for it to escape.

This ground was slimy with every kind of refuse, making her very glad of her boots. Oni drew her scarf over her mouth and nose, in case some filthy winged thing flew in by mistake, and grimly pushed on. There was nothing she could do about the smell, but if you breathed through your mouth it was easier to ignore.

After a few yards the gap between the buildings broadened slightly. She was now treading on bare, sour earth and the stink wasn't so bad. On one side the noisome, stained walls were pierced with shuttered windows, which once had looked out on something other than another wall less than two feet away. The other side was completely blank. A tiny slit of sky above permitted some indirect light, but it was hard to see. At last Oni found what she was looking for: a copper pipe, green with age, trailed uncertainly down to the ground from the roof. Oni studied it dubiously. This, apparently, was Pip's emergency back door.

She tested the pipe and found it was surprisingly stable, though slippery under her hands. She was about the same weight as Pip, so she figured it would probably hold. She took a deep breath and started to scale the pipe.

As Pip had said, it wasn't a difficult climb: there were plenty of gaps in the stonework to hang on to. The higher she got, the narrower the gap became between the buildings. By the time Oni reached the third-floor shutters, the opposite wall was little more than a foot away. Her hands were aching and she leaned back, letting the other wall take her weight, and wiped her forehead as she studied the closed shutters. According to Pip's instructions, this was the window to their bedroom.

She took out a knife from her belt and slid it up the gap between the shutters, lifting the latch that held them closed. And then, cautiously and slowly, she pulled one leaf open. This was awkward as the shutters opened outwards and she couldn't pull it all the way. To peek in the window, she was forced to climb down a little and twist herself around the shutter. She tried not to look down. It was a long way.

Pip and El's bedroom. Two pallets, for sleeping. Some pretty things El had collected – a piece of floral material pinned up on the wall, a chipped china dog, three cups painted with roses. She could see the short hallway that led to the main room. She pictured it in her head: the chest and stools for eating, a fireplace with a hob for cooking. On the mantelpiece, a silver sauce jug with a curved handle that had once belonged to Missus Pledge.

Oni studied the shadows dubiously. Was the left corner a little darker than it should be? Or was that her imagination? She dared not climb inside without first ensuring that the room was as empty as it seemed.

It was going to be difficult performing magic when she was hanging by her fingernails three storeys up, but she had no choice. She shifted herself around so she was squarely facing the window and then, making sure her feet were firmly lodged into crevices in the stonework, let go of the pipe, leaning all her weight on the opposing wall. When she was sure that her feet were stable, she drew out a little wooden box from a cloth bag that hung around her neck and flicked it open. Inside was a fine black powder that seemed to sparkle in the dim light. Oni dipped in her fingertip and put a little of the dust on each of her eyelids, and then carefully sprinkled a fine trail of it on the windowsill, mumbling the charm under her breath.

"Show these eyes what is hidden. Protect me from those who wish me harm. May all the beneficent spirits protect this child of light, who asks so humbly for their help."

She closed her eyes, waiting for the faint sting that meant the spell was beginning to work. Her pulse quickened and she felt an uncomfortable sensation of heat in her eyeballs, as if they were being cooked inside her head. It passed quickly. She breathed out, and slowly opened her eyes.

This spell always made her feel slightly nauseous. A sense other than sight kicked into focus, making her aware of every living thing in the building. Objects that had seemed solid were now blurred and insubstantial, colourless shadows that shimmered in a dim luminescence. She could see through walls, which made it hard to assess distance.

The tenement was alive with blurred, silverish

people. Some of them were sleeping, others were eating, two people seemed to be arguing. Other kinds of glows, cats, mice, rats… Up in the attic, a dead baby was lying in a crib. Two house sprites, mischiefs and ratterbags, were gathered around it. They were benign spirits who rarely meant any harm, but they were always curious about death…

Oni shook herself. She had to concentrate because she didn't have a lot of time. A Spectre, or anything else supernaturally hidden, looked different from both the living and the dead. She had never seen one before, but Amina had told her how to look for them. They weren't easy to find, Amina had said, but they were unmistakable. She said you felt them as much as you saw them.

Oni scanned the building carefully. It seemed clear, but some intuitive caution made her check again. No, nothing. Wait, there was a man near by. Oni guessed he was standing on the stairwell outside Pip and El's room. Unlike everyone else in the building, he was utterly still. She waited for a while, seeing if he would move, but he didn't twitch a muscle.

It had to be an assassin.

For a moment she regretted ignoring her mother's warning. Nobody would blame her for not going in. But she was so close, and she had to check. Before she could talk herself out of it she unlatched the window, which to her relief opened inwards, and climbed inside. Every tiny creak, every muffled movement, seemed unnaturally loud. She crouched on the floor like a lizard that had been spotted by a snake.

Hardly daring to breathe, she crept down the hallway to the main room. Pip had told her that the loose floorboard was underneath the chest. She pulled the chest as quietly as she could along the floor, her heart in her mouth, but still the man outside the room didn't move. It took a little while before she found the right board and prised it up.

She reached inside the hole in the floor and felt around. There was nothing there. She almost didn't believe it, and checked again to make sure. No parchment, no will, no deed, nothing.

She swore under her breath. And then she saw, out of the corner of her second sight, that the man was coming towards the door. For a moment she froze, and then she went to replace the floorboard. In her fear she dropped it and it clattered to the ground. Suddenly the man was moving fast. Oni scrambled backwards along the hallway. The spell had faded completely by the time she reached the bedroom so she couldn't see the assassin, but she heard the door open. Did he have a key? Of course he had a key. Assassins could get into any room they wanted, everyone knew that.

The window had swung shut on its weight while she had been in the other room, and somehow it had become stuck. Oni forgot about concealment: she was purely terrified now. Her fingers were clumsy, all thumbs, and she couldn't yank it open. Oni was still struggling with it when the man stepped into the bedroom – tall, thin, dressed all in black; dim, pitiless eyes.

She turned at bay, trapped and desperate, and drew her knife.

The assassin strode the two paces across the dark room and grabbed her arm, making her drop the knife. Oni twisted and bit him as viciously as she could. He let go, cursing, and slapped her hard across the face. She fell down and he pulled her up, twisting her arm behind her back so she cried out.

"Well, well, well," said the man. "What filthy little thief do we have here?"

Oni, bent over against the pain in her arm, felt hot tears of rage running down her face. Why hadn't she listened to her mother?

"Don't think I'll forget that bite, maggot," he said. "But luckily for you, someone wants you alive."

"Let go of me," said Oni. She kicked his shins with

her heels and he jerked her arm up so she gasped. "Let me go."

"No more struggling," he said. His voice was cold. "Or I'll ignore my orders and slit your throat from ear to ear."

He was bigger than she was, and stronger. There wasn't any point fighting. Oni let herself go limp, and the man relaxed his grip so only the threat of pain was there.

"Good boy," said the man. "Certain people are very interested in you. If you're helpful, you might even get through this with a whole skin."

Oni realized the assassin thought she was Pip. "I'm not a boy," she said scornfully. "You got the wrong person."

He grabbed her chin and pulled her face into the dim light. She saw surprise and chagrin in his eyes.

"See?" said Oni. "You might as well let me go."

"Oh, I'm not doing that," he said. "I'm curious, see? I have so many questions. Why would an Eradian be creeping into this particular apartment on this particular day? What are you looking for?"

While he spoke, Oni was trying to think what spell she could make with her hands behind her back. You can't just think spells, you have to make them with your lips or your fingers or your breath. You need time and space. She had neither. And her mind was blank; everything she knew had been wiped away by panic. Her mother was right: she wasn't ready, she had too much to learn...

But something was altering in the room, as if there were a spell happening already. She could feel magic lifting the hairs on her arms. A cold magic, cold as the assassin's eyes, but there was a strange heat in it. No, it was luminous ... something was glowing ... a green glow, getting brighter and brighter every instant.

The assassin saw the light reflected in Oni's eyes and turned around, letting her go. He straightened up, staring, his back to her. Oni came out of her trance and leapt for the window, wrenching it open. Even then the assassin didn't react; he seemed to have forgotten all about her. She scrambled over the ledge, almost falling out head first, and saved herself at the last moment by grabbing the pipe. There was a blinding flash and then the room went dark.

Oni knew, somehow, that the room was now empty.

She didn't remember how she got down the pipe, how she hurtled along the tiny alley out into the street. Her next memory was of being three blocks away, bent over, trying to catch her breath.

That was bad magic. Very bad magic. Cold like

something dead, like an absence that shouldn't be there. She felt it with every hair on her body, deep down in the marrow of her bones.

But whatever it was, it had saved her life.

Chapter Twenty

WHEN ONI TOLD THE OTHERS THAT THE PAPERS HAD gone, El started to cry, but not for long because there wasn't a lot of point.

"What are we going to do, Pip? We got nowhere to go now."

"We still got our place," said Pip stoutly. "Everybody knows it's ours."

"But Missus Pledge, she said we needed the deed, so no one could take it away."

"We can't go there now, anyway."

"I wish you never took that box. I wish I never saw that Heart. It's all spoiled."

"What, our beautiful lives?"

"It was all right," said El. She sniffed and went to wipe her nose on her sleeve and then stopped herself and took out a clean handkerchief. Amina had given them both new clothes, and she didn't want to dirty her dress.

"No, it wasn't."

The siblings started to argue. Oni rolled her eyes and for the first time looked at Amina. Their gazes locked and she went quiet for a while, and then flashed her mother a rueful smile.

"I'm sorry, Ma," she said. "You were right."

"Next time, listen," said Amina. "I've only got one of you."

"What do you think that magic was?"

Amina frowned. "I don't want to guess," she said.

"It was bad, Ma. It made me feel all sick inside."

Amina was silent for a few moments, staring at the wall. "I think it's a Rupture," she said. "And if it is, it would most likely have been caused by the Heart." She looked at Pip. "Pip?"

Pip was still in the middle of listing all his grievances, and didn't hear her.

"Shut up, Pip," said Oni, cuffing him gently. "Ma's asking you something."

"Has the Heart done anything odd today? Did anything change while Oni was out?"

"It went really cold this morning, just for a little while. Sometimes it feels like this ball of ice."

"When was that?"

"When we were shelling the beans."

Amina thought. "About an hour ago," she said. "That would have been about when Oni was in your place.'

"You think the Heart saved Oni?"

"Maybe." Amina directed her gaze at her daughter. "Did you touch it?"

Oni nodded slowly. "When Pip showed me. I felt sorry for it," she said. She glanced at Pip. "It was warm, like it was skin."

"Then maybe it has a connection to you," said Amina.

"But Pip touches it all the time!" El said. "What does that mean? Is it going to hurt him?"

"I don't know," said Amina. "It's a powerful magical artefact, which means danger. I think Pip has to be very careful. What do you feel about the Heart, Pip?"

Pip, his attention arrested, thought it over. "I feel ... that it likes me," he said slowly. "Like it's a person. It wants to be looked after. It doesn't want to be left alone, because it's lonely." His hand automatically went to his hip, where the Heart now lay in the deep buttoned pockets of his new breeches. "I think it's on our side."

"It's not on anybody's side," said Amina sharply. "You remember that."

Pip nodded, but he didn't agree. If the Heart was making assassins disappear, it was definitely on their side.

"So who do you think stole our will?" he said, to change the subject. "And why? What would assassins want with our place?"

"I don't think it is a will," said Amina.

"It is so!" said El hotly. "Missus Pledge told us! She showed us the words and everything, the squiggly shapes that meant Eleanor and Pipistrel, so we'd know what it said."

Amina smiled. "Maybe it's a will as well," she said. "Things can have more than one purpose."

"It's just an old parchment, in red and black ink and special writing," said El. "It didn't look magic. Just important."

"It might be the instructions on how to use the Heart," said Amina. "Missus Pledge might have had it from Old Missus Pledge."

"Maybe it's just what El and Pip think it is," said Oni.

"Maybe it is, maybe it isn't," said Amina. "But we won't know until we get it back."

El looked up, her eyes shining with hope. "Are we going to get our papers back, Amina?"

"If the assassins took them, they would have given them to Cardinal Lamir," said Oni.

"Exactly."

"But how would you get them back from him?"

"I don't know yet," said Amina. She drummed her fingers on the table, thinking, and then reached a decision.

"I'm going out. I need to talk to the Witches' Council. All of you, stay here – even you, Oni. I don't want you going back to your place, or to work. Don't make any noise. And don't answer the door."

"When will you be back, Ma?"

Amina, putting on a bonnet and coat, didn't answer. Instead, she turned to Pip. "Think good thoughts, boy. It might make the Heart behave itself."

As the door swung shut behind her, Pip stared at Oni. "Think good thoughts?" said Pip. "What sort of good thoughts?"

"I don't know," said Oni. "But think them anyway."

Chapter Twenty-one

THERE WAS GOING TO BE A STORM. SIBELIUS FELT THE oppressive airs bearing down on him, and he had the slight headache he always got behind his eyes when the weather changed. He stood up from his desk, stretched his arms and walked to the window, unlatching it and opening it wide. From here, an attic room on the fifth floor of the Cardinal's palace, he could see over the roofs of the city, past the smoke-stained churches and crumbling palaces of the centre of Clarel to the tangled streets beyond. The sun hung blindingly in the sky, bleaching it white.

All afternoon, since he had finished his duties at Clarel Palace, he had been staring at a grubby length of parchment. It appeared to be the Last Will and Testament of one Mistress Prunelissima Arabella Pledge, spinster and seamstress of Omiker Lane of the Chokally Quarter. She left all her worldly goods, including the key and deed to her rooms, Apartment IV on Floor III of Number II Omiker Lane, to Pipistrel and Eleanor Wastan, citizens.

There followed a list of items: a silver cream jug, thirty needles of sundry sizes and fifteen packets of pins, an itemized store of silks and velvets, a set of china missing three plates, a purse that held the money for her funeral, which was to be simple and dignified… Signed and witnessed. It was written on the back of what appeared to be the deed to the apartment. The document was very wordy for a deed, and included a plan of the apartment with its dimensions painstakingly rendered, from the heights of each wall, to the size of the bedroom window.

The will had been taken from the apartment the day before by one of Cardinal Lamir's minions. The Cardinal seemed certain it contained a clue to the workings of the Stone Heart. The document was slightly eccentric, perhaps, but it was hardly evidence of witchcraft. The woman used no witch codes; everything was written in conventional script.

But Sibelius had to find something. His life depended on it.

He had requested that someone verify the measurements of the room, just to be certain, since the numerals were likely the most fruitful place to start. He had no word back, but he was sure they would match. Doors and windows and ceilings in such buildings were generally about those sizes.

He was familiar with how cunning witches could be in hiding their nefarious practices. Perhaps this document was particularly cunning. He had no idea why Cardinal Lamir was so convinced of the sinister purpose behind the humble parchment, but he was afraid of what might happen if he reported that it meant nothing. He had to investigate every possible secret hidden in these spidery words.

Perhaps there was an invisible script which required some treatment before it became manifest. Some appeared when you heated the parchment, some when you soaked it in milk. If it was a magic text, he would need a spell to unlock it. But he didn't know any spells.

He gloomily watched the clouds gathering on the horizon. When he turned back to his desk, he realized he was hungry. He irritably rang for a servant to bring him food, and sat down with a sigh, mopping his brow.

He had to find something. Anything.

Chapter Twenty-two

AMINA RETURNED AT DUSK. SHE LOOKED PLEASED, but wouldn't talk about what she'd said to the Witches' Council, although El was burning with impatience. "You'll find out in good time," she said. "And for now, there's food to make. Get peeling those turnips."

"Did you find out how to get our will back?" asked El.

"Maybe," said Amina. "Maybe not. I've found somewhere for you to sleep for now. You can't stay here. I have work to do."

Pip, who was chopping carrots into randomly sized pieces, was interested. "Where?"

"Keep your eyes on your work, or it will be your finger that gets sliced."

Even Oni's wheedling didn't work, so they all did what they were told, and watched as Amina threw the results of their labour into an iron pot and swung it over the fire.

"Now," said Amina, and gathered the scented candles she had used the night before. She had just put the last one in place when there was a knock on the door. Everyone froze.

"Out into the garden," Amina said, sweeping up the candles and stuffing them into a drawer. "And be quiet. It's probably one of my officials wanting a window fixed or something, but I don't want you seen."

Oni, El and Pip sat on a bench against the wall, hidden from the view of the window. Out of the cool of Amina's kitchen it was stuffy and breathless, even though the sun had already set. Swarms of midges danced in the shadows. El, who didn't like the heat, sat fanning herself, uncomfortably flushed. She opened her mouth to complain and Oni put her finger over her lips. "Ma said hush, right?"

El pouted, but obeyed. Pip had a bad feeling in his gut, but he wasn't going to say so. Mind you, he had had a bad feeling ever since El had told him about old Olibrandis.

Nothing happened for a while. Then they heard muffled voices in the kitchen – men's voices. El watched Oni creep to the window and crouch beneath it so she could hear. The voices grew louder, and then there was Amina's voice, raised in indignation. Pip still couldn't hear what

140

anyone was saying, but he was suddenly aware that the Heart was growing cold against his hip.

Oni looked over to El and Pip, her eyes wide, and then flung herself at them and began pulling them towards the little gate in the garden wall. She muttered something as she opened the latch, and the gate, which usually creaked impressively, made no noise at all. She pushed the others outside and closed it behind her. They were now in the park of the Old Palace, in the suffocating darkness under the tangled trees.

"What happened?" whispered Pip.

"*Ssssh,*" said Oni. "We got to get out of here."

"Oni, I don't feel good," said El. "It's bad here. I can't breathe…"

"Hold hands so we don't lose each other," said Oni. "Quickly. Come on."

It was hard to move quickly. Oni led them through the undergrowth, avoiding open spaces. At first the Heart was so cold against Pip's hip that it hurt his skin, but the further they moved from the Old Palace the warmer it became. He felt sure they were going in circles, but at last they found the fence and, after a little difficulty, the hole in the railings. Oni pushed them through the gap and into the street.

"Now," she said. "Walk normal, like we're just out for a bit of air."

"I don't think El can walk normal, Oni," said Pip, pulling at her elbow. "I think she's going to have one of her turns."

Even in the dim light, you could see that El was very pale. She was gasping for air, and her lips were a blueish colour.

"El, we got to move on from here," said Oni. "Do you think you can?"

El nodded slowly.

"Could you do some magic on her?" asked Pip, trying to hide his anxiety. El's turns could be frightening, and they didn't have Missus Pledge's medicines, which were back in their apartment.

"I haven't got the right things," said Oni. She studied El's face, and then put her palm on El's chest, which was heaving with the effort of trying to breathe. "El, please don't panic. It makes it worse."

El didn't have the breath to answer. Oni shut her eyes, pressing lightly on her chest. To Pip's surprise, after a few moments the touch seemed to make a difference. The horrible wheezing noise abated, and El was able to stand up.

"I'm. All right," said El. "Not good. But. All right."

They walked away from the Old Palace, trying to look like a group of friends out for a stroll in the balmy evening. Oni headed towards the yellow lamps of the night markets near by, which were busy with people buying food for Midsummer Day. The Midsummer Festival was a big holiday in Clarel and, like most people they knew, Pip and El had been planning to go to the Weavers' Quarter to join in the dancing. That seemed ages ago. Pip reflected gloomily that they wouldn't be dancing this year, for sure.

All the same, he felt a little safer in a crowd. He turned to Oni. "You got to tell us what happened there," he said.

"They took Ma," she said, and he heard the tremble in her voice.

"They what? Who?"

"They were from the Office for Witchcraft Extermination. Where assassins come from. They asked about me, and then they wanted to know about you two. And when she said she didn't know what they were talking about, they said she had to come with them. And when she told them they were mistaken, they threatened her."

"Oh, Oni!" El's chest began to heave again, and Pip looked at her in concern. "I'm so sorry. It's all because of us…"

"It can't be helped now." Oni set her jaw so she wouldn't cry. "She told me to run, and that was it."

"But where can we run to?" El asked. "We can't go

home. We can't go to your place…"

Pip was frowning. "She told you to run? When?"

Oni opened her hand. On the ball of her thumb there was a faint, oddly shaped red scratch.

"It says, 'Run'."

El touched the mark with the tip of her finger, and even as she did, it faded altogether. "Is that a word, Oni? Couldn't she send other words, if she sent that one?"

"It was risky for her to even do that," said Oni. Now they could tell she was trying very hard not to cry. "They know to look for witchmarks. Maybe they'll burn her."

"They wouldn't do that, would they?"

"I don't know." Oni shook herself, and when she spoke again, her voice was hard, under control. "We can't talk here. We have to keep going."

They threaded through the crowd. As far as Pip could tell, nobody was looking at them. The Heart was cool against his skin. Why hadn't it rescued Amina, like it had rescued Oni? And what could they do now? He was in a part of the city that was outside his own territory, and that made him as nervous as anything else. He didn't have any secret boltholes here.

"Where can we go, Oni?"

"We're going to a safe house. To Missus Orphint," said Oni. Her first impulse had been to go to her aunt's house in the Weavers' Quarter, but that meant going through the Choke Alleys and she wanted to avoid anywhere near Pip and El's apartment.

"Who's Missus Orphint?"

"You'll see."

"I just want to sit down," said El. "I'm so tired."

"We can't rest yet, Ellie," said Pip, taking her hand. "But we will, I promise."

Oni was surprised by the tenderness in Pip's voice. She hadn't seen this side of him before. She held El's other hand, pressing it reassuringly. "It's a bit of a way," she said. "But we don't need to hurry now." *Much*, she added mentally.

She didn't mention that a storm was coming. They could all sense it.

Missus Orphint lived a couple of miles away, near the Brein, one of the Five Rivers. Oni prayed that they'd make it before the rain came down. El was concentrating on trying to breathe, and Pip was distracted. He was feeling disturbed about the Heart.

When he had taken El's hand the Heart had gone cold again, so suddenly and sharply that it was like it bit him. Like it was jealous.

He was trying to put together the little he knew about the Heart. It was what was left of a little boy called

145

Clovis, who was a prince. Probably a spoiled, brattish, selfish kid, who was used to having servants to wipe his arse for him. And he didn't like it when Pip felt warm towards El. Pip recalled what Amina had said: *It's not on anybody's side.*

Maybe he should try talking to it...

Don't you have sisters? he asked experimentally, inside his head.

I hate my sisters, said a voice.

Somehow Pip wasn't surprised that the Heart had answered. It was as if he already knew that it would.

Well, I don't hate mine, said Pip. *She's all I got. So you be nice, all right? Or I really will throw you in the river. You caused me enough trouble.*

The Heart went so cold that it stung him, but Pip set his teeth and ignored it.

I mean it, he said. *About the river.*

The Heart didn't answer this time. It just kept getting colder and colder. And then Pip thought he saw a tiny quiver of green light at the edge of his sight. Something like the thing Oni had described, in their own apartment: the bad magic that had swallowed up the assassin.

So that was the Heart's game, was it?

All of a sudden Pip was sick of everything. El was right: the Heart had been a terrible misfortune. They were hunted and homeless, and everyone who helped them was suffering too. Oni couldn't go back to her home, and Amina had been arrested. Who knew what would happen next?

Go on, swallow us all up, said Pip bitterly. *See if I care. Then the Spectres will get hold of you and that will be the end of all of us. But especially of you…*

The green flicker disappeared.

All right then, said Pip.

The Heart said nothing. But very slowly, so slowly that at first Pip didn't feel any difference, it began to warm up.

Chapter Twenty-three

MISSUS ORPHINT WAS A TALL, BESPECTACLED WOMAN with iron-grey hair and very white skin, as if she never went out in the sun. She looked down at the three young people who stood on her doorstep with an air of mild bewilderment.

"Oni Bemare!" she said. "What on earth are you doing here?"

"I'm sorry to just turn up, Missus Orphint. Can we come inside?"

"Of course, my dear. Of course." Missus Orphint held open the door and they filed into a tiny corridor barely wide enough for one person. They followed her into a kitchen that was surprisingly cool. A black cat, stretched out on the flagstones, opened one green eye and regarded them suspiciously.

"Sit down, all of you," said Missus Orphint, waving

vaguely towards the table. She studied them over her spectacles. "You look thirsty. Not at all surprising in this weather. I have some nice mint tea, which I'm sure you'll agree is very refreshing. And then perhaps you can tell me why you're here."

They watched in silence as she poured out a pale green drink from a tall glass jug and placed three mugs before them. El, who had been struggling for the past hour, wheezed loudly in the silence.

"I think we should do something about your breathing, child," said Missus Orphint.

"That's El," said Oni, remembering her manners. "And this is Pip. El's got short breath."

"Then we had better make it longer, yes?" Missus Orphint looked at El for permission, and then felt her pulse and her back. "Yes, it's definitely asthma. Most unpleasant. I suffer a little myself, in the season of roses."

"I think ... Missus Pledge ... called it that..." said El, between gasps.

"You knew Missus Pledge? An excellent woman. Wait here – I shall return."

She drifted out of the kitchen, and Pip and Oni exchanged glances. "Are you going to tell her about Amina?" he said.

"We have to deal with El first."

"I'm not … something … you deal with…" said El sulkily. "It's not like … I can help it."

"Don't try to talk, El, until you feel better," said Pip.

They sat in silence. Missus Orphint's kitchen was nothing like the large, orderly room that belonged to Amina. It wasn't a little room, but it seemed small because it was cluttered with all sorts of objects. The more Pip looked, the more he saw. There was cookware and crockery, of course, but every available wall space was covered with shelves. There was a row of straw dolls, a curiously carved nutcracker, a number of animals made of blown glass in different colours…

Mrs Orphint returned with a phial of clear liquid. "Drink this," she said. "It tastes a little nasty, but it will help. Luckily I had some by." She waited until El had followed her instructions, and then, as Oni had done earlier, she placed her hands on El's chest. The wheezing stopped almost at once and some colour returned to El's face. Pip had never seen El respond so quickly, even when Missus Pledge had still been alive, and he looked at Missus Orphint with respect. She must definitely be a witch.

"There," said Missus Orphint, settling herself at the table. "Now, we're all comfortable, yes?" She smiled at them myopically. "I am pretty sure I know why you're here, so we needn't discuss that just now. But am I right in thinking there are further developments?"

"They took Ma," said Oni. "They came to her place looking for us, and they took her. And now we got nowhere to go."

Mrs Orphint pushed her spectacles up her nose. "Oh dear," she said.

"Amina had made plans," said Pip. "But she didn't get to tell us what they were."

"The first thing is not to panic. Missus Bemare is a very capable woman, and I'm sure they will be forced to let her go."

"But the Office for Witchcraft Extermination never let people go," said Oni. She blinked back tears. "People go into their dungeons and you never hear from them again. Everyone knows that…"

"That's true, my dear, but the Office hasn't arrested a single real witch for more than a hundred years, except by mistake." Mrs Orphint pushed her spectacles up her nose. "They've arrested people they thought were witches, of course. Usually unfortunate old women, who deserved none of the cruelties visited upon them."

"But they took Ma away."

"My dear, your mother is very likely quite safe," said

Mrs Orphint. "I doubt they actually know anything. And she is a royal housekeeper. If they don't let her go, a lot of people in the Old Palace will complain bitterly. Nobody likes it when the privies aren't cleaned..."

Pip was finding Mrs Orphint rather disconcerting. At first she had seemed vague, a dotty old woman, but the more she spoke, the less vague she seemed. It was as if a mist were lifting. Maybe her air of bewilderment was, he thought, a kind of disguise.

She was talking of Amina's arrest as if it were only a minor problem. He had to admit that it was comforting.

"What if they don't let her go?" he said.

"Maybe things are different now," said Oni. "Because of the ... because of the..." She didn't want to name the Heart out loud.

"If they don't, we shall just have to help her get out, won't we?" Mrs Orphint smiled around the table. "But let's just see first if that happens. What we really need to think about is what to do with you three."

"Ma said she was going to see the Witches' Council," said Oni. "But we don't know what she planned."

"She wanted to ensure that the Princess could leave the palace," said Missus Orphint.

"She spoke to you about Georgie?" said Oni.

"Yes, very briefly. And obviously about *other things*."

152

"Well, we can't worry about the Princess now," said El. "She'll be all right – she's a royal. It's Amina we have to worry about."

"Unfortunately, we have to worry about everything at once," said Missus Orphint. As she spoke there was an ominous rumble of thunder, and she glanced out of the window. A few heavy drops were beginning to fall. "You made it here before the storm, well done. I was just about to have something to eat. Let's deal with the important things first."

She refilled their mugs and then opened a cupboard and took out a large pie crowned with golden pastry. A fragrant smell of cheese and herbs filled the kitchen. The cat yawned and jumped onto the chair she had just vacated.

"No, you've had your supper, Amiable," Missus Orphint said, putting the pie on the table and flicking the cat gently on her nose. She smiled at her three weary guests. "I made it this afternoon. I must have known you were coming. So eat up, and then you can tell me everything that's happened."

Later, after she had put her guests to bed in her attic, Missus Orphint poured herself a tiny glass of sherry and sat in her favourite chair listening to the rain. Amiable miaowed and leapt onto her lap, and the witch stroked her fur absently, frowning at the wall. Her air of vagueness had completely fallen away now: she looked stern and a little sad.

"Amiable, I don't like this at all," she said slowly.

The cat regarded her with her green eyes and purred.

"I don't believe we can depend on Amina Bemare being permitted to leave custody. Someone may have reported her, unlikely though that seems."

"Perhaps there are informers," said Amiable.

"Exactly. It's possible that Cardinal Lamir has information that he's been waiting to use." She sighed, and took another sip. "Or maybe it's just coincidence, because those children are friends."

Amiable nudged her hand because she had stopped stroking, and Missus Orphint smiled and scratched under her chin.

"Perhaps we should take care of the Princess tonight. Amina was insistent that we get her out of the clutches of the Spectre, and it seems to me that events are going to start moving fast."

She drained her sherry and poured herself another. "Yes, I think we should do it tonight. It would give us one less thing to do later, if everything goes wrong. I'm afraid I'll have to ask you to go out in the rain."

Amiable stopped purring, and her claws dug into

Missus Orphint's thigh. "Me?" she said. "Now?"

"I'm sorry, my dear. I don't believe it will wait. I can't do it myself."

"But rain gets in my ears. I hate it."

"I know. But it has to be done."

"All right then." The cat sounded very sulky.

Missus Orphint carefully put Amiable on the ground and stood up. "The thing is, if Amina Bemare can't talk the Office into releasing her, and if they decide to try their methods on her, it won't go well."

"I wouldn't like to stand against Missus Bemare," said Amiable.

"No. I wouldn't either. But I confess to some anxiety…"

She bent down and traced a curious pattern on Amiable's neck with the tips of her fingers. Where she touched her there was a brief silver glow which vanished into her fur.

"There. You should stay dry now."

Missus Orphint opened the kitchen window, and the smell of damp earth and breathing greenery filled the kitchen. She watched as Amiable vanished into the downpour.

She doubted that anyone would hear from Amina until she was released. The more time that passed, the more likely it was that she had been sent to the dungeons of the Office for Witchcraft Extermination. That could be disastrous.

Missus Orphint didn't doubt that Amina would be able to get herself out of there. But she might be forced to use magic… And if she did have to use magic, in the very centre of the Office for Witchcraft Extermination, it would mean that witches couldn't stay hidden any more.

It would be a declaration of war.

Chapter Twenty-four

GEORGETTE WAS SUPPOSED TO DINE IN THE GRAND hall that evening, but late in the afternoon she pleaded a sick headache. The last thing she felt like doing was talking to courtiers. Or being looked at.

Since the betrothal ceremony that morning, she had been feeling more and more depressed. Every second of her day was regulated, but now it was going to be worse: she would have to dine with her father every evening, and there would be endless dressmaking appointments. Sibelius had scheduled extra lessons about the history of Awemt, and there were rehearsals for the wedding. She wouldn't have one second alone. Not even when she slept. She couldn't see any chance of escape.

Georgette's ladies-in-waiting fluttered about her, pressing cloths soaked with lavender to her forehead and drawing the curtains in her bedchamber to keep out the harmful light. Georgette hated this kind of fuss, but for once she didn't object. Finally the Duchess dosed her with laudanum.

Georgette swallowed the bitter draught obediently and allowed herself to be put to bed. She lay in the dim room feeling light-headed, letting her thoughts tumble disjointedly through her head. What now? Maybe Amina hadn't forgotten her… And even if she had, perhaps escape wasn't impossible? *Maybe*, she thought drowsily, *there really is a way out…*

She fell into a deep sleep almost straight away and dreamed that she was making wine. Since she had no idea how wine was made, the dream consisted of her gathering huge bunches of pale green grapes, translucent as glass, and throwing them into a gigantic silver ewer where they thundered in ever-decreasing circles until, through some process she never quite could see, they turned into bottles of wine. The sun was huge and round and sounded like rain, its golden light pouring down in cataracts of fluid light—

She woke up with a jump in the middle of the night, as a particularly loud thunderclap broke over the palace. It wasn't the sun making that noise, it was the rain, pouring down in floods outside. The window shutters were rattling violently.

Lady Agathe, fast asleep in her chair, hadn't stirred.

The bedchamber was still stuffy and hot, so Georgette climbed out of bed and opened the window. A gust of wind tore the shutters from her hand, rushing into her chamber and throwing a gout of rain over her. Georgette gasped and blinked.

She leaned out and stared over the palace garden. It was almost invisible through the rain and darkness, except when jagged lightning threw harsh illuminations over the thrashing trees. She shivered, and reached out to catch the banging shutters. Finally, after a tussle, she managed to latch them again. By then her nightgown was soaked.

Lady Agathe was still fast asleep. *That's strange,* thought Georgette. *Surely all that noise would have woken her.* And then, for no reason she could trace, she began to feel frightened. There was someone in the room watching her, she was sure… She squinted through the shadows, but could see nothing. For some reason that didn't reassure her: the conviction kept growing. She stepped over to her writing table and, her hands trembling slightly, struck a flint to light a candle. In its yellow light the room seemed just as it should be. She breathed out. It was only her imagination. Nobody was here.

She was about to blow the candle out and climb back into bed when she saw a black cat sitting in the middle of the floor, gazing at her with emerald-green eyes. Somehow she hadn't seen it before. Georgette laughed. "How did you get in here?" she said. "Lady Agathe will have a fit. She loathes cats..."

"Lady Agathe clearly has no taste," said the cat. "And I should tell you that it was some business making my way through that storm."

Georgette nearly dropped the candle. She stared, her mouth open.

"We don't have a lot of time," said the cat. "So you'd better get moving."

"What?"

"If you want to leave the palace, that is. I'm told that's what you want, and I have agreed, at considerable inconvenience to myself, to help you do it."

Georgette pinched her arm, convinced that this must be an extension of her dream. But then, dreams could be real – she knew that now. She tried to gather her scattered thoughts. "Did Amina send you?"

"Missus Bemare to you, I should think."

Georgette blinked.

"At the bottom of your bed there are some clothes. I suggest you put them on." When Georgette still didn't move, the cat growled softly. "Have you forgotten how to dress yourself?"

Georgette came out of her daze to find herself possessed with an unexpected hilarity. Why not do what the cat told her? And indeed, there were clothes at the end of the bed. Boy's clothes. Linen undergarments, breeches, shirt, waistcoat, jacket, a pair of serviceable boots, a large cap. She glanced at Lady Agathe, still snoozing in her chair, and hurriedly dressed herself. Her hair was still in rags, twisted for morning ringlets, so she stuffed them under her cap. The cat watched her unblinkingly.

"Now," it said, "follow me."

"Are you magic?"

"That's a very personal question." The cat stretched. "You can ask questions later. As I have already told you, we don't have a lot of time."

"But I should call you something. I mean, you must have a name."

"Day humans always pronounce it wrong. But you can call me Amiable."

"Amiable?" Again the bubble of hilarity rose inside Georgette, but she suppressed it in case she offended her rescuer. Whoever else this cat was, it seemed more haughty than amiable. "Delighted to meet you, Amiable. I never imagined I might be rescued by a cat."

"Don't be discourteous; it's unbecoming." Amiable was already at the door, which against all protocol was standing open. The cat whisked out into the passage.

Georgette took a deep breath before she followed. This was too absurd to be true. But it felt real.

The palace at night was spooky, especially with the storm raging outside. Empty, echoing spaces stretched into shadow and tapestries billowed in stray draughts. Painted faces loomed out of the gloom when lightning flashes seared across the dark halls, making Georgette start. Despite the howling wind and thunder, no one was awake – not even the guards who were supposed to watch the doors. Everything was drowned in sleep.

All the lights were doused, but Amiable seemed to generate a sourceless illumination around her body that lit their path but threw no shadows. *How strange,* thought Georgette, *that a black cat should be luminous.* As she followed that fluid, silently padding form, Georgette thought about what she knew of witches. Very little, sadly. She had heard that witches could change their shapes, but she had never heard of talking cats, except in the children's stories that Amina had told her so many years ago now. Was Amiable a witch in cat form, or a cat who could speak? A witch, probably; after all she was powerful enough to put a spell of sleep over a whole palace.

They walked through the cavernous, deserted kitchens, past the cold storerooms where carcasses of dead animals hung from iron hooks, past tottering piles of copper pots and pans, out through the back door, straight into the storm.

As soon as Georgette stepped out of the door she was blinded by the rain and soaked through. She might as well have walked into a waterfall. Amiable was a small, dimly lit blur in front of her feet, seemingly completely unbothered by the downpour. Georgette squared her shoulders and followed. The service gates were open, with no sign of guards. They slipped out into a back lane, down a tiny street, across the Royal Plaza, down a dark boulevard, and then into a tangle of streets that Georgette didn't recognize.

For the next hour, Georgette grew colder and colder. The rain stopped, but the wind didn't. A fingernail moon slipped out through the rags of clouds, but it just made the streets seem darker. Georgette kept her eyes fixed on Amiable, fearing she might lose her guide.

They reached one of the Five Rivers – Georgette had no idea which one – and followed the cobbled path that ran beside it. It was even colder here, where the wind swept along the surface of the water, and she began to shiver uncontrollably. Just as she started to feel that there would be no end to this journey they arrived at a pipe outlet that ran into the river. Amiable jumped inside and trotted along a slimy, brick-lined tunnel without looking to check if Georgette was behind her.

Georgette hesitated for a moment, but all she wanted to do by now was get out of the wind. She scrambled after Amiable, uncomfortably stooped against the low ceiling. She wondered if there were going to be rats. She didn't like rats. She was very tired, and now she really did have a headache. And then she saw a faint yellow light spilling onto the bricks, and a sound like a roar of people talking that was becoming louder and louder. Shortly afterwards she was able to stand up, and then they turned a corner. Georgette gasped.

She blinked in the brightness, briefly forgetting how cold she was. They were in a large vaulted room like a cellar, lit with coloured lamps suspended from the ceiling. It was crowded with people of all shapes and sizes and hues.

As she looked more closely, she realized that not everyone here was human. She could see cats, dogs, a donkey, a couple of crows, a few figures she couldn't identify at all. There was a delicious smell of things cooking, and in the corner someone was playing a lute. Georgette wasn't sure, but she thought it was a dog.

Amiable spoke for the first time since they had left the palace. "Welcome to the Undercroft, the home of the night people," she said. "You're a very privileged day human to be permitted here. I hope it's worth it. For us, I mean."

Georgette swept her gaze around the cellar again. Whatever this place was, there was more life in this one room than she had seen for years in the whole palace. She remembered her manners and straightened her shoulders. "I'm honoured," she said. And she added, "I hope I don't wake up."

"Stop thinking that you're dreaming," said Amiable irritably. "It's rude."

Chapter Twenty-five

CARDINAL LAMIR HAD LONG BEEN SUSPICIOUS OF the housekeeper in the Old Palace. He was sure that Princess Georgette's regrettable early inclinations to disobedience had come from this woman's influence.

He considered it a weakness of the old regime that they had employed people who were not of pure Clarelian blood. It didn't matter how many generations southerners had lived in Clarel; as far as Cardinal Lamir was concerned, they remained foreign. Among his assassins were a few whose ancestry hailed from other countries in Continentia, but if they were to flourish in his employ, they needed to be trained from childhood, and even then they needed to be geniuses like Ariosto. He would never employ a southerner. As an educated man, the Cardinal knew that many of the techniques his assassins used had originally come from the south, but this merely proved that southerners were inherently treacherous.

And now there was a direct connection between the boy who had stolen the Stone Heart and this Bemare woman. "It's disturbing, Ariosto," he said.

"My men have brought her in," Ariosto said. "At the very least, she will divulge information about her daughter and her associates. It seems that the young thief was seen about the Old Palace quite often."

The Cardinal looked up sharply. "You should have gone yourself, Ariosto."

"I had other tasks. King Oswald's presence here has taken much of my time."

"I instructed that this investigation takes priority over everything else." The Cardinal's nostrils pinched with rage. "We can afford no more carelessness."

Ariosto considered reminding the Cardinal of King Oswald's sense of self-importance, but thought better of it. The Cardinal already knew this, but wouldn't accept it as an excuse.

"Did you confine the woman in the lower dungeon?"

Briefly, Ariosto looked startled. "No, I thought—"

"You didn't think." Again that repressed rage, that anxiety. "Did it never occur to you that this woman is very likely a witch?"

Ariosto knew Mistress Bemare. She showed none of the signs of witchcraft that he had learned in his training. He was slow to warm to any human being, but this woman had been kind to him once, a long time ago, and he hadn't forgotten. For a moment, he felt a pang of sorrow that Mistress Bemare might be subjected to the attentions of the official torturers.

He was beginning to wonder if the Cardinal was becoming slightly unhinged. He repressed the thought at once; he knew that Lamir had an unsettling ability to read his mind.

"I'll personally oversee the interrogation," said the Cardinal. He waved his hand. "And be wary. Very wary. They have wiles, these witches, that you cannot imagine."

Ariosto bowed and left Lamir's office to carry out his instructions. Cardinal Lamir watched him leave. He hadn't missed the flicker of scepticism that had crossed Ariosto's face. Like everything else in the past few days, it struck him as a bad sign.

When Sibelius had tracked down the Stone Heart at a dealer in rare items in a shabby suburb on the outskirts of Clarel, the Cardinal had felt a glow of triumph. It was the final key to his plans. But since then, things had been going wrong. Small things, to be sure, but it was on such details that empires foundered. He had been so certain that witches had been totally suppressed in Clarel: there had been no signs of real witchcraft for more than a century.

If anyone knew the signs, he did.

Chapter Twenty-six

AMINA WAS WORRYING THAT SHE HAD FORGOTTEN
to take the stew off the stove when the officials had come
to arrest her. At the best, the fire would die down, and
she would merely have a spoilt pot and a lot of smoke.
At the worst, it would burn down the kitchen. Or even
the Old Palace.

Maybe that wouldn't be a bad thing, but it would be
a nuisance.

The two men who had arrested her were clearly assassins, though of a lowly rank, so she hadn't been surprised
to be taken to the offices in the Cardinal's palace. But
now she sat in the dungeons of the Office for Witchcraft
Extermination, her arms and legs clamped to an uncomfortable metal chair. That was a bit surprising. No witch
had made it this far for almost a hundred years.

Her protests of bewilderment and outrage, reinforced

by a strong persuasion charm, had at first seemed to be working well. But then Milan Ariosto had entered the room where she was being questioned and ordered that she be taken to the dungeons. She remembered him from a long time ago, from before he had been swept up and tipped into one of Cardinal Lamir's orphanages. She had followed his career with sadness: Ariosto was one of her failures. He didn't seem to remember her, although he was careful not to meet her eyes.

Once in the dungeons she was handed over to an interrogator, a thin man with thin lips and even thinner hair. He had emotionlessly and painstakingly explained what the various torture devices did to various parts of the human body, and then left her by herself to contemplate her immediate future. A tallow candle in a dish provided illumination. Amina wrinkled her nose. It stank.

She knew that leaving prisoners alone with the tools of torture was a standard process. Often prisoners confessed before the torturers got down to business, out of sheer terror; not that it necessarily prevented them being tortured anyway.

These tools had all been used on living, breathing people for the sole purpose of causing them pain. The king called it "justice". *This,* thought Amina, *is why witches don't trust kings. Or cardinals. Or anyone at all whose idea of justice starts with the pain of another human being.*

She was trying not to worry about Oni, because there was no point. Oni, like all the children of witches, knew where the safe houses were. Amina had to trust that Oni would remember what she had been taught, and wouldn't let her fear get the better of her. In normal circumstances that would be comfort enough, but now that the Heart was released from its bonds, anything might happen.

The Heart had found Pip. She hoped that was a good thing, but she couldn't be sure. It was bad magic, even if a witch had made it for the best of purposes. In any case, what happened to the Heart was, for now, out of Amina's hands and there was no point in worrying about it. She hoped that someone would remember about Georgette. It was crucial she was taken away from King Oswald.

Her role now was to be the respectable royal housekeeper that she had appeared to be for her whole life. Since before her great-grandmother's time, the oldest Bemare daughter had been housekeeper of the Old Palace. That hadn't changed even when the King of Clarel became a Spectre. Once the royal housekeeper had been a position of high status, like the palace itself. Not any more.

In any case, when the antennae of the state began to

172

quiver with suspicion, innocence or guilt became irrelevant. As far as witchcraft was concerned, being arrested was in itself a proof of guilt. But witches had their own means of dealing with the law. Right now Amina wasn't frightened for herself, but she was worried. If the torturer followed through on his threats, she would have to use magic.

So much of the teaching of magic was all about not doing it. The more powerful magic was, the less you should use it. *Only in the last resort*, her mother had told her. *And maybe not even then.*

She had no doubt that she was being observed from some unseen spyhole, and thought that for the moment she should play along. It was important that she acted as any normal non-witch person would. She called for help, and then, when there was no answer, began to sob noisily. Then she started praying out loud. Then she whimpered for a long time.

After an hour of this, she began to get very bored. Perhaps they meant to leave her here all night. Perhaps, she thought, she might get away with falling asleep. It would pass the time. Because she was unable to move, she was increasingly uncomfortable.

Amina sobbed a bit more, and then twisted around in the chair, trying to find a more comfortable position.

There wasn't one. She relaxed all her muscles and let herself doze, as if she were exhausted. She needed to be rested for whatever was coming.

Some time later, in the darkest, coldest watches of the night, the dungeon door opened. By then the tallow candle had burned itself out, and she had been in complete darkness for about an hour.

Four men entered, all of them dressed in deepest black so their faces and hands stood out white against the shadows. Two were guards who carried pitch torches that they fixed to brackets on the wall. The sudden dazzle and smoke made Amina's eyes smart. The third was the torturer she had seen earlier.

The fourth man was Cardinal Lamir himself.

The hairs rose on the back of Amina's neck. This was serious. Maybe it was a case for last resorts, after all.

"Mistress Bemare," said the Cardinal, smiling thinly, "I must apologize for the discomfort of your accommodation. Sadly, it is sometimes necessary."

Amina stared back at him. "I beg you, sir, to release me," she said. "I have been most unjustly imprisoned, and I don't understand why. I have duties, sir, and responsibilities…"

"It has come to our attention that you practise witchcraft."

174

Amina looked shocked. "No, sir! How can that be so? I have never in my life…"

Lamir signed to one of the guards, who rolled some objects out of a small bag onto the tray of torture implements. *The muffling candles, curse it.* A selection of cooking spices. A little paring knife. An old doll of Oni's that Amina had kept long after Oni outgrew it, as a memento. They had obviously made a thorough search of her rooms. Perhaps someone had taken the stew off the fire.

"A poppet. A witchknife. Magical unguents. These are all incontrovertible evidence that under the guise of being a housekeeper in the Old Palace you have practised the evil arts of witchery." Lamir pointed to the doll with a theatrical shudder. "Which unfortunate did you curse with this poppet, eh? What devilish charms did you weave in your evil practices?"

Amina looked completely bewildered. "But … I don't understand, sir."

"Explain these evil items, witch!"

Now she wanted to laugh. "If you wish, sir. They're easily told. That doll belonged to my daughter, sir, when she was a baby, and I kept it. As a memory, if you like. The candles are for cleansing the air of unpleasant odours. That there's a paring knife. And those I think are cooking spices, sir. For the flavours." She craned her neck, trying to see. "Some of them are excellent for the digestion, too. Like the turmeric, that yellow spice there..."

Amina was using her strongest arts of persuasion, concentrating on being eager to please, homely, honest. The two guards exchanged glances, and she saw that she was swaying them, although of course they wouldn't dare to intervene. Perhaps sensing this, Lamir dismissed the guards. Amina watched the heavy door slam shut behind them.

The torturer hadn't responded in any visible way. Perhaps he was so used to seeing people pleading for their lives that he had no human responses left in him at all.

"It's well known, witch, that such as you disguise your black arts with plausible-sounding excuses that trip easily off your tongues," Lamir said. "Don't think you can deceive me."

"But, sir, there's nothing more to tell."

Lamir nodded to the torturer, who had picked up a nasty pair of pliers and was turning it over in his hands, looking thoughtfully at Amina. It was a professional kind of look, like a carpenter trying to size up the best way to saw a knotty piece of wood.

"I'm sure there's much more to tell. Let us see how a

little application – a tiny, tiny taste of what's to come – will help to refresh your memory."

"But, sir, I explained…"

Amina let panic bubble up in her voice. She wasn't pretending now. It didn't matter whether she was a witch or not; she was bound hand and foot, utterly vulnerable before two men who had every intention of doing her harm. She had seen human beings do violence to each other often, since her work with lost children meant she had spent many hours in the most desperate districts of Clarel. But this was different. The intention, in itself, was terrifying. She had never seen it so clearly in a human face before: it was cold, emotionless, devoid of anything except a conviction of its rightness.

At the best of times, Amina didn't deal well with pain. She put up with it when she had to, and avoided it when she could. She was fond of her body, and wanted it to remain the way it was.

The torturer slowly walked up to Amina and, for the first time, met her eyes. This was his moment. He was enjoying it.

Perhaps even now it wasn't too late.

"Please," she said, turning her eyes to the Cardinal. "Don't do this, I'm begging you. Why me? I've done nothing wrong."

177

"I think we both know that isn't true," said Lamir. "You are come to the place where all lies will be burned out of you. Our only desire is to save your soul."

The torturer, who had paused while the Cardinal spoke, turned his attention back to Amina. She shut her eyes.

Chapter Twenty-seven

PIP WAS JUST DRIFTING OFF TO SLEEP WHEN HE woke with a start, thinking that someone had called his name. Without knowing why, he was mortally afraid.

He sat up. The storm had passed, and a stray beam of moonlight slanted through the skylight. El was fast asleep in the next pallet, breathing easily now, and Oni was curled up next to her, snoring.

A safe house, Oni had called it. It did feel safe. The pallets smelt of lavender, and the attic was warm and clean, the walls whitewashed between dark oaken beams.

It's not safe. The voice again. It was inside his head, but it wasn't him. Clovis.

"Yes, it is," said Pip crossly. The Heart was under his pillow, and he picked it up, whispering so he wouldn't wake the others. "Did you wake me up?"

Safe for witches, maybe. Not for us. You can't trust witches.

"Who says?"

We have to leave.

Pip was too tired to argue. "We're staying here," he said flatly, and turned over to go to sleep again.

We have to leave.

"I'm not going anywhere."

I command you, as a Prince of the Realm.

The icy arrogance in the child's voice called up all Pip's truculent defiance. "You can't command me," he said. "It's not your realm. You have a better place to be, huh?"

There was a pause of naked astonishment. *You dare to defy me?* said Clovis. *You? A mere commoner like you?*

By now Pip had had enough. He told Clovis, in a few short, impolitely chosen words, that he was as good a person as any prince, and to leave him alone.

Clovis's rage struck Pip like a blow inside his skull. He reeled with a blinding headache, clutching his temples as a vicious howling drove out every thought in his head. A life of many blows meant that Pip was stoic about physical pain, but this hurt worse than anything he had experienced, as if his own brain was having a tantrum and kicking itself to bits. Tears of pain and rage forced themselves out between his closed eyelids and down his nose.

"Stop it!" said Pip. "Don't. Just stop it!"

Clovis was yelling, his voice echoing around Pip's skull. *You do what I say. That's the rule.*

"It's not my rule."

Clovis's anger was like a tempest inside Pip's skull. It went on and on. Pip gritted his teeth, scarcely aware of where he was any more, conscious only of his fury and outrage that this … this *thing* was inside his head, his own head, which was private and nobody else's business.

A brief but horribly vivid vision flashed through his mind. A face spattered with blood. A woman holding a dripping knife in one hand, and a clump of meat in the other, speaking words he didn't understand but which filled him with loathing and terror. Clovis's voice, screaming, *I hate you I hate you I hate you…*

The sickness of nightmare clutched Pip's throat. He convulsed with nausea and threw up his dinner over the pristine coverlet. But still some small, stubborn part of him refused to give in.

And then, blessed relief. A hand on his forehead, a voice that wasn't him and wasn't Clovis. Oni. She sounded as if she were a long way away.

"Pip? Are you all right? What's wrong?"

The pain lessened, as if the Heart had grown tired, like a sulky toddler. Pip opened his eyes and saw that

Oni and El, woken by his shouting, were crouched beside him. Oni's hand cupped his brow, cool and soothing. He sat up, wiping his mouth with a trembling hand. Although Clovis had quietened down, Pip could still sense his anger, simmering dangerously.

"It's Clovis," he said thickly.

Oni's forehead wrinkled in puzzlement, but before she could ask him what he meant Pip saw, with a clutch of foreboding, that the light had changed, as if the moon had come out from behind a cloud. But it wasn't moonlight, it was a greenish glow. It rapidly grew so bright that it threw harsh shadows around the room. El looked over her shoulder, her eyes widening, and half stood up, her mouth open in fear. Pip reached for her hand but she was pulled away by some invisible force, falling backwards towards the light. And in the next moment, she vanished before his eyes.

Oni was being pulled away too. Screaming for El, Pip grabbed Oni's hand, holding her fast against the awful gravity of the green light. He could see the Rupture now, an impossible hole in the middle of the room. He felt as if Oni's hand was blurring, as if already she wasn't quite there.

Neither Oni nor he had heard the door open, but suddenly Missus Orphint was next to them. She held a branch of sweet-smelling candles that flamed straight up without guttering, although she was moving swiftly. She thrust her hands into the centre of the uncanny green light, but even as she reached, the light snuffed out.

Her head sagged for a moment in defeat, and then she turned to the other two. "What happened here?"

"It's El," said Oni. "She's … she…" She covered her face with her hands, unable to speak.

Pip grabbed the Heart from where it lay beneath his pillow and threw it against the wall. It hit the plaster with a light thud and rebounded onto the floor.

"Bring her back!" Pip was so angry that he scarcely knew what he was saying. "Where is she, you dead horrible worm! How dare you! How dare you take my sister?"

"Hush," said Missus Orphint, and she lightly touched his shoulder. "Hush, Pip. Anger is no use now."

"He took El." Pip burst into tears. "He took El because I wouldn't do what he said."

"How do you know that?"

Her voice was very calm, and as she spoke Pip felt his fury die down, to be replaced by an awful grief. He knuckled his eyes and took a breath before answering.

"He told me," he said. "Clovis."

"The Heart? Clovis has been speaking to you?" Oni looked horrified. "Why didn't you say so?"

183

Pip didn't answer. He shrugged and walked over to where the Heart lay on the floor, and picked it up. Missus Orphint watched him carefully but made no move to stop him. The Heart felt neither warm nor cold, and there was no responsive pulse when he touched it. Clovis was nowhere – not in Pip's head, not in the Heart. Pip weighed the Heart in his hand, staring down at it.

"I was too late, Pip," Missus Orphint said. "I'm sorry."

"Can we get her back?"

Missus Orphint didn't answer. She was looking at Oni. "You all right, Oni?"

Oni nodded. She was trembling now. "Is she … is El dead?"

"I don't believe so," said Missus Orphint. "But it's hard to know."

There was a heavy silence, broken by Oni.

"What are we going to do?"

"First," said Missus Orphint, "Pip will tell me exactly what happened before that Rupture opened in this room. And then we will think about what is best to do next."

Pip looked at his feet. "He wanted to leave here. He ordered me; he said he was a prince and I had to do what he said." The anger flared inside Pip again as he spoke. "He said he doesn't trust witches."

"He might have some reason for that distrust." There was a dryness in Missus Orphint's voice that made Oni glance up at her.

"He shouldn't have took El." Pip wiped his face with his sleeve. "She didn't deserve that. She did nobody any harm, not ever. I wish I never picked this thing up. El was right. I should have thrown it in the river."

"Throwing it in the river wouldn't have made any difference," said Missus Orphint.

"It might have stopped it from taking El."

"It might. It might not have. You had already touched it, remember." She sighed. "The first human touch, after all those years…"

She took Oni and Pip's hands, as if they were very small children. Somehow Pip didn't resent the gesture, although normally he would have prickled with insult. "Come downstairs, you two. I'll make us a hot drink." She glanced at the ruined coverlet, where Pip had thrown up his dinner. "And then I'll clean up that mess."

Chapter Twenty-eight

DESPITE AMIABLE'S REBUKE, GEORGETTE STILL wasn't sure if she was awake. She was rarely ill, but laudanum draughts were routinely prescribed by the court physician for any kind of sickness. Over the years the taste of laudanum laced with sherry and honey had become inextricably bound with her memories of the sickroom. She was familiar with the dreams it brought: vivid, strange, absurd visions.

Like the Undercroft.

On the other hand, her recurring dream of her mother and the dragon and the crying little boy had never come with laudanum. And even though that was definitely a dream, it had also been real.

Perhaps, she thought, *I will soon wake up in the palace, still betrothed to King Oswald.*

The only thing that made her wonder if she wasn't

hallucinating after all was the cold. Her clothes were soaked through and clung to her skin: even in the warm fug of the Undercroft her teeth were chattering.

The Undercroft was as large as a market square. In fact, it was very like a market, from what she remembered of following Amina on her shopping trips when she was small. Or maybe, she thought, it was more like some huge, chaotic party.

She followed Amiable closely, afraid she would lose her in the crowd. The cat threaded purposefully through a miscellany of stalls where people were dancing, or arguing, or playing complicated games, or simply watching everyone else. She had never seen such a variety of forms and figures.

There were many animals like cats and birds, who were, against everything she knew about their natural inclinations, not only tolerating each other but seemed to be, in one case at least, having tea together. She almost trod on a small terrier-like dog, who told her sharply to watch where she was putting her clumsy feet, and she was sure she saw two foxes playing dice. There were other creatures too: sprites, or people who looked like sprites; a shadowy figure she couldn't quite see even when she looked at it directly, and which gave her a hollow feeling in her insides.

At the far end of the Undercroft was a tent, a smaller version of the pavilions that were set in the palace grounds for special occasions like tournaments or fencing matches between the nobles. This one was made of bright green silk, with yellow stripes. Georgette followed Amiable inside, bending her head to enter, and stopped short, blinking with surprise. Inside, the tent was much bigger than it looked from the outside.

A group of about half a dozen people, who were seated around a table deep in conversation, turned their heads and stared at her in surprise.

"I brought the Princess early," said Amiable, jumping onto a chair. "Plurabella Orphint thought we ought to do that first, to get it out of the way."

A tiny old woman, so old she was bent almost double, stood up slowly and shuffled down the middle of the tent towards Georgette. Her eyes were two different colours, blue and brown, and her long white hair was piled up into a bun on the back of her head. "A good idea," she said to Amiable. "Plurabella always thinks ahead."

She turned to Georgette and studied her, as if she were some exotic specimen. Georgette felt a strange awe, a prickle a little like fear. She curtsied without even thinking, trying to think of the polite thing to say.

"Welcome, child," said the old woman.

"I've never even heard of this place," Georgette said. She bit her lip, because that wasn't what she had meant to say at all. "I mean ... thank you..."

"You shouldn't have heard of it," said the old woman. "It isn't always this crowded, mind. Tonight is the Solstice Carnival, to celebrate Midsummer. Which perhaps is fortunate, since the Witches' Council is here already."

She studied the Princess again with that clear, unsettling gaze, and despite herself Georgette blushed. She felt as if she had a smut on her nose.

"My name is Missus Clay," said the old woman. "We're no friends of the kingdom, I can tell you now. But since one of our respected colleagues requested that we take you from the palace, we are happy to welcome you to the Undercroft."

Georgette was beginning to feel dizzy, but she tried to pull herself together. "It's an honour to meet you," she said.

"We would not normally interfere in royal business," said Missus Clay. "But it seems that the Spectres are moving, and Amina says that you are one of the major pawns. So it is better that we remove you from the board altogether."

Georgette didn't know how to answer. She didn't much like the idea that she was a pawn.

"What a poor miserable scrap," said a man at the table. "She's wet through. Didn't you give her a rain charm, Amiable?"

"Do you think I had the energy, after putting a whole palace to sleep?" said Amiable sulkily. "I would have thought a simple thank you would suffice."

She stretched and yawned. And then her form blurred, and before Georgette's eyes Amiable transformed into a young, dark-haired woman. She was wearing no clothes, but this didn't seem to embarrass Amiable or anyone else. She stretched again. "That's better," she said.

Georgette's dizziness was getting worse and there was a roaring in her ears, as if she might faint. It was true, she was cold and miserable. Her clothes clung damply around her body. She could see steam rising from them in the warmth of the tent. But she was a princess, and princesses don't faint. She swayed and almost fell, clutching at the cloth wall of the tent.

The old woman took her elbow and led her to a chair. For all her apparent frailty, her hand was very strong. "First a change of clothes, and a hot drink," she said. "She's freezing."

It was amazing how much better Georgette felt when she was dry and warm. She was given some different clothes, breeches and a shirt and a waistcoat as before, and had changed hurriedly at the back of the pavilion. Nobody was looking, but that didn't make her feel any less self-conscious.

By the time she returned to the others, Amiable had put on a crimson dress. She was disconcertingly pretty, with the same black hair and green eyes she had as a cat, except that now her pupils were round. Georgette felt more shy and uncertain than she ever had in her life.

There was a silence as everyone there studied her with open curiosity, aside from a sprite who was seated on the table itself. It was deeply absorbed in a game of knuckles. The bones it was using were tiny. Georgette stared at it distractedly. Were they rat knuckles? Did rats have knuckles?

The sprite felt her gaze and glanced up at her. She just had time to see that its eyes were bright yellow before it vanished. Georgette blinked. The knuckles kept bouncing up and down by themselves.

"Stop it, Bottomly," said the man who had spoken earlier. "The poor thing's already confused enough."

Georgette blinked again, and politely averted her eyes from the levitating knuckles. The sprite popped back into sight. "Sorry, Helios," it said.

Helios smiled reassuringly at Georgette, and she gave a wavering smile back. He had golden hair, and was wearing a high top hat, a yellow waistcoat and a long red skirt. His eyes were deeply kind.

"Better now?" said Amiable. "I'm sorry about the rain. It couldn't be helped."

"Yes, thank you," said Georgette.

"Good," said Amiable. "So how, may I ask, are you going to help us?"

Everyone at the table, including the sprite, looked at her as if she had an answer. Georgette felt herself blushing again. "I don't know," she said. "I don't know who you are. I don't even know if all this is real."

"I told you that was rude." Amiable pouted.

"Hush, Amiable," said Missus Clay.

By now Georgette was scarlet, but she sat up as straight as she could. "Did Amina ask you to rescue me?"

"Missus Bemare to you," said Amiable sharply, a flash of green fire in her eyes. "I'm still not sure that it wasn't you that got Missus Bemare arrested by the Office for Witchcraft Extermination."

"Amin— Missus Bemare has been arrested?" said Georgette, shocked. "I would never in a thousand years do anything to hurt Am— Missus Bemare. Not for anything. She's like … she's like my *mother*."

"Missus Bemare was your wet-nurse," Amiable snapped. "Do you think she had any choice about that?"

"Darling, you're embarrassing us," said Helios.

"Speak for yourself, sunboy," said Amiable.

"I don't believe the Princess informed on Missus Bemare," said Missus Clay. "There are many things at play in the city. Although it's always possible that I'm wrong."

Georgette was quiet. Perhaps it was her fault, even if she hadn't intended harm. She shouldn't have gone to Amina for help. But there was no one else.

"We should never let outsiders in," said Amiable. "And this one's a *royal* outsider..."

The dark-skinned man next to Amiable patted her hand. "This is the safest place, Amy," he said. "We talked it over with Amina, remember?"

"I still think it's wrong, Potier. But I got her here, didn't I?"

"Enough." Missus Clay's voice cut across the murmurs that were rising around the table. "For better or worse, and I hope for better, we decided to bring the Princess here. I think it is likely for the better."

Georgette's heart was sinking into her boots. She had no idea why she had been brought to this place, or what these people expected of her. The only person who could guide her through this was Amina, and Amina wasn't here. "How do you know she was taken?"

"She sent word," said Missus Clay. "Before she went

into shutdown. Probably when they had her in the wagon, all in chains."

"She's not back yet," said a very short man who hadn't yet spoken. "And nobody's heard anything. It's a bad sign. They probably took her to the torture chambers."

"Juin, the voice of doom," said Potier mockingly. "Of course we've heard nothing. That's protocol, isn't it?"

Georgette swallowed hard. She wasn't supposed to, but she knew what happened in the torture chambers of the Office for Witchcraft Extermination.

"If they've put her in the dungeons, I don't think she can get out," she said, so quietly that she was almost inaudible. "Nobody does. It's too late…"

"Missus Bemare is more than able to deal with prisons," said Amiable scornfully. "We're not worried about *that*."

"Oh." Georgette remembered that Amina had said that Cardinal Lamir was a Spectre himself. "But isn't the Cardinal a … a…?"

"She's more than a match for a Spectre," said Amiable, and sniffed. "If he is a Spectre. Which he probably is."

"One Spectre, anyway," said Missus Clay. "We must hope that she doesn't have to deal with any more of them. My concern is that if Missus Bemare is forced to use her powers, it will expose us."

"And that's bad," said Juin, nodding gloomily. "That's very bad indeed."

"Maybe it isn't," said Missus Clay. "Maybe it's time we stepped out of the shadows. Maybe we've lived too long dominated by fear."

Bottomly, who had been playing knuckles all through the discussion, looked up at this and gave a tiny cheer. Georgette glanced at him involuntarily and he vanished at once, but almost immediately reappeared again. This time, Georgette remembered to avert her eyes.

"It's rules to disappear," he said with a touch of defiance. "Ratterbags aren't *supposed* to be seen."

"Of course it's rules," said Helios. He looked as if he were trying not to laugh. "But my name means the sun. I am supposed never to live in the shadows. And all my life, I have never lived anywhere else."

Chapter Twenty-nine

AMINA SHUT HER EYES. THE TORTURER LIFTED HER middle finger from the arm of the chair and attached the pliers to her nail.

Even after all the hours she had spent in this cell preparing herself, Amina didn't feel quite ready. She plucked some stolen moments out of the flow of time.

She wanted to think about her Aunt Tobia.

Aunt Tobia had taught Amina the rules of magic when she was knee-high, counting them off on Amina's stubby little fingers. "First," she would say, "Do No Harm. Second: Everything Is Connected. Third: Never Use Magic for Selfish Ends." Then she'd pause. "The Fourth Law. Well, that is more difficult. This is a law that takes a lifetime to understand. Fourth: You May Break the First Three Laws, But Only If You Follow Them With All Your Mind and All Your Heart."

Like all simple things, magic is deeply complex. Amina bent her mind to the Fourth Law.

Amina's craft came from a different tradition than from most of the witches in Clarel. Her Eradian ancestors were master weavers who had moved north on the trading routes hundreds of years before, bringing with them spices, amber, gold and silk. Some settled in Clarel, which was then an important trading centre. It was less important now, since the wealth had moved elsewhere, but the Eradian weavers of Clarel were still famous throughout Continentia. Every Eradian child was taught the secrets of textiles.

Weaving the fibres of reality into new patterns: that, for both good and ill, is what magic is.

"It can be hard to see, because it will often cloak itself in honey and spice, or wall off eyes with deceptive words," Aunt Tobia had said once. "But if a witch makes horror where once there was beauty, and suffering where once there was pleasure, and shame where once there was innocence, then you will know it as bad magic. Beware the bad magic."

From the moment the Cardinal had entered the room, Amina could smell the bad magic in Lamir. It was rotting underneath his robes, like decomposing meat. Until that moment, Amina had never been completely sure if

Lamir was a Spectre. It was a persistent rumour among witches, but it was always possible that Lamir was merely an ordinarily cruel and ambitious man.

Her stolen moments were slipping past.

Amina cleared her mind, permitting her thoughts to drift where they desired. She remembered the sweet golden air of a summer dawn. She remembered the first time she had ever kissed a boy she loved, the first kick of her daughter inside her womb. All moments of profound change, in which sadness was knitted up into joy. Joy. That was what she needed.

At last. Now I know what to do.

Amina re-entered the river of time and opened her eyes.

The torturer was still lightly holding her middle finger. He was extending the moment of apprehension, letting his victim know that he was about to inflict unbearable agony. The iron clamp held her wrist to the arm of the chair. His eyes flickered to her face, again with that almost imperceptible smile.

Amina smiled back, as radiantly as the early sun.

The torturer blinked and hesitated, taken aback, and turned to Cardinal Lamir. As Amina smiled, the torture chamber filled with the golden light of dawn.

Cardinal Lamir looked astonished, and Amina

realized then that he hadn't really believed that she was a witch at all. None of the poor souls who had been tormented in this chamber of horrors had been witches. Lamir had known that, and he had tortured them anyway. As the light poured out of her, Amina's witch senses opened: she could hear voices, the vibrations of unimaginable suffering that had soaked over years and years into the naked stone walls. She felt a surge of bright, merciless fury.

She concentrated briefly and the clamps on her arms and legs snapped open, releasing her. The torturer paled and stepped back, crooking his fingers by his temples in the sign against the evil eye. Her gaze swept over him with contempt and he became rigid and fell voicelessly, like a block of wood, to the floor.

Lamir overcame his shock almost at once and began to shout for the guards. He lifted his hands, readying himself to cast some kind of spell. Amina almost choked on the magical aura around him. It was a corpse smell, a stench like death but much, much worse. Rot and decay are part of the natural way of things, the fertilizer that feeds the roses of next season; but this was death arrested, the decay that promises no roses... For an instant her rage faltered, as if the light inside her was being sucked into an enormous, ravenous vacuum.

She didn't have time to think. Every moment Lamir became more dangerous, and she had never before faced the magic of a Spectre. She lunged forward with all the force of her anger and punched Lamir on the nose.

Amina was a big, well-muscled woman, and Lamir, although tall, had a skeletal build and the strength of one who never had to perform any physical task for himself. The last thing he expected was this kind of direct assault. He went down like a sack of turnips and didn't move.

She bent over the Cardinal with a shudder and touched his temple with her forefinger. The feel of his skin was obscene, loathsome, but she forced herself to concentrate. She could feel a pulse. She hadn't quite destroyed his body.

As she focused her mind, she felt his consciousness flicker. Lamir was coming back. She might have the power to wrestle with him, but she doubted it. Not on her own.

Somebody was already rattling the bolt of the torture chamber. She wavered, wondering whether to take the risk of fighting the Cardinal. No, she couldn't. Her first duty was to escape.

Amina shut her eyes, remembering everything she loved. When she opened them, she was a rat. Her tunic had collapsed around her, like a tent.

She just had time to wriggle out and hide under the chair before the cell door slammed open and the two guards came running in, pikes at the ready. They halted when they saw the two prone bodies and the empty chair, their mouths round "o"s of astonishment. One poked the tunic cautiously, as if it were a dead body that might spring into life at any moment, and the other knelt down and checked the Cardinal's pulse.

Amina scuttled behind them, hidden by the flickering shadows of torchlight, and out of the open door.

And then she ran for her life.

Chapter Thirty

FOR THE FIRST TIME EVER, ONI FELT SORRY FOR PIP. Her sympathy was mixed. She couldn't help blaming Pip for getting them all into such trouble. It was his fault that her mother had been taken away by the Cardinal's assassins, and his fault that El had vanished into a Rupture. If he hadn't stolen the Heart, Oni would be asleep in her own apartment that she paid for with her own money. But she had never seen him look as forlorn as he was now.

Missus Orphint made tea and disappeared to clean up Pip's vomit. Oni noticed muffling candles were placed around the kitchen. In a safe house like Missus Orphint's, where the walls were already thick with wards and charms, it was a sign of her anxiety.

Pip sat twisting his hands in his lap, his head bowed, his tea untouched. Oni knew that he was trying not to cry in front of her. She wanted to cry herself. El was her dearest friend.

They had liked each other from the start. When they were younger, other kids had called El names, teasing her for her short breath, or calling her "simple" or worse. Oni had always stood up for El, and in turn El stood up for Oni when she was teased for being a raggedy-arse weaver kid. They had fought side by side and laughed together; they had told each other their secrets, their fears and wishes and jokes. And now El was gone. It didn't seem real.

She couldn't help worrying about her mother, too. She wasn't as confident in Amina's ability to escape the dungeons of the Office for Witchcraft Extermination as Missus Orphint seemed to be, and that made her feel disloyal. Amina was one of the most powerful witches in Clarel, everyone knew that. Well, all the witches knew that, anyway. In the ordinary way of things, she should be fine. But nothing was ordinary any more.

Since Pip had turned up in the Crosseyes the day before – was it really only a day? – Oni's world had fallen to pieces. Witches spoke about Spectres in secret behind muffling candles, because even to think of them was dangerous, but Oni had always regarded them as frightening stories, not real things that would affect her real life. Then Pip had taken the Heart out of his pocket and put it on the table in her little apartment, and Oni had known at once what it was. Every witch in Clarel knew about Old Missus Pledge and what she had done when she tried to destroy the Spectres.

At the centre of everything, the heart of a dead boy, who had been trapped by a witch between life and death and made into a counterspell. And a grubby little thief called Pip.

"Oni," said Pip, breaking her thoughts. "What's a Rupture?"

"I don't know a lot about this stuff," she said. "Ma told me some things…"

"Does it mean like … something breaking open? Like, one place breaking into another place? And that other place, that's where El is, right?"

Oni glanced over at him. He was staring straight ahead now, frowning. "Kind of," she said cautiously. These were deep waters. "There's this place, and the In Between, and then other places as well…"

"So why can't we go there and get her back?"

"I don't think it's a place that you can just go to."

Pip was quiet for a few moments. "What if I make Clovis take me there?"

"How would you do that?"

More silence. "I don't know. But maybe I could."

"Why didn't you say he was talking to you?"

Pip hunched his shoulders, scowling. "It didn't seem important."

Oni knew that he felt guilty, so she didn't push it. "Is he talking to you now?"

"No," said Pip. "Not a word. Not since El went." He pulled the Heart out of his pocket and held it in front of his eyes. "Maybe he's not inside this any more. The Heart's just a thing now."

"What do you mean?"

"Like any other thing. Like a stick or an old shoe or something. It didn't feel like that before. It felt alive. Maybe Clovis has gone away."

"I don't think he can go away, because of what Old Missus Pledge did," said Oni. "He's locked in there."

Pip didn't answer. He was staring at the Heart, and Oni knew he wasn't listening to her. His expression changed, hardened: his eyes seemed to become shining surfaces, hiding whatever was behind them. He turned to Oni.

"How much do you actually know about Spectres?"

"A bit. What all witches know. Not a lot."

"Maybe you got it wrong. You're a witch, and witches are evil. Probably even more evil than Spectres."

All the air went out of Oni as if he had punched her in the stomach. It seemed ages before she breathed it back in, and then she could barely see for rage.

"How dare you say that? How *dare* you? When my own mother picked you up off the street when you might have died? When Missus Pledge gave you a home? When you've known me all my life and you know how much I love El? When Ma is in the dungeons because you can't keep your filthy hands off anything shiny?"

Pip hunched his shoulders up, turning away from her, and she pulled him back roughly, still shaking with anger. "Look at me when you insult me," she said. "*Look* at me."

He slowly dragged up his head and met her gaze, his expression still hard. Oni clenched her hand, wanting to punch him. And then something melted, and his eyes were red-rimmed and wet, desolate.

Oni's anger vanished at once, leaving in its wake an overwhelming tiredness. "Aren't you going to say sorry?"

Pip looked at his feet, and then up. He seemed like Pip again. "I'm sorry, Oni."

"You should be."

"I didn't mean you or Amina," said Pip. "But maybe there are evil witches, like in the stories. Maybe Old

Missus Pledge was really evil."

"That's not true!" said Oni hotly. "Old Missus Pledge was trying to get rid of the Spectres."

"Many witches at the time thought what she did was bad magic," said Missus Orphint. Oni and Pip jumped, startled: they had been too intent on their argument to notice that Missus Orphint had been standing by the door, listening. She entered the kitchen, carrying a bucket, and tipped its contents outside the back door. "Arabella Pledge told me that her mother said that twisting blood magic was the worst thing she had ever done. Blood magic is for healing and life, and Old Missus Pledge said she made it into an abomination."

"But maybe it wasn't wrong," said Oni, in a small voice. "If it was to destroy the Spectres..."

"It didn't destroy them, though," said Missus Orphint.

"That's only because she couldn't finish the spell."

"Maybe. We'll never know if it would have destroyed the Spectres unless we can find out how to use the spell."

"The Spectres seem to think it's dangerous," said Oni.

"Maybe they know more about the Heart than we do." Missus Orphint paused. "Old Missus Pledge used Spectre magic to make the Heart, Oni. Don't forget that. If Clovis is terrified of witches, perhaps he has reason."

"What can we do, then?" said Oni.

"Perhaps the first thing to do is to make Clovis less frightened. Maybe he needs a friend."

"I want to find El," said Pip. "I don't care about the spell. I don't care about some silly dead prince or Spectres or anything. I just want El back."

Missus Orphint hesitated, and then spoke very gently. "I don't know if we can get her back, Pip."

"She's somewhere," said Pip. "If she's not dead, she's somewhere, and that means she can come back."

Missus Orphint opened her mouth to reply, but Oni let out a squeak, as if she had been pinched, and then held out her hand, palm open, so Missus Orphint could see. Words were scratching themselves on Oni's skin, fading almost as soon as they could be read.

Out. You safe?

"Is that your ma?" said Pip.

"Yes," said Oni, with a warm rush of relief that made her eyes prickle with tears. "Yes, it is."

Missus Orphint let out a breath, and Oni realized that she had been as anxious about Amina as she was.

"Well, at least Amina can look after herself," said Pip bitterly. "El can't. She's alone and frightened and she won't know what to do, any more than a baby kitten."

"Stop it, Pip," said Oni. "It doesn't help." She was tracing an answer on her palm. "Ma says she's going to the

Undercroft. Why doesn't she come here?"

"The Midsummer Carnival's on tonight," said Missus Orphint. "Some of us were going to meet there, before your ma was arrested and our plans got upturned."

"Are we going to the Undercroft, then?"

"I think I should," said Missus Orphint. "I was supposed to be there hours ago. And now, it's even more urgent I speak to the council. They need to know what happened here. But I shouldn't leave you two alone…"

"I'm not a baby," said Oni sharply. "Why can't we come too?"

"I daren't take you out of the safe house. Not until we know what's going on." Missus Orphint tapped her fingers on the table, frowning in thought. All trace of the mild, vague woman who had greeted them at the door the evening before had vanished entirely: she looked stern and sharp. Pip realized that her vagueness really was a kind of disguise.

"I think I must go," she said at last. "I'll be as quick as I can be. Don't do anything rash, either of you. I mean it. Oni, you will have to be on guard, and Pip, you listen to what she says." Here she looked hard at Pip.

"I want to see Ma," said Oni, her jaw jutting ominously. "You can't tell me what to do."

"No, I can't. You're quite right." Missus Orphint put

on her hat. "I'm requesting you as politely as I can to heed my words. You two should go to bed and get some sleep. We've already lost El, and Amina would never forgive me if I lost her daughter too."

She opened the kitchen door and stood for a moment, looking out. The moon was peeping out from behind the swags of clouds, letting down a silvery light. She stepped outside, and disappeared into the darkness. They heard her footsteps retreating, followed by a long silence that was punctuated by the *drip drip drip* of rain from the trees.

Oni stood up and shut the back door. "I thought she was going to fly. Missus Pledge is an owl-shaper," she said, as she returned to her chair.

"A what?"

"She turns into an owl. Maybe she thought it was too dangerous to use magic."

Two hours before, Pip would have been amazed and fascinated, but now he didn't care what witches could do. None of it was any use if they couldn't rescue El. It was witches that had caused all this trouble, anyway. It was a witch that had made the Heart.

"Pip."

He ignored her, so Oni plucked at his sleeve.

"Pip, I'm really sorry. I'm sorry about El. I'm sorry about everything."

"Like that does any good."

"Maybe we could try to look for her."

"You just said you didn't know how. And anyway Missus Orphint said not to do anything."

"Missus Orphint said you should try to talk to Clovis."

"He's not there. And why would I talk to someone who probably murdered my sister?"

"Try, Pip. Surely it's worth a try? For El's sake?"

Pip met her eyes. "Why?"

"You heard what Missus Orphint said. Maybe he needs to be less frightened. Maybe he needs a friend."

Oni didn't say out loud what she was thinking, because she was too afraid. Pip was more than sad and angry: he didn't seem quite himself. And Oni had begun to wonder why.

Maybe Clovis had disappeared from the Heart because he was now inside Pip. Maybe Clovis was beginning to take over Pip's body, just like Clovis's father had planned to take over Clovis's body.

Oni bit her lip, trying to think clearly, instead of panicking. All the stories she knew about the Heart said that the child prince wasn't yet a Spectre. They said he had been touched by the Spectre's blood magic, but not devoured by it. But now Oni had begun to wonder if it was already too late when Old Missus Pledge made the spell. Maybe the soul trapped inside the Heart wasn't a little boy: or at least, it wasn't only a little boy. Maybe Prince Clovis was also the Spectre King, and now both of them were inside Pip.

If that were so, then Clovis's father hadn't been killed after all. Not properly. Maybe, Oni thought, the Cardinal didn't want the Heart because he was afraid it would destroy the Spectres. Maybe he wanted it because it was a way of bringing back the Spectre King.

Or something worse.

The longer she thought, the worse the possibilities that unravelled before her. If she could find out more about what was happening inside Pip's mind...

"Pip," she said, clasping his arm. "Maybe we can help El."

Pip brushed her hand off irritably. "Don't *do* that, Oni. It's annoying. Of course I'll try it. I just don't know where to start."

Oni sighed with relief. Her fears suddenly seemed silly. He was just Pip; rude, sharp-faced, irritating Pip, the same as always.

"All right," she said. "Let's try."

Chapter Thirty-one

MISSUS ORPHINT ARRIVED AT THE UNDERCROFT shortly after Amina. The carnival was still in full swing, but Missus Orphint was not in a carnival mood. The disappearance of El had shaken her more than she had permitted Oni and Pip to see. A Rupture in her own safe house? That was bad. That was very bad.

She didn't like leaving those two children alone, either. Oni was smart, very much her mother's daughter, but not even the most experienced witch knew much about Ruptures. Ruptures were what happened when magic strained the fibres of reality too far and broke them, and they were completely unpredictable. Spectre magic, which ignored all the Laws, made small Ruptures all the time, although even Spectres tried to avoid them. A Rupture that was driven by a mind, let alone the mind of a damaged child – that was something else. Something much more dangerous.

Missus Orphint had some very strong views on what Old Missus Pledge had done when she made the Heart, and none of them were complimentary to Old Missus Pledge. She understood why the witch had taken the risk, but that didn't mean she approved. But whether she approved or not, it was imperative that the witches find Old Missus Pledge's spell before the Office for Witchcraft Extermination got hold of it.

At the Council Tent, a slim, fair girl with deep shadows under her eyes was standing a little distance away from the others. She was dressed in breeches and a shirt, and her hair was wound into ringlet rags. She was obviously the Princess Georgette, but she didn't look much like a princess without all her finery; she looked forlorn, exhausted and lost.

Missus Orphint didn't approve of royals either, and she especially didn't approve of royals descended from the Spectre. But despite herself, she felt a pang of compassion.

"I promise that I wouldn't betray anyone here," Georgette was saying. She was holding herself very straight. "I just *wouldn't*."

"How do we know that?" said Amiable. She seemed

in an irritable mood. If she had been in cat form, her tail would have been thrashing. "That's exactly what a traitor would say."

"Hush, Amiable," said Amina. "Georgie has no love for our enemies."

Georgette pressed her hands hard together, trying to control the wobble in her jaw. "They are my enemies too," she said. "None of them wish me good. My father wants me to marry a Spectre and to send me away to another country where I'll be all by myself, totally in his power."

Helios looked sad. "Your own father?"

"He said he'd have me beheaded if I didn't," she said. "I don't think he would really, but if he catches me now, after I've run away, I'll be locked up and forced to marry King Oswald. I'd much rather have my head cut off."

All the witches could hear the suppressed terror in Georgette's voice. Even Amiable looked taken aback.

Amina, seeing that Georgette was on the brink of tears, stepped forward and took her hand. "It's all right, Georgie," she said. "Of course people are going to be suspicious. We all have suffered greatly at the hands of the royals. And trust is hard to earn."

Georgette swallowed. "Of course," she said, trying to speak proudly, as a princess would.

215

"Well, I understand why she wants our help. I still don't get why we're helping her," said Amiable. "What's in it for us?" A couple of others murmured in agreement.

Amina was about to answer when she saw the look on Missus Orphint's face. "Something's happened, hasn't it?"

Missus Orphint nodded. "Yes. I'm afraid Eleanor Wastan has been taken by a Rupture."

Amina went still, and her jaw tightened. "This happened in your house? You left them alone, after *that*?"

"I'm sorry, Amina. I had no choice. I didn't dare to take them out of the safe house. It was imperative that the council knew, and I came as fast as I could. I think we must find Old Missus Pledge's spell now, as a matter of urgency."

"But how?" said Helios. "It's been missing all these years, and no one knows where to find it…"

"Oni told me about Missus Pledge's papers," said Missus Orphint. "I think she had the spell in her house all that time."

"I do, too," said Amina. "But if we are right, those papers are now in the hands of Cardinal Lamir, at the Office for Witchcraft Extermination."

"Then we really are in the basket," said Juin. "Even if they haven't worked out how to read the spell, how under heaven do we find it, let alone get it back?"

A desolate silence fell. Georgette, who was still standing a little aside, spoke hesitantly. "I think I know where it might be," she said.

"You?" said Amiable. "Why?"

Georgette lifted her chin. She was getting a little tired of Amiable's needling. "A couple of years ago I found out that my tutor, Sibelius d'Artan, works for Cardinal Lamir. He translates papers for him, and various other things… I was curious, so I went to the palace library and looked up a monograph he wrote. It was in the locked section, but I managed to get in there by stealing the librarian's keys. It said that Sibelius was the world's foremost authority on the witch script."

Missus Clay snorted. "Aside from witches, of course," she said.

"Yes. So my guess is that if anybody is investigating secret papers, it will be Sibelius."

Missus Orphint looked thoughtful. "It's worth a try," she said. "A simple finding spell could pinpoint where this Sibelius is."

Amina had been listening, but in an abstracted way. "I don't like the thought of those young people all on their own with all this Spectre magic," she said abruptly.

"Neither do I," said Missus Orphint. "Although Oni is, after all, very capable."

"Yes, she is, but…" Amina bit back what she was planning to say. "Perhaps I can leave retrieving the papers up to you? I want to make sure my daughter is safe."

"Of course." Missus Orphint rummaged in her bag until she found a key, and held it out.

Amina took the key and hurried off, kissing Georgette hastily on the forehead in farewell. The Princess watched her leave, feeling abandoned again. In the palace she knew that nobody really cared about her, but even so, she was always looked after. Nobody here seemed to care about her at all. Not even Amina.

"All right," said Amiable. "Let's see if this princess really is of any use."

Chapter Thirty-two

SIBELIUS HAD SPENT THE ENTIRE NIGHT IN HIS DINGY
room at the Office for Witchcraft Extermination, trying
to save his neck.

For the past two years, Sibelius's biggest ambition
had been to survive his employment and get home to
his modest estate. He kept his head down and concentrated on pleasing his master as best he could. He
tried not to think too hard about what he was doing.
He wasn't sure any more that he was helping to prevent evil. He had a horrible feeling that he was doing
the reverse. And that was even before all the business
with the Stone Heart...

Survival seemed a very slim chance now.

His eyes ached from staring at the Last Will and
Testament and Property Deeds of Prunelissima Arabella
Pledge, spinster and seamstress of Omiker Lane. He had

examined it from every possible angle. He had compared the measurements of her humble apartment with the measurements recorded on the page. They accorded exactly. He cautiously held the parchments over a candle flame to reveal any invisible writing. He had tried dribbling grape and lemon juice on the pages. He had taken out every second, third, fourth, fifth, sixth and seventh word, to see if they made any hidden sentences. He turned them into numbers and read them backwards and sideways and diagonally.

He had fallen asleep at the desk and had horrible dreams about Prunelissima's meagre possessions: pins and needles danced around bonfires, and armies of china cups came to arrest him. No matter what he did, he couldn't find anything to show that these documents were anything more than what they appeared to be. And he knew he couldn't get away with making something up. The Cardinal would know instantly if he tried to deceive him.

His eyes felt as if they had been rolled in sand. He walked over to the window, pulled it open and stared out over the sleeping city. Perhaps his only recourse was to throw himself out. It would be a kinder death than disembowelment.

As he returned to his desk, his gaze fell on his shoes

and he felt a lurch of contempt. Had he really sold his soul for a pair of silver buckles?

"Yes, that's exactly what you did," said a voice.

Sibelius looked in the direction of the voice. An owl was sitting on his windowsill, its eyes reflecting back the candlelight in the room. He was too exhausted to be afraid, or even surprised.

"You're in a bit of a mess now, aren't you, Sibelius?"

Obviously, Sibelius thought, he was hallucinating. He had read that this could happen in states of extreme exhaustion and stress. He laughed humourlessly and sat down, staring at the owl. It looked quite solid, for a hallucination. Although he had never had a hallucination before, so he didn't know what they were like.

"What choice do I have?" he said bitterly. "What choice did I ever have? It's not like anyone can say no to the Cardinal."

"Of course you had a choice," said the owl. It sounded impatient, even contemptuous. "You were greedy and ambitious and, I'm afraid, very, very foolish."

Even through his self-pity, Sibelius felt a twinge of shame. "Are you my conscience?" he said at last.

"No," snapped the owl. "I wouldn't want to be anything so filthy."

Sibelius stared gloomily at his silver buckles. "Anyway,

even if I had a choice in the beginning, I don't any more."

"Of course you do. You could, for example, run away."

"Everybody knows that you can't hide from the assassins."

"What everybody knows isn't the same as what is true. All you need is the courage to stand up for what you believe, in your secret heart, to be right. I think you knew what you were doing was deeply wrong."

Sibelius shifted uncomfortably in his chair. "It's too late now."

The owl said nothing. He found its unblinking gaze unnerving.

"Anyway," he added. "I know you're not real. You're just a figment of my imagination."

"You know nothing of the sort," said the owl. "I can tell from here that you know I'm real." It fluffed out its feathers. "Which, of course, I am."

"Owls don't talk."

"There has been no reason, up to now, for any owl to speak to you."

"Then why now?" Sibelius was beginning to feel a little frightened. Hallucinations, he felt, ought not to be so insulting.

"You have excited our interest," said the owl. "I would, for example, be very interested in looking at

222

those documents that you are investigating."

"They're nothing," said Sibelius sadly. "I can't find a single sign of witchery."

"They would be very important to the unfortunate people who own them," said the owl, with some asperity. "But maybe you're wrong. Perhaps you're looking in the wrong place. Or in the wrong way."

"How would you know?" Sibelius was beginning to get angry now. "I am the foremost expert in the witch script in the entire kingdom and I can't find a single mark."

"You are not the foremost expert. You are just the best at guessing," said the owl. "I, on the other hand, am an expert. Maybe I could show you. But first you'd have to abandon your task here."

"If I don't do what the Cardinal commands, I'll be executed. It's not like I care whether it's a witch document or not. I just don't want to be killed."

The owl thought it over. "Good point," it said. "Why not just come with me, and forget the whole thing? As long as you bring the will, of course."

Sibelius rubbed his eyes. He really was very tired.

"Coming with me will be less risky than remaining here and waiting for the Cardinal to draw your entrails. Which he almost certainly will, when you present him with nothing."

"You're right," said Sibelius sarcastically. "I might as well seek the protection of a nocturnal bird. Or I could save time and jump out of the window."

"I think you are being unnecessarily pessimistic," said the owl. "Although, true, given that you are being guarded by assassins, this window is our only means of egress."

Sibelius shook his head. No doubt his mind was tricking him into ending it all. His mind was probably right. The Cardinal wanted results by lunchtime and it was almost dawn already. He didn't have a hope. He was so tired he didn't care any more what happened to him.

He laughed mirthlessly. "All right then, owl. I'll come with you." He stepped towards the window.

"Excellent. But don't forget the will!"

Sibelius grabbed the parchments from the table and stuffed them into his pocket. "Now what?"

"Climb onto the sill. This might be a little tricky, so don't fall off."

"I thought falling off was the point?" The owl didn't respond so he shrugged and climbed clumsily onto the broad stone ledge. The owl hopped to the side to give him space. The night sky was cloudless, and the stars twinkled white and clear in the distance. There was a faint glimmer of dawn in the eastern sky. It occurred to

Sibelius that these would be the last stars he ever saw. For a moment he felt a stab of sorrow.

"I hope it doesn't hurt too much," he said.

"You might feel a bit of a sting, but only for a short time," said the owl. "Just be quiet for a while, while I get prepared."

Sibelius shut his eyes and nodded. He felt completely passive and resigned. Any moment now the hard stone ground beneath would come rushing up towards him and then there would be … what?

He wondered confusedly whether he would get into heaven. He had always tried to do the right thing, even when he knew underneath that what people said was the right thing was actually the wrong thing. If he were God, would he let himself in?

He thought he probably wouldn't.

He tried to remember a prayer, any prayer, but his mind had gone blank.

"Ready?" said the owl. It didn't wait for an answer.

"Ow!" said Sibelius.

The owl was correct. It stung. Quite a lot.

Chapter Thirty-three

RIGHT NOW, PIP HATED CLOVIS WITH EVERY FIBRE IN his being. That arrogant, spiteful little worm deserved nothing better than a good kick in the shins. Although, of course, being dead, he didn't have any shins.

Since the moment Pip had touched the Heart he had sensed Clovis's presence, but now, when Pip most needed to speak to him, the Prince had gone silent. He couldn't feel him anywhere.

Oni was frowning, staring at the table and plucking her lip. "Maybe he's just hiding, Pip," she said. "Maybe he's scared."

"He should be."

"Well, think about it. Maybe he didn't mean to take El."

"He *did* mean it. He wanted to take you, too."

"But maybe it was like, you know, when you lose your

temper and do something awful, but then afterwards you're sorry."

"Why would he be sorry?"

"I don't know. But when he was killed, he was just a little boy. And, you know, he was lonely. I could feel it when I touched the Heart. He was a lonely, frightened little boy."

"Like I care."

Oni looked up. "Do you want to get El back?"

Pip didn't answer. Of course he did.

"Well, then. Stop being angry, and *think*. I know it's hard for you, Pip, because you're not very clever, but we got to think."

Pip opened his mouth to object to the insult, but ended up saying nothing. He didn't have the heart to fight with Oni.

Where had Clovis gone?

Inside his head, maybe, where he was before. But hiding. Pip closed his eyes.

All right, Clovis, he said. *I'm not angry any more.*

He waited, but nobody answered.

We need to talk. Are you there? I promise I'm not angry.

He waited again, watching the pendulum on Missus Orphint's wall clock swing back and forth. One, two, three, four, five. No answer. This wasn't going to work.

You are *angry,* said Clovis. *I can feel it.*

Pip took a breath, trying to suppress his mounting rage. *Can you blame me? You hurt my sister. She never did you any harm. She never did anyone any harm. And look what you done. It's not fair.*

She didn't like me. Clovis sounded sulky. *Why should I care?*

If you want to be friends with me, you should care. You hurt El, you hurt me. You hurt me really bad, Clovis.

Silence. But this silence felt different. It had a tinge of surprise, as if Clovis had encountered a novel thought.

Princes don't have friends, he said, after a while. *Princes can't afford the weakness of sentimental bonds.* He sounded as if he were quoting a lesson learned by rote.

Who says? said Pip. *Everybody needs a friend. Anyway, you're not even a prince any more. You're just dead. Sort of.*

That was a mistake. Pip felt a lash of hurt, and Clovis vanished.

Hey, Clovis. Come back. Pip waited. *I'm sorry,* he said. *I just want to talk.*

Nothing.

He opened his eyes and jumped. Oni was closer than he had realized, staring straight into his face.

"I can hear Clovis," she said, her eyes wide. "I couldn't before, but now I can hear him too."

228

"He's gone again," said Pip.

"Yes, but he's probably listening."

Pip hunched his shoulders. "This is weird," he said. "I don't like it."

"Let's try again."

Oni shut her eyes. Pip noticed how her long eyelashes rested on her cheek, how the candlelight threw warm shadows on her skin.

This time Clovis spoke first. *I don't like being dead,* he said. *It's cold here.*

Pip couldn't think of what to say. For the first time since El had vanished, he felt a tiny stab of compassion.

I miss the taste of food, said Clovis. *I'm not hungry, but I miss it all the same. Sometimes I try to remember what plums taste like ... and roast goose. Roast goose was one of my favourites.*

Oni's voice, a whisper. "Are you all alone?"

Yes.

"That must make you sad," she said.

A silence. *Yes.*

"Can you imagine how sad Pip is now that El is gone? Now he's all alone, too."

A pause. *He can talk to me,* said Clovis. *I'll be his friend instead.*

"It doesn't work like that," said Oni. "You can't just

229

replace one person with another. Every friend is special, like no other person in the whole world. And you can have more than one friend."

I'll order him. He'll have to be my friend.

Pip felt his anger rising again. This was hopeless. "You can't order people to be your friend. That's not what friends do."

Then how can you be sure that they'll stay your friend?

For a moment Pip felt a sense of disbelief: was he really trying to teach a dead prince about friendship?

Yes. Yes, he was.

"They just do," he said. "If you're proper friends."

"When you're friends, you trust each other," said Oni. "Everyone makes mistakes. You learn to forgive mistakes. But you never order friends around. Never. You never punish them. You learn to trust each other. You keep your word."

Another pause.

"Friendship takes time," she said. Oni's voice was as soft and sweet as honey. "And sometimes it doesn't work. But when it does work, it's the best thing in the world. El is my friend. My best friend. And I miss her. I miss her really badly."

This time there was a long silence. Pip held his breath.

If I bring her back, will we be friends?

Suddenly, heartbreakingly, there was an emotion in Clovis's voice that Pip hadn't heard before.

Hope.

"We can try," said Oni.

"Yes," said Pip. "We can try."

Chapter Thirty-four

SIBELIUS HAD GIVEN UP ON REALITY. WAS THIS REALLY a hallucination? Maybe, he thought dazedly, he was actually dead, and had entered some kind of afterlife that none of the books talked about.

He was standing in a yellow-and-green striped tent. He had no recollection of how he had got there. He didn't remember anything after the blinding pain, which had felt exactly as bad as if he had been stung all over by wasps. At least that had passed now, but he still felt extremely shaky.

The owl seemed to have disappeared, but a tall woman with a gentle, bland face and greying hair was holding his elbow. Another woman, so bent with age that she barely reached his breastbone, was standing right in front of him, inspecting him intently. As he was a shy man, he blushed to the roots of his hair and looked away, only to find that the tent was full of other people seated around a table where they had clearly been eating breakfast. All of them were staring at him. His gaze fell to his feet, where he kept it fixed on his buckles.

Those silver buckles, he thought, had brought him much more trouble than they could possibly be worth.

"Greetings, Sibelius d'Artan," said the crone in front of him. "My name is Missus Clay. If you wish to be sick, there is a bucket to your left."

Sibelius was very nauseous, but even feeling as bad as he did, the thought of throwing up in front of all these people filled him with embarrassment. He pressed his lips tightly together and shook his head.

"Sadly, transmogrification is a little discombobulating to the internal organs," said a tall, grey-haired woman who was holding his elbow. Sibelius noted, with an increasing sense of unreality, that she sounded exactly like the owl. "We've never been able to get rid of it. And I was in a hurry. Well, if you're not going to be sick, you might as well sit down. But keep that bucket handy."

When Sibelius didn't move, she gently led him to the table in the centre of the tent and pressed him into a chair. A fair-haired boy with his hair pulled back in a ponytail was sitting opposite. He looked unsettlingly familiar. Distracted, Sibelius tried to place his face.

"It's nice to see you, Sibelius," said the boy, smiling a little tremulously. Sibelius realized with a start that it wasn't a boy at all. It was Princess Georgette, dressed up as a commoner. What was she doing here?

"I suppose I've gone mad," he said. He drew out a handkerchief and mopped his brow. "It was only a matter of time…"

"The will, if you please," said Missus Clay.

Sibelius looked around the table. "I suppose you're all witches?"

The grey-haired woman nodded. "Yes," she said. "That's right. And we want the will."

"I can tell you that there's not a skerrick of witch magic anywhere in that parchment." Sibelius laughed with a note of hysteria. "I've looked and looked and looked."

"We'll be the judges of that, thank you," said the woman. "My name is Missus Orphint, by the way. You've met Missus Clay, chief witch of the Witches' Council. And these are the senior members." She gestured around the table. "Aside from Princess Georgette, of course."

Sibelius blinked. He had definitely gone mad. He thought he might as well accept it. It was, in any case, better here than sitting in his dusty chamber on the fifth floor of the Office for Witchcraft Extermination thinking about disembowelment.

He smiled weakly. "How very lovely to meet you," he said.

"It won't be lovely, if you didn't bring the will," said a pretty, dark-haired woman to his right.

"Hush, Amiable," hissed a golden-haired man next to her. "Be nice. The poor man's in shock."

"You want the Last Will and Testament of Mistress Prunelissima Arabella Pledge, spinster and seamstress of Omiker Lane of the Chokally Quarter? Or maybe I should just quote it to you. I know it all by heart." Sibelius drew the will out of his pocket and threw it onto the table. "You can have it, with my blessings."

Suddenly nobody was looking at Sibelius. Everyone's gaze was fixed on the shabby parchment. For a few moments, nobody moved a muscle.

"Do you think it really is the spell?" said Georgette doubtfully. "It just looks like an ordinary will."

"What would you know?" said Amiable.

Georgette cast her a look of dislike. "I know what official documents look like, if that's what you mean," she said.

Missus Clay shuffled forwards. She picked up the will and held it in front of her with the tips of her fingers. When she let go, the parchment hung in the air, as if it had been pinned to an invisible board. She leaned forward and breathed on it.

Sibelius heard a bar of music, violin music he thought, played on an old, out-of-tune violin by a very bad musician. And then he heard a voice. A woman's voice, that held traces of strength but was also worn and scratchy. He looked around, trying to see who it was, but it was no one in the room. It was coming from the parchment.

Sibelius's jaw dropped open. He had never even considered that the spell might be audible.

"I, Prunelissima Arabella Pledge, witch of Clarel, speaking in the Year of the Oak Apple, on the sixth day of the Month of Rejoicing, here make confession on my deathbed. I have done a dark thing, in a time of terrible darkness. I speak before you in humility and sorrow, both for what I have done and for what is to come. I cannot undo what I have done, forgive me. But I beg you to heal the wound, and to close this evil, the evil that came before me and the evil that I have unwittingly created."

The unseen witch paused. There was a stirring around the table, as if everyone drew breath at the same time.

"Firstly, it is imperative that the Heart is never taken from the casket that keeps it insulated from outside influences."

"That's torn it," said Amiable. The others turned and hushed her.

"Secondly, it is crucial that the Stone Heart is not touched

by a living soul. I cannot tell what would happen to any unfortunate who enters the sphere of its influence. Thirdly, and most important of all, it must be kept from the Spectres."

Old Missus Pledge paused again, struggling for breath.

"I sought to find a way to destroy the Spectres for ever. But alas, I failed. By abstracting the Heart from the Infant Vessel, I created a new kind of Rupture. And now I know that if the Stone Heart fell into the hands of a Spectre, it could instead multiply their power to an unimaginable extent."

"I knew it!" said Missus Orphint under her breath.

The old witch coughed. "It's too late to destroy this evil artefact. Destroying the object would only release the spell into the diurnal world. The Ruptures that resulted could tear apart the whole of reality. So this evil thing must, at all costs, be kept safe and secret."

Her voice was fading, but her urgency grew. Everyone leaned closer, trying to hear every word.

"The Stone Heart must never be permitted to land in the clutches of the Spectres. I ask you, my siblings, to exert yourselves in all the ways you know to keep the future safe from these dread possibilities. I beg your forgiveness again for my terrible failure. May the powers of eternal love have mercy upon my soul."

The scratchy violin chords sounded again, and the

sheet of parchment slowly peeled itself out of the air and fluttered to the ground.

Everyone at the table, including Georgette and Sibelius, stared at each other in horror.

It left the witches no hope at all of destroying the Spectres, and precious little of surviving if the Cardinal or Oswald found the Heart. The only solution now was to find the casket that Old Missus Pledge had made to imprison it. The casket that Pip had sold to Olibrandis, and that had almost certainly been taken by the assassin who murdered him.

"Damn," said Amiable.

Chapter Thirty-five

ALLOWING HIMSELF TO BE TAKEN BY THE RUPTURE
was the bravest thing that Pip had ever done.

Now it was right in front of him, he felt nakedly
frightened. The hole was almost as big as he was. It was
like looking into a green, glowing cave that stretched
into depths he couldn't see. The walls rippled as if they
were made of thick vapour, moving in hypnotic spirals
and waves. He could feel a terrible gravity pulling him
closer and closer, and every single bit of him shouted
that he should run away. It was too strange, too uncanny.
It didn't belong in Missus Orphint's cosy kitchen.

"If I go in," he said out loud, "will you bring me back?"

I think so, said Clovis.

"What do you mean, you *think* so?"

You dare to question me? The arrogance was back in
Clovis's voice. *Me? A prince of the realm?*

"I don't think you should go," said Oni quickly. She was pressed against the wall, as far away as she could get, her eyes wide with fear. "I think it's a trap."

Pip set his jaw. It probably was a trap. But it was the only chance of getting El back.

"I want you to promise me. I want to be able to *trust* you."

"On your word as a prince," added Oni.

The Rupture became agitated, the rolls of vapour churning rapidly. *It's insulting for such as you to make demands of me*, said Clovis.

"It's no good," said Oni. "He'll just betray us."

Pip shook off her hand. "Clovis, if you don't bring me and El back I will never be your friend. I'll hate you for ever and ever. I don't care what you do. You can hurt me as much as you like, it won't make any difference. You'll be all alone and you'll deserve it."

He took a deep breath. "That's *my* promise," he said. "And me, I keep my promises."

He moved forward and put his hand into the Rupture. It was slightly cool, but otherwise he felt nothing except an increasingly insistent tug. This close, he could hear a faint, high humming. His heart was beating so hard it felt as if it were jumping in his throat, trying to throttle him.

He looked back over his shoulder. Oni was staring

at him, her hands clasped tightly together, and he felt a twinge of sorrow within his fear. Perhaps he would never see her again. He opened his mouth to say goodbye, but there was a sudden jerk and he was pulled inside. The faint humming became a rushing noise that grew louder and louder, until it hurt his eardrums, and the dim glow was now a pulsing flash that was so dazzlingly bright that he could see it even when he closed his eyes.

It was unbearable, and it seemed to go on for an eternity, a bruising assault on all his senses that drove every thought out of his head except the desire for it to stop. He lost all track of time. It could have been hours, or just a few moments; he had no way of telling.

But at last it did stop. No more rushing, no more flashing lights. At first the relief was overwhelming. He stayed very still, his eyes jammed shut, afraid that it might begin all over again.

Where was he?

It was still cool, but he wasn't cold. His cheek was pressed hard against some kind of soft fabric, a carpet maybe. Very cautiously, he opened his eyes.

Right in front of his face stood a pair of polished black boots.

Pip scrambled to his feet. The movement made his head swim. He swayed and blinked, staring around in bewilderment. The black boots belonged to an assassin, who stepped back as he rose, but that was the least of Pip's astonishment.

He was in a bedchamber, unlike any he had ever imagined. It blazed with light. Pip had never seen so many candles in one place. They burned in a crystal chandelier that hung from the ceiling and in huge candelabras placed about the room. The ceiling and walls were painted with pictures of fantastic animals – dragons and unicorns and griffins – framed by ornate gilt cornices. All the furniture seemed to be made of gold.

Pip turned in a full circle, his mouth open in astonishment. On a table with spindly gold legs was a golden platter piled high with purple plums, and a gold decanter surrounded by long-stemmed glasses. At one end of the room was an enormous bed with red and gold curtains of heavy brocade. The room was so big it made the bed look small.

The assassin wasn't the only person there. Sitting against the opposite wall was El, on a chair with legs so spindly that they looked as if they would snap under the slightest pressure. Her hair was elaborately styled in ringlets and she was wearing the same dress that Princess Georgette had worn on the day that she came to Amina's place.

"Pip!" she said, her face shining. "Are you come to rescue me?"

"I think so," said Pip. "But who are all these people?"

"This is Heironomo Blaise," said El chattily, gesturing towards the assassin. "He's quite nice, really, you wouldn't have thought so, would you? And that's Harpin Shtum." She waved her hand at a man dressed in a green velvet jacket with soiled lace at the cuffs, who bowed. Pip recognized him as a card-sharp he had seen around the Crosseyes. "I don't know who the other person is. He just turned up when you did."

Pip stared at the last person, a small, fair-haired boy. He was too thin, and under his eyes were huge shadows. He was dressed all in gold, from head to foot: golden jacket, golden waistcoat, golden breeches, golden buckles on his golden shoes. All the glitter somehow made him look smaller than he really was.

The boy was looking at Pip with a mixture of uncertainty and hauteur, his chin high. "Do you like my room?" he said. "I made it just for you."

Clovis. Pip swallowed, trying to gather his thoughts. "You what?"

"It's much nicer here now," said El. "Before it was…" She trailed off, frowning. "How odd!" she said. "I can't remember. It's like we only just got here and also as if we've been here all the time having a party. Maybe it was always like this."

"No, it wasn't," said Harpin Shtum. "Floating around in the dark, and all that sobbing…"

"Oh yes, that was so frightening! But it's lovely now." El looked at Clovis. "Did you make my dress? It's so pretty."

"This is my eternal kingdom," said Clovis grandly. "My word is law."

Pip glanced at the walls of the room. He was sure they were moving, like sheets rippling in a slight breeze. Everything seemed somehow not quite right: the plums were too purple, the gold too bright. He had a hollow feeling in his chest, as if he were in the middle of a dream that at any moment might turn nasty.

"You just made this up?"

"It's for my friends," said Clovis. "See how happy your sister is?"

"You promised you would take us back," said Pip. "I want to go home. Don't you, El?"

El smiled sunnily at him. "It's so nice here, Pip," she said. "Much nicer than Clarel."

"See?" said Clovis. "Why would you want to go back there? It's much better here."

Pip ignored the Prince. "With an assassin?" He flung out his arm, his voice high with incredulity. "An actual assassin is in this room, and you want to stay here? I bet you my right hand that this is the man that tried to capture Oni."

The assassin smiled wolfishly.

"I told you, Pip, he's quite nice really," said El.

"He's *nice*?"

"He was an orphan like us, Pip. He didn't have a choice."

"But you and me, we didn't become assassins."

"We didn't get put in the orphanage. That's what the orphanages are for, so the Cardinal can get assassins. He'd whip them if they didn't obey. Sometimes they were *killed*."

Heironomo started and, to Pip's surprise, blushed. Pip looked at him properly for the first time, and realized that the assassin wasn't much older than El was.

"I didn't tell you that," the assassin said.

"Yes, you did," said El, and went back to admiring her dress.

El didn't seem like El. There was something odd about her eyes, as if she wasn't really focusing on anything, as if she wasn't quite there. Pip strode forward and shook her shoulders. "El, wake up. We got to get out of here. That's the only thing that's important right now."

"But your sister doesn't want to leave," said Clovis, with a little smile of triumph.

"Yes, she does," said Pip belligerently.

El looked up into Pip's eyes, and blinked.

"Yes, I do want to go home. Oni's not here. And I miss our place." She smoothed out the lace on her sleeves. "I know this dress is really pretty, and it was really nice of you to make it for me, but maybe it's time to go now."

The walls began to shake. Harpin, looking worried, plucked at Pip's sleeve. "Maybe, young sir, you shouldn't…"

"Clovis," said Pip, looking him right in the eye. "You promised. Were you planning to be a dirty traitor all along?"

Clovis went white. "You dare…"

"You said you wanted to be friends. No wonder people hate the royals. Whether you're a prince or not, you're just a low-bellied cockroach if you break your word."

Pip just had time to see Clovis's lip wobble before all the candles went dark. He heard El cry out in terror and the assassin cursing, but then their voices were drowned in a roaring that grew louder and louder. Above the roar, he could hear Clovis's voice shrieking with rage. "I hate you!" he shouted. "I hate you, I hate you, I hate you!"

Inside Pip something snapped. He lost his temper, but not in the way he usually did. Perhaps as a reaction to Clovis's loss of control, he felt himself become cold and calm. And absolutely furious.

"Yes, you hate everybody," he said. He didn't shout, he didn't even know if Clovis could hear him. "You hate everybody and everything. And you know why? Because you're a coward."

The roaring stopped with disconcerting suddenness, leaving a silence so heavy Pip felt as if his ears were stuffed with wool.

"I'm not a coward," said Clovis.

"Yes, you are." Pip remembered what Oni had said before he went into the Rupture. "A coward is a person who bullies other people to do what they want, because they don't have the courage to trust." He took a deep breath. "You know what's brave? Trusting your friends. That's what someone with courage does. You're just a snivelling, spoilt *coward*."

He spat out the final word with all the force of his rage. It echoed in the darkness, each repetition a little louder than the last, becoming so loud that Pip covered his ears, and then it died slowly into silence.

"I'm *not*." There was a sob in Clovis's voice, and for a moment he sounded like an ordinary seven-year-old boy.

Pip took a deep breath. "Prove it."

Chapter Thirty-six

AS SHE LEFT THE UNDERCROFT, AMINA SENT A scrawl to Oni to let her know she was on her way. Then, as an afterthought, she sent another forbidding her to make any attempt to rescue El. She knew her daughter well: of course that would be the first thing Oni would think of.

Normally Oni would have responded at once. When she didn't answer, a cold dread began to spread in the pit of Amina's stomach. Oni's silence could mean that she was already in the midst of an attempt to rescue El and didn't want to lie to her mother. Or it could mean that she hadn't received the message.

Oni might have been taken by the Rupture. She might be dead. Plurabella shouldn't have left those children alone with that monstrous Heart.

Missus Orphint's house was only a short distance

from the entrance to the Undercroft. There were no flambeaux in this part of town, and the streets were plunged into shadow. Amina briefly weighed the risks of her magic being sensed by a Spectre, and decided haste was the priority. She cast a small candle charm to light her way and hurried to Missus Orphint's house, her fears crowding in her throat.

By the time she arrived at Missus Orphint's front door, Amina was in a flat panic. She almost dropped the key as she tried to open the door, and then she turned it the wrong way, cursing as she jammed it into the lock, but at last the tumblers clicked over. She slammed the door behind her and stepped into the narrow hallway where a lamp burned on a small table, waiting for Missus Orphint to come home.

Amina heard Oni's voice at the other end of the house. Relief rushed through her whole body, leaving her legs shaking. In its wake came a surge of anger. She had been almost sure that Oni was dead. How dare she not answer her message? How could she be so thoughtless? She would have known how worried her mother would be...

Amina gave herself a few moments. This wasn't like her. In an emergency, she was the person who always kept her head. People turned to her because she was never flustered: she was the one who knew how to stop the bleeding, what to say to the newly bereaved, how to comfort the dying. The shock that everybody else felt in disaster happened later in private, when she had time to deal with it. What was wrong with her?

I guess it's been a hard night, she thought.

She breathed in deeply through her nose and out again, emptying her mind of its jittering. And then she snapped out the candle spell, marched down the hall-way and threw open the kitchen door.

She halted, blinking in surprise. The kitchen was more crowded than she'd expected, and everyone seemed to be in the middle of an argument. Oni was standing at the far wall, her eyes sparkling with indig-nation. Pip was next to her, his mouth set in a stubborn line. At the table El leaned forward on a chair, looking more pale than usual. Opposite El sat two men: one, clad in the black uniform of his trade, clearly an assas-sin. Oni had used a spell to bind the strangers; Amina could see the magical shackles from where she stood.

They were all too intent on their argument to notice Amina's entrance. She cleared her throat. "What, by the grace of the good earth, is an assassin doing here?"

Oni's face lit up. "Ma!"

"You had better tell me what's been going on here,

250

young lady." Amina moved ominously into the kitchen. "How could an assassin get past Plurabella's wards? Did you let him in?"

"Oh, no!" said El. "He came back from the other place, when Pip came to rescue me. He ended up rescuing everybody else by mistake, including Heironomo. And then Oni put a spell on him and now he's really cross."

Amina had a sudden absurd desire to laugh. She frowned to cover it and glanced across at the assassin. "You mean that this is the man who tried to capture Oni and was swallowed by the Rupture?"

"I keep telling them, he's quite nice really," said El.

Pip was clearly trying to keep his temper. "El, I know you like to think the best of people, but even you know that assassins…"

"I could see inside people, back in that place. I saw inside Heironomo."

"He tried to arrest me," said Oni.

The assassin looked nervously at Amina and licked his lips. He was very young. Amina reflected that assassins often didn't last very long in the Cardinal's service. He was always looking for new blood.

"I'm sorry," he said. "I was just … doing my job…"

"You're sorry that you can't go to the Cardinal and

betray us all to the Spectres," said Oni, tossing her head. "I know your sort."

Amina looked at the other man. "And who is this?"

"Harpin Shtum, at your service, ma'am," said Harpin unexpectedly. "A pleasure to see you, Missus Bemare, even in such peculiar circumstances."

Amina regarded him narrowly. She thought he did look a little familiar, but she couldn't place his face. But then, she met so many people...

She took a deep breath. "I think that you had better tell me everything that has been going on here," she said. "And yes, leave the strangers tied up for the present. We really have no idea who they are."

She glanced around the kitchen. Everybody looked exhausted.

"And then we'd all better get some sleep. It's been a hard night, and right now I can't see that today is going to be any better."

Oni laughed, with a little sob. "Oh, Ma, that is such a you thing to say!" She ran up to Amina and threw her arms around her neck and hid her face in her shoulder, hugging her as tightly as she could.

"I'm sorry I didn't write you back," Oni whispered, her voice muffled. "I knew you'd worry. But I didn't know what to say..."

Amina felt the last of her anger drain out of her. "I'm just glad you're not dead." She breathed in the smell of Oni's hair, a faint scent of rosemary and sweat. "So glad."

Chapter Thirty-seven

WHEN LADY AGATHE DREW BACK THE BROCADE curtains on the Princess's bed and discovered it empty, she let out a shriek and ran to the Duchess in the dressing room, who was preparing the Princess's wardrobe. "Don't be ridiculous," said the Duchess, shaking out a skirt. "Of course she's here."

"But, ma'am, she's nowhere to be seen," wailed Lady Agathe. "I looked everywhere in the chamber, and under her bed... And her nightdress on the floor, like she just dropped it there..."

At that the Duchess came to see for herself, followed by the rest of Georgette's ladies-in-waiting. It was true: there was no sign of the Princess anywhere, in her bed-chamber or anywhere else in the royal rooms. The Duchess said some unladylike words under her breath.

"Where could she be?" said one of the younger ladies.

"Maybe she climbed out of the window again?"

"It's not unlikely," said the Duchess coldly. "Even though she pretended to be as sweet as pie, she was always abominably disobedient."

"But, ma'am, it's three floors up," said another lady doubtfully. They all looked at the window, which had been opened to let in the morning sun, sparkling and clean after the overnight tempest. There were no useful vines or trees that would have aided any erring princess bent on fleeing the palace, and even if Georgette had succeeded in climbing down three floors, she would have landed in an enclosed garden in the centre of the palace. After some early adventures, Princess Georgette's chambers had been chosen with particular care to foil any thoughts of escape.

"Why would she do that, and her just betrothed?" Lady Agathe clasped her hands together. "And how could she get past the guards?"

"I shall have something to say about your dereliction of duty later, Agathe," said the Duchess. "But first, we must find her."

Lady Agathe paled. As the lady-in-waiting charged that night with ensuring Princess Georgette's safety, she would be the first one blamed for the disappearance.

"Maybe she got up earlier," said another lady, "and

was hungry or something, so went to the kitchen. I mean, she's done that before."

"And nobody saw her?" said the Duchess. "Not a guard? Not a servant? Have you checked?"

A half-hour later, they had ascertained that the guards who stood all night outside the royal chambers had seen nothing. Nor had any servants. Some guards reported feeling cramps and headaches in the night watches, and one said he was sure he had been put under some kind of spell. None of the Princess's clothes were missing, nor any of her possessions. She had simply vanished into thin air.

By now all the ladies were in a panic. A couple of them, like Lady Agathe, were genuinely fond of Georgette, and were worried about what had happened to her; but all of them were most worried about what might happen to them.

"Witchcraft," said one of the ladies at last. "It must be witches."

"Witches!" cried another, who prided herself on her sensitive nature, and swooned. Everybody rushed to revive her with smelling salts except Lady Agathe, who was looking thoughtful.

"It's the only explanation," she said. "I was cast into an enchanted sleep by some foul magic…"

The Duchess didn't believe in witches, although she

never said so aloud. She had always considered that a belief in magic was base and vulgar superstition and besides, she had never seen a witch with her own eyes. But she did believe sincerely in the punishments that would come her way when she had to tell King Axel that his only daughter – the jewel of his kingdom, and the seal of his alliance with the kingdom of Awemt – had gone missing.

She blamed Princess Georgette. She had never trusted that girl, not ever. She was sly enough to have crept out through the palace disguised as a servant or some such, fooling everybody. And everyone knew that Lady Agathe had the brains of a pigeon. It would take nothing to deceive her.

"I agree," said the Duchess. "I cannot think of any other way that Princess Georgette could have vanished so completely, without anyone noticing." She drew a shuddering breath and added ominously, "A great evil is afoot in this palace."

She crossed her scrawny chest and squared her shoulders. As senior lady-in-waiting, it was her unpleasant duty to tell the King the terrible news. She imagined his response and shuddered. Perhaps, she reflected, it would be wiser to get the ordeal over as quickly as possible.

She hurried through the palace to the King's chambers,

flustered and upset, foreseeing disaster for herself and her family unless she could absolve herself from blame. The King was still dressing, but when she said it was an emergency she was permitted into his room.

He was every bit as angry as she had expected. She braced herself against his rage, blinking fast.

"Perhaps, sire, the Princess disguised herself as a servant," said one of his lackeys, once the first gust passed. "She may be suffering from pre-nuptial nerves, as delicate females are known to do."

"Delicate female? Deceitful, lying little hussy, more like," growled the King. "You can't trust the female sex. You never know what's going on inside those heads."

The Duchess decided it was time to divert his rage. "We very much fear she has been taken away by supernatural means," said the Duchess. She didn't dare to say the word "witch" in the King's presence. "Several guards told us that something strange happened in the palace last night. As if it were put under an evil spell."

"Witchcraft?" The King's eyebrows bristled. "Witchcraft in my kingdom? In this very palace?"

"She has vanished without trace, sire. It seems like the only explanation."

"Hmmm." The King began to look thoughtful. Like his father, he was an unimaginative, pragmatic man, and he didn't really believe in witches. Axel I had kept the Office for Witchcraft Extermination going after he took power, because it was useful: its assassins were skilful at spycraft and were deadly. Axel II himself had used the office to get rid of quite a few troublesome peasants. In this case, blaming witchcraft might be a handy way of avoiding diplomatic repercussions with Awemt.

He called to mind Georgette's disobedience when she first arrived at the palace. He had honestly thought that the Princess was reformed. She had appeared so biddable, her youthful rebellions tamed to a charming liveliness, and she had always displayed a proper meekness when the occasion required. But even so, there was always something he had never quite liked, a sense that she kept her own counsel and had her own plans. She was too clever for a mere girl.

For a moment, with a pang of apprehension, he had a vision of the Princess dressed in silver armour, a sword raised, leading an army against the palace. What army? The thought was ridiculous.

He was personally almost sure the Princess had left the palace willingly, but perhaps it would be more politic to pretend that she had been abducted. Traitress or no, the palace needed the Princess back. The alliance between Clarel and Awemt could still go ahead

259

without the marriage, but King Oswald would consider an absconding bride a mortal insult.

The important thing was to ensure that Oswald punished the person who deserved it, Princess Georgette, and not the Kingdom of Clarel. When he married her, he could make her as miserable as he liked.

Chapter Thirty-eight

A BRISK BREEZE SWEPT THE LAST STORM CLOUDS from the sky and then died down, its task completed. On the eastern horizon an amber glow presaged the coming dawn. High above, stars twinkled in a deep azure field as if they had been newly washed.

Across the city of Clarel, roosters fluffed their feathers, threw out their chests and began their morning announcements. It was going to be a beautiful Midsummer Day.

In the Weavers' Quarter, it was the best day of the year. Everyone prepared for weeks: homes were polished until they sparkled and everyone practised their steps for the midsummer dances that wound through the streets, blessing all the houses. Bakers worked from midnight, kneading the traditional sweet pastries and breads. The almond bonbons that were distributed to all the children of Clarel had been long prepared, and were stacked in muslin bags tied up with yellow ribbons.

But this year there would be no festival.

In the small hours, under cover of darkness, the Cardinal's soldiers set up roadblocks on all the major streets. Then hundreds of them marched into the Weavers' Quarter, their chain mail clinking ominously, and stationed themselves in the squares.

Although the soldiers thought the quarter was asleep, many eyes watched them arrive. Rats watched from the gutters, dogs barked in the workshop yards, cats hissed and leapt onto walls, their hackles bristling. Some of those animals weren't what they appeared to be.

The raids began just before dawn. The Eradians weren't unprepared. Amina had sent word of her arrest to her sister Zoa the night before, and within an hour the news had reached every home in the Weavers' Quarter. The senior members of the Weavers' Guild had held a midnight meeting.

Everyone was alarmed that such a respected citizen as Amina Bemare had been arrested. It had been at least a hundred years since any Eradian had been accused of witchcraft. Every family had stories of the bad old days, when the Weavers' Quarter had suffered under regular persecutions, and evil memories die hard.

Not many people slept that night. Zoa, who had a sharp nose for trouble, advised that all children be sent elsewhere in the city. In the quiet hours before the soldiers arrived, carts rumbled all over Clarel, taking sleepy children to safe houses for surprise visits. Precious possessions were hidden in secret caches and witches were posted to every street in the Weavers' Quarter, to provide as much protection as possible. Witches could calm people down and ensure that people weren't hurt. And in the last resort, they could fight.

The first houses to be hit were, as everyone had suspected, those belonging to the Bemare family. The soldiers were greeted by outraged citizens, already washed and dressed for the day. They were bundled at swordpoint into closed wagons and sent to the Office for Witchcraft Extermination, and then their houses were searched and pillaged by the soldiers. Once all the Bemare houses were dealt with, the troops moved on to the rest of the Weavers' Quarter, working methodically, street by street.

It didn't occur to the soldiers until much later that it was strange that they found no children.

Even the most pessimistic of the guild hadn't expected that the raids would spread beyond the Bemares. As the sun rose higher and the raids spread, anger grew. In some streets, punches were thrown. One old man was beaten up badly by soldiers, prompting the entire crowd to turn on the troops despite the best calming spells the witch could muster.

As the day broadened, the people of Clarel, expecting the usual midsummer festivities, began to crowd along the blocked streets. When they were stopped, they demanded to know why they were being prevented from entering the Weavers' Quarter. Criers announced that it was because the Eradians had used witchcraft to kidnap Princess Georgette.

It didn't go down well. Most people scoffed openly. One party of soldiers was pelted with eggs by disappointed citizens.

Meanwhile, hundreds of people were being delivered to the Office for Witchcraft Extermination. There were far too many to be held in the dungeons, and harassed officials were forced to let many of them go. A crowd began to gather outside Clarel Palace, shouting for the King to stop the raids. Soldiers tried to turn them away, but the crowd kept swelling.

The Cardinal stood at his window and watched the rabble, clouds gathering on his brow. The palace might be suspicious of the Weavers' Quarter, but everyone in Clarel knew the Eradians. They worked with them, or they were their neighbours. And everyone wanted to get jobs with the Weavers' Guild because they paid on time, and much more generously than the nobles.

If Lamir had remembered that today was the Midsummer Festival, he might have delayed these raids. But he hadn't even thought about it, because it was an event attended only by the city's commoners. No nobles celebrated Midsummer Day, and therefore it was of no importance. He had forgotten, if he ever knew, that for most ordinary people in Clarel, the Midsummer Festival in the Weavers' Quarter was the high point of the year.

The mood in the city was turning ugly.

The Cardinal scratched his chin, pondering. Perhaps, after all, this unrest could be turned to his own advantage. Maybe the King could be toppled off his throne without the Cardinal having to lift a finger.

Chapter Thirty-nine

GEORGETTE LIKED TO THINK THAT SHE WASN'T CON-ceited. For years she had despised her father's touchy pride, and she had vowed that when she was Queen, she would never be like him. It was humbling to discover that she was, after all, not above the vice of vanity.

For years, ever since she had left the Old Palace, she had been treated as a princess, which meant that, for good and ill, she was always the centre of attention. When she walked through the palace, everyone, even the Cardinal, bowed or curtsied. If she spoke, people listened (or at least, they pretended to). She had always held a secret contempt for court protocols, but now that nobody observed them, she felt offended.

She woke up after retreating in the small hours, limp with exhaustion, to the dormitory that extended from the back of the council pavilion. She was almost certain that the tent expanded as more people entered it, but if it did, she never saw the transitions. Sibelius was still fast asleep, snoring under a purple coverlet. After Missus Pledge's will had been decoded he had gone into some kind of daze, and Missus Clay had given him a warm drink that Georgette was sure contained some kind of sleeping potion. In any case, he had gone straight to bed, and hadn't stirred since.

According to Georgette's pocket watch, it was a quarter past eleven. In the Undercroft, she had no way of telling whether it was day or night, and she seemed to have lost her sense of time. She slipped out of the dormitory into the main room of the tent to find that it was a hive of activity.

She then discovered that nobody can ignore people as well as witches. They can ignore people so hard that it's like they're invisible. (In extreme cases, they actually do become invisible, but that's another issue.) She sat on a chair at the edge of the tent and unrolled the rags from her hair, keeping her ears open. She thought of waking up Sibelius just to have someone to talk to, and then decided that would be too humiliating. She was a princess; she didn't need company.

Being unimportant was a novel sensation. For one thing, it was really dull. Nobody had even thanked her for being right about Sibelius d'Artan and tracking down the spell. When she'd asked Amiable what was happening, Amiable had simply answered that it was nothing that concerned princesses, and strolled away. Even Helios, the nicest person on the Witches' Council, was too busy running around organizing people to take much notice of her. He said vaguely that there had been raids and that people had been injured and at least one person had been killed.

"Where?" asked Georgette.

"The Weavers' Quarter, but it's spreading. It's going to be civil war out there…"

Georgette's ears pricked up. "Maybe I can help," she said. "I mean…"

"I think the most important thing you can do is to remain here, where the Spectres can't find you," said Helios. "Excuse me…" He hurried off, and Georgette watched him talking animatedly to a dog that had entered the tent. A dog was more important than she was?

She was ashamed of that thought, but it didn't stop her thinking it.

So, there was some kind of rebellion happening in the City of Clarel? She sat on a stool, out of the way, and kept her ears open as strangers arrived and gave reports.

She had one single, overwhelming conviction: she, Princess Georgette, ought to be leading any rebellion. This was her chance to actually take over the palace and become Queen in her own right. The people would follow her for certain: they were always excited to see her when she made public appearances. Her grandfather had led a revolt that deposed the Old Royals. Why couldn't she do the same thing?

When Missus Clay plumped down at the central table to grab a quick bite of bread and honey, Georgette took a deep breath, squared her shoulders and politely asked if she could sit next to her. Missus Clay licked a drip of honey from her hand. "If you wish, my dear," she said. "Do you want some bread?"

Georgette wasn't hungry, so she shook her head. "I just wanted to ask what I can do to help the revolt," she said.

Missus Clay looked Georgette up and down. "I know it's hard for you, being used to being at the centre of royal affairs and so on," she said. She spoke quite kindly. "At the moment, there's nothing for you to do, except make sure that you keep out of the way of Spectres. That's the most important thing of all."

"But ... I could really help with the rebellion." Georgette tried to keep the frustration out of her voice, but even she could hear it. "It's ridiculous just to hide here when I could be out, you know…"

"On a white horse leading the charge, like your grandfather in all the paintings?" Missus Clay's gaze was discomfittingly sharp. "I can tell you for a fact there was no white horse. He didn't even have a sword. Your grandfather just went into the palace with an axe and a lot of angry people and chopped off the King's head."

Georgette blushed. "No, I wasn't thinking that. But surely if a princess of the blood stepped forwards and said…"

"See, there's the problem," said Missus Clay. "All this stuff about blood. It's all very well, Axel the Blacksmith chopping off people's heads, but it's not like it actually stopped the Spectres, did it? And after he took over, things were no better for witches than they were before." She took out a huge yellow handkerchief and dabbed her mouth. "We learned never to trust princes. Or princesses, for that matter."

"You can trust me," said Georgette hotly. "I'd never betray Amina."

Again that sharp look. "Maybe," said Missus Clay. "Maybe we could trust you now. But could we trust you in a year's time? In five years' time? That's the real question."

"Why would I change?" Georgette tried to keep her voice reasonable. "Especially if the witches helped me. That would be breaking my word."

Missus Clay briskly brushed the crumbs off the table and stood up. "My dear, I don't want to be harsh. But we know through bitter experience that the word of a royal isn't worth the air it stains."

"Then why bother to take me from the palace? Why bring me here?"

"That was Amina's notion, my dear. She was right, because it would be bad if you married Oswald. But it does leave us with the puzzle of what to do with you in the meantime…"

"But…" Georgette started to say, and then she bit her lip and stared down at her hands. She felt like crying.

All she had ever been was something that nobody knew what to do with. For her father, she was a nuisance – at best a bargaining chip. The Queen hated her, because the Princess held a rival court. For Amina, she had just been a burden, a task that the palace had told her to do. She had always thought that Amina loved her, or at least liked her, but now she wasn't even sure of that.

Nobody wanted her. Nobody needed her.

Missus Clay took her hand and squeezed it. "Don't think I don't feel for you," she said. "I know it's hard and strange for you here, girl, but things are very dangerous. I think you'll manage fine with us, once you get used to it. But right now we have Spectres to deal with, and then we need to get rid of the royals, because that's where the rot begins. I can tell you have a good heart, that's why I'm straight with you. Now, I've got things to do."

Georgette watched Missus Clay walk off. She felt a bit stunned.

In her wildest dreams, she hadn't even imagined that the witches might want to get rid of royalty altogether. How could you have a kingdom without a monarch? Who would be in charge? There had to be someone in charge. And you couldn't have witches running things. All they did was argue with each other.

The witches didn't know they needed her, yet. But they did.

Georgette went back to her out-of-the-way stool and brooded deeply. Since nobody was going to help her, she figured that she would have to help herself. She tied her hair up and put on her cap.

If she remained down here, she was only a pawn in somebody else's game. It was no different to being stuck in the palace. So she should just leave. Since everybody was ignoring her, maybe she could creep out without anybody noticing. She wasn't wearing a princess dress, so once she was out of the tent she would look like anybody else.

In all the histories she had read, rebellions always had an inspiring figurehead. She should be that inspiring figurehead. She had trained her whole life for it. The first thing, she thought, was to find the leaders of the rebellion. She would have to avoid the witches, because they would bring her back here. She had to make the witches see how they needed her.

She listened to the conversations going on around her and tried to piece together the information she overheard. The Undercroft entrance was near the Furrier's Bridge. She summoned to memory the city maps she had studied in the palace library. If she crossed the bridge, she would be very near the Weavers' Quarter, which was where the main rebellion was happening. She could ask her way, if she got lost.

She yawned and stood up. Helios was passing and glanced at her.

"I think I'll find some breakfast," she said.

"Good idea," Helios replied vaguely, as he hurried off. "Get some food while you can."

Georgette walked out of the tent. Nobody stopped her. Once she was out, she kept walking.

It took her some time to find the exit. The Undercroft

was more crowded than it had been the night before, but now it wasn't like a party at all. At one stall a short, stout man was telling a story to a group of small children. At another, she saw people tending to the wounded: a man with a bleeding hand, a boy with a broken arm, an old woman with a whiplash across her eyes. Clearly there was trouble in the city of Clarel.

At last she found the tunnel that led to the river. There were two people guarding the entrance and she halted, wondering what to say to them. It wasn't completely clear if she was a prisoner in the Undercroft. She observed them for a while, trying to see what protocol she should follow, and realized they were only questioning people who entered the Undercroft. They didn't seem to be too worried about who was leaving.

She took a deep breath, and then sauntered casually towards them.

"Take care out there," said one of the guards. "We're hearing bad reports."

"I will," said Georgette, nodding pleasantly as she entered the tunnel.

It seemed almost no time at all before she was standing by the edge of the river, blinking in the sunshine. She scrambled up to the street and walked until the Undercroft entrance was out of sight. She searched along the river for the Furrier's Bridge. That must be it, over there.

She breathed in and out, trying to stop the trembling in her legs. She didn't know whether she was more frightened or excited.

Excited, she thought. *That's what I am.*

Princess Georgette was out in the city of Clarel. And for the first time in her whole life, she was out by herself.

Chapter Forty

A TERSE NOTE FROM THE PALACE ABOUT THE DISAP-
pearance of the Princess arrived just after Cardinal
Lamir's breakfast. He threw his plate across the dining
room and swept to his office in a state of frigid rage. The
sight of Milan Ariosto waiting for him in the corridor did
nothing to abate it.

Ariosto was paler than usual and his expression was
wary. He took note of the Cardinal's blackened eye but
had no visible reaction. Of course Ariosto would know
that a witch had escaped their clutches and, worse,
knocked the Cardinal out. Normally he would have
betrayed at least a twitch of secret amusement.

"Well?" Lamir snapped, as he locked the chamber
door behind them. "Out with it. I know already that it's
not good tidings."

"Yes, my lord." Ariosto nervously licked his lips, another bad sign. "It seems that your translator has gone missing."

"My translator?" For a second the Cardinal didn't know who Ariosto meant.

"Sibelius d'Artan, my lord."

"What do you mean, he's gone missing? He gave you the slip? I told you to keep him under surveillance."

"We did as you ordered, my lord. We had a guard outside his chamber here, and of course all the usual security in the office. There is no sign of him anywhere this morning."

"You mean that he's vanished into thin air?"

"It seems so, my lord."

"But the man's a fool. How could he possibly have got past the assassins?"

"I agree that he's a fool, my lord." Ariosto licked his lips again. His mouth was very dry. "Nevertheless, he is certainly absent."

There was a long, pregnant silence. Ariosto stared at his shoes, awaiting the Cardinal's punishment. There was no point defending himself. Losing track of a surveillance target was unforgivable. It had never happened before under Ariosto's command. Not once.

The Cardinal drew in a long, audible breath, and then

spoke in an alarmingly even tone. "Tell me exactly what you know," he said.

"Yes, my lord." Ariosto's voice was drained of all expression. "D'Artan was last seen when an orderly brought him a late supper at a quarter to midnight. All seemed normal. This morning at the prime bell the lamp was still burning. The guard assumed that he was working, or that he had perhaps fallen asleep. By the terce bell, he began to be worried. He knocked on the door to see if d'Artan wanted to break his fast, and received no response. He then entered the room and found it empty."

"Who was the guard?"

Ariosto decided to evade the answer. "One of my best men."

"And the document d'Artan was investigating?"

"There is no sign of it either, my lord."

Ariosto could feel the Cardinal containing his rage.

"So. How did this d'Artan escape?"

"We presume he left by way of the window. It was found open."

"I thought I told you to put d'Artan in an office that offered no chance of climbing out."

"He was in one of the fifth-floor chambers. Even an assassin would be seriously challenged to climb down."

"Are there bars on the window?"

Ariosto swallowed. "No, my lord. They didn't appear to be necessary."

"And you checked the ground below?"

"Naturally we considered that he might have taken his own life," said Ariosto. "There is no sign of a corpse, nor of any violence."

"Then it is definitely witchcraft. Again! In the centre of the Office of Witchcraft Extermination!"

There was a long silence. Ariosto could feel the pressure building in the room. Shadows coalesced in the corners as if demonic shapes were forming there. He could almost hear them shifting in the darkness, slavering, unsheathing their claws. His throat tightened, but he couldn't tell if that was the Cardinal's doing or his own fear.

He was ten years old again, back in the orphanage.

The worst thing that could happen to an orphan was to be called to the Cardinal's office on Visiting Day. Orphans who committed the worst transgressions were put on the List. Every week there would be three or four terrified boys standing in the corridor outside the office, waiting for judgment. Some boys never came out of that room, and nobody ever knew what happened to them.

Ariosto had only been in that queue once. Once was

more than enough. It occurred to him, as he stood with downcast eyes in front of the Cardinal, that his whole life had been formed around his desire never to stand in that corridor again. And yet, here he was…

"Let me summarize for you. In the past few hours there have been three incidents. A witch has escaped our custody. Princess Georgette has vanished from the palace. And now it seems one of the office staff, working on a high-level investigation, has also inexplicably disappeared?"

Ariosto blinked. The Princess had run away? After days spent guarding King Oswald, he didn't really blame her. Impossible though it seemed at the present moment, Oswald was even more unpleasant than the Cardinal.

"I understand that the situation is deeply serious, my lord."

"Good." For a moment the Cardinal's tension was audible in his voice. "You realize that the kingdom is under the most serious attack in living memory? The smallest slip now, in such a time of crisis, is unforgivable."

"Yes, my lord."

"I am disappointed, Milan," said the Cardinal softly. His voice was thick oil filling Ariosto's ears. "I am very, very disappointed. You seem to be losing your edge."

"I am ashamed, my lord—"

An invisible pressure, fast as a whiplash. Ariosto cried out. He was cast face down onto the floor, his cheek pressed into the stone flags, his arms pinned, his legs. It was as if a hundredweight of rocks pushed down on every inch of his body. He couldn't move; he couldn't breathe. Every second it grew heavier. He could feel his ribs cracking. He only had space for a single thought: he was going to die.

Just as he was about to black out, the pressure lifted. His starved lungs made a whistling noise as the air rushed back in. He lay there for a measureless time, unable to feel anything except an incredulous relief that the weight had gone.

"Get up."

The Cardinal's voice was absolutely cold.

Ariosto found to his surprise that he could move. He lifted himself onto his knees, and then to his feet. He was shaking all over, and he almost fell again because of his dizziness.

"I will spare you, for now," said the Cardinal. "But this is your final chance."

Ariosto nodded. He was still unable to speak.

"I want you to find d'Artan. I want you especially to find the documents he absconded with. I want you to do this within the next day and night."

Ariosto nodded again.

"I expect both are concealed in the Weavers' Quarter. I expect the raids to be thorough and executed with speed and efficiency."

"Yes, my lord. The raids are progressing well…"

"I have my own reports, fool. Get your disgusting presence out of my chamber."

Ariosto bowed and walked backwards out of the room, bent over as if he were leaving the presence of a king. He closed the door softly behind him and straightened up slowly. He didn't care that one of the office guards was staring at him with a mixture of fear and mockery. Right now Ariosto was beyond pride. He hurt viciously all over, from the hairs on his head to his toenails.

He felt astonished that he was still alive. He walked to his office, feeling the surprise ebb away. In its place was a liberating clarity. Without realizing it, he had been afraid his whole life. And now, for the first time he could remember, he wasn't afraid.

The worst the Cardinal could do was to kill him. Well, this time Lamir had made a mistake. Ariosto was alive. And every living cell inside him vibrated with hatred.

Chapter Forty-one

PIP WAS ALMOST TOO TIRED TO BE AMAZED, BUT EVEN
so, the Undercroft took him aback. The past few days
had been a series of successive shocks, but somehow the
Undercroft was the biggest. It was as if he had looked up at
the sky and discovered a populous city hanging just over
his head, only to be told that it had been there all his life.

"All these people live in Clarel?" he said. "And they're
all witches?"

"I think there are people here now who aren't witches,"
said Oni, looking around. "But just because you don't
know about something doesn't mean it doesn't exist."

"I know, but so many...?"

"Imagine having to hide for your whole life in case
someone decided to burn you to death. That's why."

Pip was silenced by the edge in her voice, but El took
Oni's hand.

"That's awful," she said. "I'm sorry you couldn't even tell me."

"I know," said Oni. "But I couldn't."

"But now it doesn't matter?"

Oni shrugged. "Things are changing," she said. "Though maybe they're changing for the worse."

It was almost lunchtime. They had snatched a few hours' sleep, but it wasn't enough: Pip could feel tiredness dragging at his shoulders. More than anything he wanted to go back to sleep, but not just because he was still tired. Clovis was inside his head, and he wouldn't shut up. It was driving him up the wall.

We're friends now, aren't we? Clovis had said, when they had been vomited back out of the Rupture into Missus Orphint's kitchen.

Yes, we're friends, said Pip.

So, what do friends do? Do we play? Do we?

Clovis sounded very young, much younger than when they had first spoken. Like he was about three. The arrogant child prince seemed to have disappeared altogether.

We be friends, said Pip. *That's what friends do.*

Oh. The disappointment in Clovis's voice gave Pip a twinge of conscience. *I thought we might do something special.*

Just being friends is special, said Pip, unable to think of anything better to say. Even to his own ears it sounded like a sop. But it seemed to please Clovis. As they lay down to sleep on Missus Orphint's pallets, he had the strangest feeling that Clovis was cuddling trustingly against him.

And then Amina had woken them and said she was taking them all to the Undercroft, even the assassin. Heironomo had given up arguing, but at this he looked frightened. Oni told him that he was lucky that Pip hadn't left him behind in the Rupture. "Nobody's going to turn you into a frog," she said scornfully. "Even if you deserve it."

Heironomo, all his braggadocio gone, didn't answer. All he knew was that he was being taken to a place full of people with very good reasons to hate him. Neither he nor Harpin resisted when Amina shook their magical shackles and told them to follow her quick smart. They just looked resigned.

Now El was back, Pip didn't feel angry with Clovis any more. All that rage had been replaced with an uncomfortable sense of being *responsible*. He didn't like that very much; he wasn't used to it.

Well, he had always felt a responsibility for El, but that was different. There had only ever been El and him.

Now there was Clovis and him, and Clovis was inside his head. Sometimes it was a bit difficult to tell which were his thoughts, and which belonged to Clovis.

Clovis's inconsequential chitchat ceased abruptly the moment they entered the Undercroft. Pip knew why at once: he could feel Clovis's fear as if it was his own.

As far as Clovis was concerned, this was his worst nightmare. They were walking through a pit full of witches. If Clovis had been a puppy, he would be huddling into Pip's ankles, shaking all over.

Nobody will hurt you here, Pip said, hoping it was true. *I won't let them. Fair's fair. You kept your promise.*

Witches are cruel, said Clovis. *They say they're going to help you and then…*

The memory tore through Pip's mind like sudden fire. A woman, not very old, brown-haired, quite plump. She looked a little like a younger version of their Missus Pledge. She was smiling, holding out a ripe apple. He was very hungry. He reached out for the apple, heard his voice thanking the kind lady.

And then, a merciless grip, and terrible pain. A knife plunging into his chest, blood splashing on his face, on her face, screams filling his ears that he knew were his own screams…

So Old Missus Pledge had lied. She hadn't found

Clovis after he had been killed by the executioners. She had killed him herself.

No wonder he's frightened of witches, Pip thought. *Imagine being able to remember your own death. And dying like* that…

"You all right, Pip?" El was pulling at his elbow. "You going to be sick? You've gone all green."

Pip swallowed, trying to contain his nausea. "I'm all right," he said gruffly.

"We better catch the others up. You stopped, just like that, and…"

He shrugged El off, quickening his pace. "I said, I'm all right."

He began dimly to perceive what it meant that Clovis had decided to trust him. If the story that Amina had told them were true, Clovis's father had decided to devour his son's soul. His own father. And then Old Missus Pledge had cut out his heart. While he was still alive. That same Heart that Pip still carried, almost forgotten, in his pocket.

If Pip let Clovis down too, it would be a disaster. And not just for Clovis and Pip, but for everyone else as well.

Most witches are good people, Pip said to Clovis as he hurried after Amina. *Oni's not like that. You know that, you must know that. You stopped the assassin from hurting her.*

287

Silence.

Spectres are worse than witches. Much worse.

More silence. A growing feeling of confusion, sadness, fear.

At last Clovis spoke. *Yes. No. I don't know.*

I won't let them hurt you, said Pip again. *Even if they want to.* To his surprise, this time he meant it. He added, as an afterthought, *They won't want to, though. I'm sure.*

He felt, rather than heard, Clovis's response: a little leap of relief. A secret, troubled part of Pip's mind whispered that perhaps he was being a little dishonest, that maybe the witches wouldn't care about Clovis. And after all, he and Clovis weren't really friends. He really didn't want Clovis to be hurt, but he still wasn't sure if he actually liked him.

Chapter Forty-two

KING OSWALD — OR, MORE ACCURATELY, KING Rudolph – was an old hand at court politics. As his valet clipped his nails after morning chapel, he sniffed the air in the palace. He could tell by the itch in his bones that something was wrong. He had noticed that the Princess was absent from her usual pew in the service. At first he had accepted the explanation that she had been taken ill, but now he was beginning to wonder. Had the girl absconded? Of course nobody would dare to tell him if she had.

Patience, he said to himself. *Patience…*

Patience was his chief – perhaps his only – virtue. The alliance with Clarel was the first major step in a strategy that he had been working on for fifty years. Ever since the Spectres had lost power across Continentia and all the quarrelling kingdoms had banded together to declare war on Awemt, Oswald-Rudolph had been quietly rebuilding alliances. He had rewritten histories and silenced the witches. He had bided his time. And now everybody had forgotten about the Spectres, or thought that they were just a legend. The time was ripe.

In less than a year, King Oswald would be Emperor of Continentia. He might even adopt his old name again: Emperor Rudolph. It had a nice ring. And a new age would dawn. An age of endless power...

The servant finished filing his nails and bowed. Oswald waved a hand to dismiss him, still pondering deeply. He needed that princess. She had the right bloodlines. Axel was a buffoon, but a little vulgar breeding was needed now and then to bring strength to the line; otherwise it became progressively weaker and the blood magic failed.

Through her father, Georgette was the only link left to the line of King Odo of Clarel. Spectre blood on both sides would ensure that the magic took properly. There could be no more failed vessels. Every one of his sons so far had died soon after he began the procedure. He needed stronger children.

The Princess was, of course, terrified of him, but that didn't bother Oswald. Had she run away? How was that possible? Should he pressure Axel to reveal what he was hiding? It annoyed Oswald that he was forced to dance around the petty deceptions of this primitive kingdom.

He was still pacing up and down in his sunny guest chamber pondering his options when the Cardinal was announced to his presence. Oswald noted with amusement that he had an impressive black eye.

Without asking permission, Lamir dismissed Oswald's servants. When the door closed on their heels, the Cardinal lifted his hand, speaking a word in a forgotten language. The chamber vanished: now both men stood in a dim, columned hall that seemed to stretch for infinite distances on every side.

"Do we really need these theatrics, old friend?" asked Oswald coldly.

"I do not wish to be overheard."

"There are more subtle measures. It's still too early for such open power."

"Is it, Rudolph, my oldest of allies?" Lamir approached him, as if even now he feared being overheard, and spoke close to Oswald's ear. "Is it really? Me, I fear if we don't move soon, it will be too late. The witches are rising."

"What do you mean?"

"I was openly attacked last night in my own dungeon." Lamir lifted a finger, and an image appeared in the air between them. It was of the dungeon chair where the witch had been held; the manacles twisted and broken.

"And you permitted this to happen?"

"It wasn't *permitted*," hissed the Cardinal. "There is more. My chief translator of witch script has disappeared. And this morning it has been reported that Princess Georgette has also vanished. All in the space of one night. Now the commoners are rioting. It's a conspiracy, without doubt."

"Ah." So the Princess *had* absconded. "Perhaps the Princess simply ran away, given the very lax standards of security that exist in this palace. I'm sure she can be easily found.'

"I have already asked the Void where the Princess is. It couldn't tell me. That should give you pause."

There was a short silence. "You assured me that there was no witch problem in Clarel."

"I told you that because I believed it to be true."

"I passed on to you all my knowledge of the signs." Oswald inspected his left hand and noted with irritation that his manservant had overlooked a tiny hangnail. "If you paid no proper heed, you are a bigger fool than I realized."

The Cardinal's lips tightened. "Perhaps it's no

coincidence that the witches are rising precisely at the same time that you have entered Clarel," he said.

"What are you insinuating? That I brought the witches with me?"

Lamir said nothing for a few moments, as if he were striving with himself. "No," he said at last. "Although I wonder how serious you are about our alliance."

"I am very serious, believe me." *You will find out how serious I am,* Oswald thought to himself, *when I return as Emperor Rudolph and absorb your pathetic essence into my own power...*

The Cardinal stiffened, as if he had picked up the edge of Oswald's thought. He forced himself to relax. Of course he didn't trust this man. But for the moment he needed Oswald, just as Oswald needed him. In return for promoting the alliance between Clarel and Awemt, Oswald had promised to unseat King Axel, putting the Cardinal on the throne in his stead.

The two men studied each other, each hiding their dislike.

"If we don't reach for power now, it will be too late."

"I think your fears overcome you. The existence of witches is no reason for panic. They remain weak. But the Princess must be found, as a matter of urgency. Of course no one in the palace has seen fit to tell me of her absence. But I will set my own investigations in train."

"I think that would be wise."

"We're suffering a few potholes on our journey, but it strikes me as nothing worse. It is only to be expected."

"I hope you're correct."

"I usually am." Oswald snapped his fingers, and his chamber returned to its former state, the morning sunshine streaming through the window. "Thank you for your visit."

The Cardinal bowed unsmilingly. "My pleasure, your Grace." He turned and left.

Oswald stared after him thoughtfully, wondering how much of a threat the Cardinal really was. He was hiding something. Lamir was an ambitious leftover from the court of Odo the Fifth, and as a Spectre he had some ability. But it didn't compare to Oswald's own. Nobody's did. He was the first and the greatest of them all.

He had no doubt, however, that Lamir was a treacherous snake. It would do to watch him.

Oswald thought idly of visiting the King and telling him that he knew that the Princess had run away, dealing him a mortal insult. It might be amusing. With any luck, Axel would burst a vein and drop dead on the spot. That would be extraordinarily convenient.

Then he frowned. Lamir was correct on one point. Oswald was wary of haste: yet one could be too cautious, and miss the tide in its flood.

Maybe now was the time to take power.

Chapter Forty-three

PIP WAS FEELING MORE AND MORE UNCOMFORTABLE.

He was sitting in the Witches' Council tent. El was next to him with her bewildered look, picking her nails. Oni was opposite, next to her mother. He couldn't tell what Oni was thinking, and she was unusually quiet. Meanwhile, about half a dozen people he didn't know and whose names he mostly couldn't remember were all in a deep discussion about whether there were any spells that could help to deal with the Heart.

One of the council members was invisible. A tiny book was suspended in mid-air on one side of the table. Every now and then a page was flipped over and the invisible person read something out about spells in a squeaky voice.

"It's only Bottomly," Oni said, when she saw that El, who was staring hard at the floating book, was getting anxious. "He's a ratterbag – they don't like day people looking at them."

"Day people?" said El.

"People like you, who don't know about magic."

El looked hurt. "I might know something. Just a little bit."

"It's nothing personal."

At first Pip liked the oldest witch, Missus Clay. Her spine was so bent that she seemed even smaller than she really was, but her smile had genuine warmth. A man called Helios also seemed friendly. Everyone else was … not exactly rude, but not exactly welcoming, either. He could see the glances that they cast at him when they thought he wasn't looking.

There was a lot of talk about different types of spells and magic, which began to bore him, and his mind drifted off. He had a slight headache, which was gradually getting worse, but mostly he was worried that Clovis might start panicking. The last thing they needed was for Clovis to cause another Rupture.

The first request the witches had made was that he show them the Heart. He had taken it out of his pocket and slowly placed it in the middle of the table. All the witches stared at it as if he had put a scorpion in front of them. Amiable hissed.

"It doesn't look like anything, does it?" said Oni, to break the silence.

"An evil thing," said Juin in a hollow voice. "An evil, evil thing."

Pip had an overwhelming feeling that he ought to defend the Heart. "It's not its fault," he objected.

"One of us destroyed herself to make this," said Potier. He was looking very sombre.

"And Clovis," said Pip. "She destroyed Clovis, too. She cut out his heart while he was still *alive*."

Helios blinked. "That can't be true," he said. "No witch would do that."

"It *is* true," said Pip. "I *saw* it." His jaw jutted out belligerently as he stared at the witches around the table.

"That's ... that's terrible," said Potier. He sounded shocked.

"We all heard her," said Missus Clay harshly. "*I have done a dark thing, in a time of terrible darkness.*"

All the witches stared down at their hands, as if they were ashamed.

"He was just a vessel for the Spectres," said Amiable. "And who cares what happens to royals, anyway?"

"Amiable, be quiet," said Potier.

"Now is not the time to argue," said Missus Clay. "Yes, Old Missus Pledge did an awful thing, but the good and the bad of it doesn't concern us here." She looked at the Heart, her expression unreadable, and then looked away. "What we have to decide now is what to do about it."

The witches then cross-examined Pip about the casket. They were particularly interested in how he had taken out the Heart.

"I just opened it," said Pip. "It was a bit tricky—"

"A bit tricky?" said Amiable. "It was spell-shut by one of our best witches!"

"Nobody could have opened that casket without a counterspell," said Missus Clay.

Now everyone was looking at him suspiciously. Pip flushed. "I don't know about that," he said, shrugging. "I just opened it."

"Maybe the spell was about keeping the Heart in, rather than keeping anybody out," said Missus Clay.

"Maybe there wasn't a spell at all. I just told you what I did. Don't believe me if you don't want to."

"How do we know that he's not with the Spectres?" said Juin. "We don't know anything about him."

Pip flushed with anger and opened his mouth to argue.

"He just asked the box nicely," said El, before he could say anything. "And then it opened up for him." There was a short, sceptical silence.

Amina gave Pip a warning look. "That's a ridiculous suggestion, Juin," she said. "I've known this boy for years."

"We have to destroy it," said Amiable. "And with it, everything the Spectres are."

"But we can't," said Missus Clay patiently. "Destroying the Heart would have no effect on the Spectres, and it could open a Rupture that swallows everything."

"We have to get the casket back, and return the Heart to it," said Amina. "It will be in the Office for Witchcraft Extermination, most likely. Though there's a tiny chance that it might still be at Olibrandis's shop."

No, said Clovis. *No, no, no…* And he started to cry.

Pip's mind flooded with fear and sorrow. He felt, as sharply as if he had been punched in the stomach, the desolation of the imprisonment that Clovis had suffered for years, trapped inside Old Missus Pledge's spell.

"Someone should check the shop. What does it look like?" Helios turned to Pip.

Pip, struggling with Clovis's despair, didn't respond at first.

"Pip?" said Amina. "What does the casket look like?"

He started. "I can't remember," he said.

"Yes, you do, Pip," said El. "It was silver, with a red dragon on it, and purple stones. It was very pretty. About so big." She measured out a space with her hands.

Pip glared at her. He could feel Clovis trembling, like a small animal crouched inside a burrow hearing a predator scratch at the entrance. The Prince's fear was like a heart beating inside his own heart.

He was beginning to realize that the witches were more afraid of Clovis than sorry for him. Amina had said, when she first told them about the Spectres, that what happened to Clovis wasn't his fault, but even she was ready to punish him with the cruellest thing in the world. Worse, most of the witches were looking at Pip with horror and pity in their eyes, as if Pip himself were part monster.

This led to an even more uncomfortable thought. Pip was pretty sure the Heart had become an empty shell since the night before. It wasn't changing temperature any more, and there was no responsive pulse when he touched it. As he had told Oni, it was just an ordinary unliving thing. He thought now that Clovis wasn't just *talking* inside his head: maybe, after Pip broke Old Missus Pledge's binding spell, Clovis could move wherever he liked. And perhaps he had moved house, and now lived inside Pip.

Which sounded a lot like what Spectres did, except that Pip didn't think that Clovis was trying to eat his soul. He was just there, kind of being a nuisance.

If the witches suspected this, they'd want to destroy Pip as well as Clovis. He glanced around the table, feeling hunted, and briefly caught Oni's eye. She was watching him closely. He was suddenly sure that Oni suspected the same thing.

"Maybe we don't have to lock up the Heart," he said hoarsely. "Maybe we just need to…" He trailed off.

"Need to what?" said Amiable. "Tell it to be nice to us? Tell it to stop being a Spectre?"

"He's not a Spectre, though, is he? And maybe he just needs, you know, to be looked after…"

Amina spoke gently. "I understand what you feel, Pip. Sometimes we have to do unjust acts, so even more terrible things don't happen."

"But that's not fair. How are witches any better than Spectres if that's how they behave? I mean, that's what Old Missus Pledge did, and look what happened!"

El was sitting up very straight. Pip could hear her breath rasping. "Everything is horrible since you found the Heart, Pip. Maybe Amina knows best…"

"Nobody knows best!" said Pip angrily. "And especially not witches."

"I think Pip has a point," said Oni. "If we can't destroy the Heart, and the other alternative is to imprison it with spells, that doesn't solve anything. Even if we hid it now from Oswald, who's to say that another Spectre mightn't come along later and use it? We got to think about that, too."

"But there is no other way," said Potier. "We already went through all this. There's no magic anyone knows that can solve this."

"Maybe we don't need magic," said Oni. She had on her stubborn look. "Maybe we need another way."

"What way?" said Helios.

"Maybe we need to think about the First Law," she said. "First, do no harm. Forgetting that got us into this mess in the first place."

"Yes, I know," said Helios. "I agree with you. But now that we are in this mess, it's too late. Sometimes there are only bad choices."

Pip stirred uneasily. He was liking this conversation less and less. "Maybe we should just be kind," he suggested. It sounded pathetic even to his ears.

Juin laughed straight out, but without mirth. "Witches always used to be kind," he said. "And then we got betrayed. I think we're already being too kind, letting all these day people into the Undercroft. Bad mistake."

Missus Clay told Juin to be quiet, and then she leaned over the table and took Pip's hand. "I realize this is upsetting," she said. "But these are bad times, and maybe there is no good choice. If the Spectres find the Heart, we will all suffer, whether we are witches or not. There will be no escape. Not for anyone."

"Yes, but…"

It was no use. Pip couldn't argue against that logic. He fell silent, listening to Oni arguing that they had to find another way. He already knew that she was losing.

I told you, said Clovis. *Didn't I tell you?*

Oni gave him a curious look, and he wondered if she could still hear Clovis talking to him.

Pip stared at the Heart. It lay on the table, black and shrivelled. A horrible thing, as El had said when she first looked at it. Evidence of a terrible act.

Let them have it, said Clovis inside his head. *It doesn't matter any more. We have to run away. If we don't, they'll do the same thing to you as they did to me.*

The witches were now arguing about how best to break into the Office for Witchcraft Extermination and search for the casket. All they seemed to do was argue.

Pip met Oni's eye. He was almost sure that she knew what he was going to do. He wanted to tell her to look after El, but he didn't dare say anything of the kind out loud.

"Where's the privy?" he said.

Helios told him it was at the other end of the Undercroft and offered to show him the way.

"I'll be all right," said Pip, standing up. "I'll find it on my own."

Chapter Forty-four

AN ORDER HAD ARRIVED FROM THE PALACE THAT King Oswald required a formal guard of assassins to accompany him on a visit to a private club that was popular with nobles in the city. Today, Ariosto thought, he would take care of the guard duty himself.

He changed into his best livery, and walked slowly to the palace. He arrived half an hour early and requested a personal interview, which earned him a puzzled glance from Oswald's private secretary.

"This is a rare honour," said King Oswald, as he entered the guest chambers.

Ariosto bowed. "At your service, your grace." He took the liberty of looking directly at Oswald and blinked. He hadn't looked into his eyes before, and they were deeply unsettling.

"I hear that it has been an unusually busy time at the

Office for Witchcraft Extermination," said Oswald.

"Yes, sire. The Cardinal has been most anxious."

Oswald turned towards the window. "I hear that witches are abroad. I don't know why this should alarm Lamir so much. After all, isn't witchcraft his domain?"

"I'm sure, your grace, that you have your own ways of dealing with witches in Awemt."

"We are … very efficient. Perhaps Lamir could take a few feathers from our cap. But he is sadly incurious. He seemed to believe there was no problem in Clarel at all."

Ariosto's heart was beating fast, but he showed no sign of it. "For all that, he is deeply interested in witch-craft. Certainly, some of the artefacts we have secretly recovered seem to me of a dubious nature."

"Really?" Oswald looked amused. "I thought you believed that he was merely professionally interested. What kind of artefacts do you mean?"

"In recent years, it's been an item he called the Stone Heart." Out of the corner of his eye, Ariosto saw Oswald stiffen. "We managed to track it down, through the offices of a young witchcraft expert called Sibelius d'Artan. But then it was lost."

"Lost?"

"Our men were returning to the office when they were, apparently, robbed by some riff-raff. We're fairly certain it was taken by a young pickpocket with links to witches. The entire office has since been devoted to its recovery."

Oswald was silent, staring out of the window. Finally he turned around. "Do you know what this Stone Heart is?"

"No," said Ariosto.

"But I think you can guess," said Oswald.

"My guesses, sire, are at best stabs in the dark. I know it is a magical artefact. I know that it was made by a witch from the heart of the crown Prince Clovis, just after Axel the First seized the throne. I suspect it has great power."

Oswald turned again to the window. It seemed to Ariosto that he was suppressing agitation, but it was hard to tell. Like most nobles, Oswald was adept at hiding his feelings.

The assassin waited, wondering how his gamble would pay off.

At last Oswald turned to face him. "Why are you telling me this?"

"I thought it may interest you." Ariosto permitted himself another direct glance, and looked away. There was a red flame in Oswald's eyes. Or perhaps he was imagining it.

"As it happens, it interests me deeply. What do you wish to gain by telling me this?"

Ariosto cleared his throat. "I am the best assassin in

all Continentia. Perhaps you might be keen to employ someone of my skills in your personal retinue."

At this, Oswald laughed. "Had enough of Lamir, eh?"

"I believe he is not the man I thought he was," said Ariosto. *Or maybe,* he added privately, *he is exactly the man I knew he was.*

"Do you know where the Stone Heart is?"

"No, sire. We're assuming that it is in the possession of witches. Most likely a witch called Amina Bemare, who escaped from the office last night through magical means."

"And do you have any idea why Lamir wanted it?"

"No, sire." Ariosto cleared his throat again. "I assume that it may serve his personal ambition in some way."

Another silence. Ariosto simply waited.

"So why this sudden transfer of allegiance? I wonder," said Oswald.

"I hate Lamir." Ariosto spoke coldly, without expression. "With every part of my body and every part of my soul."

"Dear me. Lamir must be in a state, if he's alienating his most loyal staff."

"Yes, sire."

Another pause.

"I'm surprised that Lamir never made you a Spectre," said Oswald conversationally. "You would have made a most excellent vessel."

Ariosto felt a stab of terror as everything fell into place and his mouth went dry. He had known, of course, that Lamir had unusual powers, but he had never suspected that he was a Spectre himself. His licked his lips, trying to think of what to say.

Oswald examined his face, a cold smile on his lips. "Dear me, you had no idea, did you? In any case, one has to begin in childhood. No doubt your breeding is vulgar, and the thought caused Lamir distaste. I confess I have similar distaste. One only wants the finest vessels for one's soul, after all."

He walked up to Ariosto and forced up the assassin's chin with his finger. Ariosto stared into his eyes, unable to move.

There was no warning, none of the theatrics that the Cardinal was so fond of. There wasn't time to feel afraid. Ariosto only had time to note that he hadn't imagined the red fire in Oswald's eyes.

Oswald said a single word in a low voice, and Ariosto burned up instantly from inside. It was too quick for pain. For an instant he was a blazing column of fire, which went out almost as quickly as it appeared. Then a grey, man-shaped shell crumbled into a small pile of ash on the expensive carpet.

It was, by Oswald's standards, a merciful death. He

glanced down, his face expressionless.

A shame, he thought. A criminal waste of some truly exceptional talents. But he couldn't trust that the man wouldn't do something foolish. Despite everything, the chief assassin Ariosto, the most feared man in the kingdom of Clarel, was an innocent.

What he had revealed certainly explained a few things about the Cardinal's conduct. Oswald walked over to the window and gazed out blankly, digesting the information Ariosto had just given him.

The Stone Heart. Was it everything that repute made it? It was hard to say, since it had been made by a witch.

Oswald-Rudolph understood everything there was to know about blood magic. He doubted that witches had an equal understanding of Spectres to his own, although it was difficult to be certain. Witches were, in the end, blinded by their own short-sightedness, their vain desire to do good.

If the rumours held any truth, the Stone Heart was a tool of unsurpassed power. But equally, it could be used to destroy every single Spectre... And the Cardinal, fool that he was, had let the witches get hold of it.

Oswald-Rudolph's first impulse was to leave Clarel, pleading urgent affairs at home, and leave these incompetents to their own mess.

On the other hand, he was reluctant to leave without the Princess, since he needed her for his next vessel. And if the Cardinal did find the Stone Heart and succeeded in unlocking its powers, he could be unstoppable. Oswald turned on his heel, thinking deeply. Perhaps he should find the Princess first. He could trace her fairly easily with some simple magic. And secondly, he must find the Stone Heart. That might be a little more difficult, but surely not impossible, if he reached for his powers.

He ought to tell his staff to prepare for departure from Clarel, just in case. But in the meantime…

He summoned his secretary. "I have," he said, "a sentimental request."

"At your service, sire," said the secretary. A well-trained servant, he pretended not to notice the pile of ash on the carpet.

"I am afire with love for Princess Georgette, as you know. And I find I have the fancy to hold something that belongs to the Princess. Something that she values, something that is precious to her, so I may the better summon her to mind."

His secretary bowed. "I shall enquire of her ladies-in-waiting, sire," he said.

"Make sure you're quick," said Oswald. "My passion is impatient."

Chapter Forty-five

GEORGETTE'S COURAGE BEGAN TO FAIL THE MOMENT
she crossed the Furrier's Bridge. As a child she had often
ventured into the streets by the Old Palace with Oni and
the other servant children, but that was a long time ago.
At Clarel Palace, she had been far more strictly confined.
On the rare occasions that she went beyond into the city
streets, she was either carried in a sedan by four strong
men, or travelled in one of the palace carriages. And she
never went anywhere without an escort of guards.

She hadn't realized that the city was so hard to find
your way around in. She exited the narrow bridge, which
was lined with dilapidated and grimy shops that sold
animal skins and smelt terrible, and set off confidently
down the wide street that ran before her, sure that it was
heading in the right direction. But then it turned and
twisted and somehow she found herself at a dead end,

being eyed speculatively by an old man in rags who was sitting on a doorstep. She beat a hasty retreat, doing her best to look as if she weren't lost, and tried another street. This grew narrower and narrower and at last dived into a dim alley, which she was reluctant to enter.

The witches had said there was trouble brewing, but Georgette couldn't see any sign of it. If anything, the streets seemed emptier than usual. Either people were exaggerating, or she was in the wrong place. She thought of asking for directions, but the few people she saw seemed sinister and she walked past them quickly. She doubled back again and saw some Midsummer Festival ribbons on a corner lamp post. She peeked down the road: it was lined with midsummer stalls, although again the street was empty. And then she began to hear a faint roar, as if there were a crowd in the distance. She bent her steps that way, guiding herself by the sound.

Georgette didn't want to admit it, but she was beginning to feel that she had made a mistake. What had she been thinking? How would she find the leaders of the rebellion? And even if she did, would anyone really believe that she was Princess Georgette? She was dressed like a street boy, a commoner, and most of being a princess is looking like one. And by now she was thoroughly lost. She didn't think she could find her way back to the Undercroft even if she wanted to.

At the end of the street she ran into her first patrol of soldiers. About half a dozen men in armour were leading an old woman away in chains, but she wasn't going quietly. She was scolding one of the soldiers, a scrawny young man with pimples, at the top of her voice. Several spectators were hooting in derision, shouting at the soldiers to let her go.

"What would your ma say, Inias? She would be ashamed of you. Ashamed! Arresting one of her oldest friends."

The soldier, whose ears were bright red, muttered that they were just following orders.

"Following orders!" retorted the woman in chains. "That's a puny excuse. I helped bring you into the world, boy. It was a difficult birth too, and were you worth the trouble? I saved your mother's life, and yours too. And this is the thanks I get?" She lifted her chained hands and shook them at him. "You're a disgrace!" She turned around to the other soldiers. "All of you. You're disgraceful!"

More people were gathering, standing out of range of the weapons and heckling. Georgette, lingering despite herself, could see that the soldiers were growing afraid

315

of the crowd. And she knew that frightened soldiers were dangerous.

"Shut up, woman, or you'll get the back of my hand," said one of them.

"Go on," said the old woman. "Hit an old woman who barely reaches your chest, you mangy cowardly weasel."

"Yeah, do that," said a burly man with a red face in the crowd. "Proud, are you?"

"Put down your arms!" Georgette hadn't intended to say anything at all. She couldn't believe that it was her voice speaking, but it was: her princess voice, trained in commanding inferiors, crisp and authoritative. "And unchain that woman! At once!"

Everyone turned around and stared at her. She raised her chin. "I am Princess Georgette of Clarel Palace," she said, as arrogantly as she could. "And I do not countenance this behaviour."

The soldiers stared at her and hesitated.

"That's not a princess," said one. "It's just some kid."

"She sounds posh though," said one of the bystanders.

"He's wearing trews," said another.

Georgette took off her cap with a flourish and shook out her golden ringlets. "Of course I'm your princess," she said. Now she was committed to this, she thought, she had no choice but to play it to the end. "I am going among my people in disguise, to see the hardship they endure. I find much injustice." She turned a stern glance on the soldiers. "And those who commit injustice will pay for it."

The soldiers looked flummoxed. A couple of people started cheering, and then the cheering was picked up by others. More and more people were gathering around the soldiers, and Georgette could see that some of them were armed.

"You heard the lady," someone said. "Didn't you say you were following orders?"

"Those who do not obey will feel the wrath of the palace," said Georgette fiercely.

The issue wavered in the balance for a few moments. At last the man called Inias jerkily unlocked the chains around the old woman's wrists with a muttered apology and pushed her into the crowd. Then, without a word, the soldiers turned and marched away, taking their tattered dignity with them.

The crowd whistled and hooted at their retreat. A couple of burly men hoisted Georgette onto their shoulders and she punched up in victory, her golden hair gleaming in the sunshine. Everyone started cheering. Georgette flushed with triumph.

The old woman hobbled through the crowd and

stood in front of Georgette, her arms folded. "You put the girl down, boys," she said. To Georgette's chagrin, they instantly obeyed.

The old woman was studying her with rather too sharp a gaze. "Granny Golovier, at your service," she said. "I thank you, Your Highness."

Georgette nodded graciously, hiding a sudden wariness. Was this woman a witch? "My pleasure," she said.

"I don't know if you are who you say you are, but I'm grateful," Granny Golovier went on. "My advice is, princess or no, you go home now."

"My place is with my people," said Georgette.

"I'm not sure who your people are, but I'm pretty sure these aren't them."

"I'm not going anywhere," said Georgette, glancing around at the crowd. "I must speak to the leaders of the rebellion."

The old woman frowned, her face collapsing into a web of wrinkles, and then beckoned Georgette closer. Georgette, deciding again to be gracious, took the woman's hand and leaned down until she could feel her whiskers tickling her face.

"I think you'll be needing to talk to the Witches' Council, my dear," the old woman whispered in her ear. "That's if you're really serious about talking to leaders."

Georgette jerked back, but the woman kept hold of her hand with surprising strength. "Listen, my girl. I can see right plainly that the way you're going you're headed for trouble."

"I don't need witches," hissed Georgette. "I want to talk to the *people*."

"Witches are people, girl. All kinds of people. It's what nobles never quite understood..."

"Are you a witch?"

At this, the old woman let out a crack of laughter. "Me? No! But I've been around this world a good bit longer than you, and I know a thing or two."

Georgette bit her lip, and straightened up, withdrawing her hand. For a moment she wavered. Perhaps Granny Golovier was right. Perhaps she really should go back to the Undercroft.

But that would be humiliating. She imagined how Amiable would sneer. It would be admitting defeat before she had even tried.

This was her chance to be Queen. Leading the riots was how Axel I had become king, after all. Why couldn't she do the same? All she needed was courage...

"Thank you, my good woman," she said loudly, for the benefit of the bystanders. "I will always fight for justice."

Some of the crowd, Georgette saw, were losing interest

now the soldiers had gone and were wandering off. She had to gain their attention. She took a deep breath, as she had been taught to do in her deportment classes.

"Arise, my people!" she cried. "We must cast down the tyrants!"

Some laughed, but others started cheering.

Georgette lifted her hand. "To the palace!"

More people started cheering, and a few began to chant, "To the palace!" She was hoisted up again by the burly men and swept off in a wave of enthusiasm.

It was a little difficult to keep her balance and dignity as she bobbed above the heads of the crowd, but Georgette did her best, holding her chin high. As they proceeded up the street, more people joined the crowd, attracted by the shouting and cheering. She looked over her shoulder. There were dozens of people now.

This was more like it. It was exactly as she had imagined, like the uprisings she had read about in history books.

Granny Golovier stared after Georgette until her bearers turned a corner and disappeared, and then she shook her head at a couple of chickens that were scratching in the dirt. "Poor silly child," she said. "Sometimes you just can't tell them."

Chapter Forty-six

IN HIS PRIVATE LIBRARY, CARDINAL LAMIR SAT ALONE
at his writing desk, staring at the wall. Something was
amiss in the fabric of things. The riots in the city – *pffff* –
who cared? A little bloodletting didn't do any harm. The
King would send in the army, there'd be a massacre and
then everybody would go home. But riots along with the
disappearing Princess, the loss of the Stone Heart and
revolting witches: those were more serious matters.

He had an uncomfortable feeling that King Oswald
knew more about his plans than he would have liked.
And it had been a mistake to use the office to hunt down
the Stone Heart. He realized that now. It had drawn
attention.

He checked his pocket watch. Ariosto was late.

The Cardinal was still the only person who knew how
to use the Stone Heart. That was a comfort. Not even the

witches knew. The Oracle of the Void, whom he summoned through the mirror in his library, had shown him the exact spell the witch had used to make it, and in that instant he had seen how to take this half-formed soul, this Spectre-who-was-not-a-Spectre, and incorporate it into his own being.

Once he did that, he could control Ruptures. And once he could control Ruptures, he could control reality. He could, if he wished, destroy King Oswald.

Destroying King Oswald was very much part of the Cardinal's plan. From there it would be a simple matter to take over all of Continentia. There would be nothing and no one to stop him.

One careless decision. That's all it had taken. He should have sent assassins to collect the Stone Heart. They wouldn't have lost it. But at that stage he was hoping to keep it secret even from assassins. He still held out hope that he could wrest it back from the witches. It would have to be found quickly if everything were not to be lost. Or worse...

So near, and yet so far.

The hair prickled on the back of the Cardinal's neck. That wasn't his own thought. Or was it?

Low laughter echoed through the room. The Cardinal knew that laugh. He whirled in his chair, looking wildly around. The chamber was empty. But then he saw that the surface of the mirror was shimmering, like the surface of a dark pond. His mirror. The mirror that no other being, living or dead, should be able to unlock.

Before Lamir's appalled eyes, King Oswald slowly stepped out of the mirror. Only it wasn't King Oswald: he had put away his earthly form. Now he was a skeletal Spectre, Oswald-Rudolph, his form glowing in the shadowed room, his robes flickering with tongues of cold flame.

"Rudolph," said Lamir. His mouth was suddenly very dry. "How ... delightful to see you..."

"An informal visit, merely," said the Spectre. His urbane manner was completely incongruous with his demonic appearance. "I thought you'd be relieved to hear that I am on my way to pick up Princess Georgette."

"You've found her?" Lamir said, attempting a smile. "That is excellent news."

"Indeed. I am fortunate in that I have some skill with primitive location spells. There are certain witch techniques of which you could have taken more notice. There are many things of which you should have taken more notice." Oswald floated towards Lamir, transfixing him with his empty eyes. "So unfortunate. One mistake after another..."

The Cardinal's eyes narrowed. "I have no idea what you mean."

"To think it was your most loyal servant who betrayed you. So sad. I'm afraid I had to get rid of Ariosto. Such a talented man. And yet … so frail in the end."

Lamir blinked. Even in his wildest dreams, he hadn't imagined that Ariosto might turn against him. He had nourished him from childhood, he had given him everything…

"Alas," said King Rudolph. "Betrayal breeds betrayal. And I do not countenance disloyalty, Lamir. However, you had your uses. On one point I agreed with you: now is the time to take power."

Lamir snapped out of his shock and stepped menacingly towards Rudolph. "I am thinking that this disloyalty you speak of isn't mine," he said. As he stood up his form dissolved, and now two Spectres faced each other, rippling with cold fire. "You know as well as I do that servants are prone to lying."

"Your assassin wasn't lying," snapped Rudolph. "I could see his thoughts. As I can see yours, despite your pathetic attempts to hide them from me."

Out of nowhere, a black-tongued sword appeared in Lamir's hand. Before Rudolph could react, he swung its blade in a wide arc at his rival's neck. There was a flash of red light, a crack of bone, and Rudolph's head fell onto the patterned carpet with a dull thump and rolled beneath Lamir's desk.

Lamir relaxed, thinking for a moment that he had triumphed; but a low snicker echoed through the room. The skull kept rolling, out from beneath the desk and then around the room in ever-increasing circles, faster and faster. The headless skeleton seemed to be watching the skull with interest. As it orbited Lamir, the walls of the office wavered and vanished.

Lamir slashed viciously at the skeleton, but it caught his blade in its bony hands. The Cardinal flinched back as if the weapon had shocked him, letting go of the hilt, and the black sword wavered and dissolved into a wisp of smoke.

By now the skull was moving so swiftly it was barely visible, and its cold laughter was the only thing that Lamir could hear. He spun wildly, trying to keep his eyes on it, speaking words that tumbled one into another – spell words for death, destruction, maiming; but they seemed to have no effect at all on the nightmare head.

Then, quite suddenly, the skull stopped in mid-air, its empty glare focused on Lamir. Its stillness was even more dreadful than its movement. The Cardinal watched as it moved slowly towards him, closer and closer, until it was a hand's breath from his face.

"I know you have it, Lamir," said the skull softly. "I want that spell."

"I don't know which spell you speak of."

"The spell that unlocks the power of the Stone Heart. The key to your grimy little dreams."

"I … do … not…"

The skull floated even closer. "I had hoped that, out of our long friendship, you would give this knowledge to me," it whispered. "But no. Lamir, fool that he is, thinks he can resist even *me*."

The flames around Lamir's form flared up in a sudden blaze, as if he were making one final, supreme effort. But even as the blaze lit up the darkness, Rudolph's skull melded into Lamir's, the two heads becoming one: and the flames of both Spectres were snuffed out, vanishing into the darkness of complete void, where even time doesn't exist. And in the void, Rudolph devoured Lamir's memory.

After an unmeasurable moment, a light reappeared: the flames that clothed the headless skeleton flared up redly, illuminating the shelves of Lamir's library. Rudolph's skull was back with the rest of his body, studying the man who slumped before him: Lamir, stripped of his Spectral form, his face drained of all blood, his eyes wide with horror.

"I am grateful for your assistance, Lamir," said the Spectre mockingly. "However reluctantly given. But now, I fear, this is the end of our long alliance."

Lamir lifted his arms in one last gesture of defiance or despair, but even as he did he could feel his bones dissolving, his hands crumbling, his torso collapsing inwards. His face hung in the air for an instant, and then trickled down to the carpet in rivulets of dust.

Rudolph walked to the mirror without looking back at the small heap of dust and vanished through its shimmering surface.

There was a long silence, as if the chamber itself were holding its breath. It was broken by a tiny snap. A crack appeared in the centre of the mirror and began to lengthen across the glass. And then there was another, and another, until the entire surface was a spider web of cracks.

Finally, with a musical tinkle, the mirror ballooned outwards and collapsed from its gilt frame, covering the floor with thousands of tiny glass splinters.

Chapter Forty-seven

IT WAS A LONG TIME SINCE HE HAD USED HIS FULL power. How many centuries? He couldn't remember exactly; in his mind the past collapsed into a single gaping absence. All those years he had been forced to hide his true nature in the flesh of his descendants. All those moments in which he had bitten down his rage, concealed his strength, patiently building the foundations of his immortal realm, so he would never be cast down again.

For the first time in an age he felt … joy. Yes, that was it. Joy. The exhilaration of absolute power. He could destroy this entire pathetic city if he wished. He could grind its every palace and hovel into dust. He could see the thoughts of each person inside its walls, shimmering knots of feeling that illuminated every winding street. All he had to do was swoop down, out of the shadowy realm where his soul soared, and any one of those flickering, living thoughts would be blotted out for ever.

He had come to Clarel to ensure his mortal reign, to strengthen the line of heirs whose bodies would house his soul. The last thing he had expected to discover here was the key to absolute power in the realms of magic. But there it was: the soul of little Prince Clovis, melded by the witches into a spell that he himself was incapable of forging; the very spell that would cause their own downfall and his triumph.

The irony was delicious.

His heightened perceptions searching through the busy city of Clarel, he paused to savour the moment. Every life beneath his gaze was subject to his whim. Already his power was greater than anything imagined in the puny dreams of any emperor in history. Even inside the confinements of mortal bodies, his precious life constantly endangered by the frailty of flesh, he had always been the most puissant of them all: the first and the greatest of the Spectres. And soon he would be far greater. Soon even death would have no dominion.

All he needed to set the keystone into the arch of his ambition were two souls: one flesh, one unfleshed. Once they were his, and his alone, no other Spectre could begin to challenge him.

And even now those two souls hurried together through the tangled streets of Clarel, unaware of how he tilted above them on invisible ethereal currents, sensing his way ever closer to the soft chiming of their terror.

Nothing could stop him now.

Chapter Forty-eight

AFTER PIP ABSCONDED FROM THE UNDERCROFT, HE remembered all his earlier fears about assassins. He didn't want witches to cast some terrible spell on him, but he didn't want to have his throat cut like poor old Olibrandis, either. And then there were the Spectres. Amina seemed to think that Spectres could track people down wherever they wanted.

Pip rubbed his temples. His head was aching: tiredness, he guessed. He really hadn't had enough sleep. He wished he had a safe house to go to now. Pip had spent almost his whole life learning how to slip unnoticed through the streets of Clarel, but he knew nothing about protecting himself from Spectres.

He was lost. Not totally lost, because he had a good sense of direction – like a homing pigeon, El said – but he wasn't quite sure where he was. He knew it was somewhere near the Weavers' Quarter, but he couldn't seem to find a landmark: he was winding through small, anonymous streets and tiny squares, but there were no familiar buildings or statues. In the Choke Alleys he knew every blind close, every escape route, every hole. He was much less familiar with this part of the city.

The further he went, the more uneasy he felt. Thoroughfares that he expected to be crowded were spookily empty, and sometimes the wind carried a faint noise which sounded like people shouting or even the clash of weapons. He began to have an uneasy feeling that something was leading him astray. There was, he thought, something weird going on: none of the paths he chose were leading him in the direction he wanted. He was trying to get as far away from trouble as he could, but every street he entered seemed to bring him closer instead, as if the roads twisted as soon as he entered them.

He began to wonder if it was the witches, or maybe even Spectre magic confusing him somehow. Then he shook himself. It was probably because he didn't have a destination in mind. His strongest instinct was to go home, but he knew he couldn't. He didn't have a home any more. Maybe his best bet was to scarper out of town altogether.

Find a little country village, like the place he'd been born.

We should hide in the other place, suggested Clovis.

What other place?

Where we were before you made me bring everyone back. It's safer there.

I'm damned if I'm going back into that Rupture, said Pip, with an effort. It was getting hard to argue with someone inside his own head. *It's horrible there.*

El liked it, didn't she? We could bring El and Oni with us, and then we wouldn't be lonely. We would all be friends.

You did something to El to make her like it, said Pip. *That wasn't nice.*

Nobody can find us there, said Clovis. *Not even my father.*

What's your father got to do with it?

I think he's looking for us, said Clovis.

What? Pip pulled up short outside an abandoned butcher's shop. *How do you know?*

A rush of feeling tore through him: mostly fear, but mixed with longing. It took him a moment to realize that it was Clovis. It was getting more and more difficult to tell his own thoughts from Clovis's.

I can hear someone calling me, said Clovis.

This is bad, thought Pip, and for a moment the confusion lifted: that was definitely his own thought. *This is very bad…*

333

Isn't your father dead? asked Pip.

He misses me, said Clovis.

He doesn't miss you, said Pip. *He just wants to use you. Didn't you listen to the witches?*

You only think that my father is bad because of what the witches said. But you can't trust witches.

You're talking to your father?

No. Again a pause. *But I can hear him. He's calling me…*

As if a door had opened inside his head, Pip could suddenly hear him too. If it was hearing. He couldn't understand any actual words, but he didn't need to: the meaning was clear. A soft, melodious voice, full of love and regret, calling to Pip. No, not Pip. Calling to Clovis. Come home, be safe, be happy, be loved, you will never again be alone…

For a moment, Pip almost fell into the lure of the enchantment, feeling the seduction of its promise. But the streetwise part of him flicked alert. And then he did hear a voice, speaking as clearly as if there was a person just ten feet away.

Come home, Clovis, my dear boy. Come home…

Underneath its bewitching music, Pip sensed something hard and chilling. Something … deadly.

He's lying, said Pip sharply. *Don't even think about it. Don't you dare tell him where I am.*

Who are you to question the honour of a royal? And suddenly the trusting child that Clovis had been for the past few hours was gone, and the princely arrogance was back.

I'm me, said Pip. *Your friend. Pip. Remember?*

Come home... The voice was even stronger now, and Pip struggled with an overpowering longing to answer that voice, to say yes, to give in and run towards it. He could feel the aching void inside Clovis, the desire for a father who loved him. Clovis was shutting himself against Pip, turning away.

Don't answer him, Pip said to Clovis. *Don't. It will be the end of us both. Don't you care about me?*

Pip's headache was getting worse and worse, a throbbing pain. He clutched his brow, stumbled against the wall of a house, and slid down.

Princes have no friends, said Clovis.

No wonder, thought Pip bitterly.

Come home, my son. Come home and be with those who love and understand you.

Pip gasped and bit his lip, trying to will the voice out of his head. It was bad enough having Clovis there, but this as well? He could feel its malignance: it beat against him as heat beats out of a fireplace. At the same time, he could feel Clovis surrendering. He was drowning in a wash of confused feelings that weren't his own, that were somehow wound through the very fibre of his being.

I'm Pip, he told himself. *Me. Pip. Me. Not anybody else.*

He tried to push everything away, to think.

It's a trick, he said desperately. *Your father's dead.* Even as he said it, he thought that was a ridiculous thing to say to a dead boy. *It can't be your father…*

Don't be a clod, said Clovis. *Don't you think I remember my own father?*

I don't remember mine, said Pip. *He died of typhus. Anyway, they killed King Odo. The witches said he was destroyed. They cut his head off with an axe. This isn't him.*

It is my father, said Clovis, but now there was doubt in his voice.

Can't you feel it, you pea-brain? It just wants to eat you. In any case, your real father never gave a spit for you. He just wanted to eat you as well.

He felt Clovis's anger like a spike in his temple. *My father is a king,* said Clovis indignantly. *It's different for kings. You don't understand. You can't, you're just a commoner.*

"I am full of love for my son," said the voice. This time it wasn't inside Pip's skull.

In the street before them stood a tall man with a pale face, clad in a dark green cloak. He had a simple gold chain about his neck, and a gold brooch on his shoulder, and he was smiling.

Father!

The gladness in Clovis's voice made Pip's heart lurch with unexpected pity. This must be the semblance of Clovis's father. The man who had been turning Clovis into a vessel for the Spectre's soul. He had never loved Clovis, no matter how much Clovis longed for his love. Surely Clovis knew that. How lonely did you have to be?

Pip looked up into the man's eyes. All he saw there was cold, bottomless greed. His insides dissolved in naked terror.

In that moment, he knew that Clovis felt what he was feeling.

No, said Clovis.

The vision shimmered and reformed. The King's face shrivelled to a skull, with empty sockets where his eyes should have been. He was clothed in livid flame, and through the fire Pip could see his skeletal form. He was floating closer, his bony hands stretching out, and around Pip there was only darkness, swallowing everything else.

So that's what a Spectre looks like, Pip thought. *I wish I hadn't seen it.*

He closed his eyes, but it made no difference: he could still see the terrible vision before him. He felt as if his soul were being sucked out of his body, as if the Spectre were a spider, already draining the fluids of its victim.

Pip screamed. There was a flash of searing green light and a weird jolt, as if the ground itself had jumped. *Oh no,* thought Pip. *The Rupture.* Then he blacked out.

When he came to, his eyes were still squeezed shut. Very slowly, he opened them and blinked, dazzled. Had Clovis thrown him into the Rupture again? Which was worse, the Rupture or the Spectre?

He decided that the Spectre was definitely worse.

He was crouched on the cobbles of a tiny lane that ran between two shabby, crooked buildings. A beam of sunlight, finding its way unsullied through the leaning hovels and walls of Clarel, struck him straight in the face.

It didn't seem like being in the Rupture. And anyway, there hadn't been that weird flashing tunnel. Somehow it felt … solid. Gingerly Pip reached out and touched the cobbles with his fingers. There was a pile of dried horse dung just next to him. The fragrance filled his nostrils. He had never thought that he could be so happy to see good honest horse droppings.

I'm sorry, said Clovis, in a tiny voice.

What happened?

I took us to another place. Not the other place. This place.

Pip shook his head. *You're gabbling, Clovis. I don't understand…*

I couldn't take us far. We're round the corner from where we were. But he can't see us now.

It wasn't your father, was it? Pip said it as a statement.

No. Clovis's voice broke. *But even if it had been…* He went silent again.

Even if it had been … what? said Pip.

You were right. My father never cared for me. Not like you do. You left the witches for me and you put yourself in deadly peril. It was dishonourable to bring you into danger after your sacrifice.

Dishonourable, thought Pip. *Right. I suppose so.*

Spectres are worse than witches, Pip said. *Much worse. Much, much, much worse.*

Clovis didn't say anything for a long time. Pip stood up slowly, brushing off his clothes. Every muscle was sore, as if he had been beaten all over, and his head was still aching, but it felt different from before. Then he had felt like his skull might burst, as if something was trying to prise open the bones and force itself inside.

He looked around, trying to work out where he was. Some nameless little alley, with shuttered windows and a bad smell. It definitely *seemed* like Clarel. A mangy dog fossicking for scraps in a midden stared at him and sniffed curiously, but there was nobody else close by.

Are we still friends?

Pip took a deep breath. *Yes, Clovis,* he said. *Yes. We're still friends.*

He stood for a couple more moments, trying to clear his head.

We have to get somewhere safe, he said. *A place where that ... thing ... can't find us.*

Chapter Forty-nine

AFTER THE ENCOUNTER WITH THE SPECTRE, PIP
seemed to have lost what little sense of direction he had
left. Once his pulse stopped racing, he stepped out of
the laneway and ventured cautiously down a side street,
which led to a large thoroughfare he didn't recognize. It
was packed with people, all of them heading one way,
and he had unwarily stepped into the flow, thinking the
crowd would make him harder to find, even for a Spectre.
But now he couldn't get out: the street had turned into a
river of people that bore him along, and no matter how
hard he fought, he couldn't seem to reach the edge of it.

Many people, Pip saw uneasily, carried weapons:
knives, mallets, hammers, even old swords. There was
going to be trouble. And the push was getting tighter
and tighter as more people joined. He began to be afraid
that he might fall and be trampled.

He didn't even know which way the Undercroft was now. Clovis was no help at all. When Pip asked him where they were, he just repeated that he had moved them a street away from where they had been before, and then he went very quiet and refused to answer.

Pip was beginning to suspect that Clovis's ideas of distance bore very little relationship to his own. It was probably something to do with having been locked up in a tiny box for fifty years. Or maybe princes didn't know anything about cities because they spent all their lives inside palaces having their arses wiped by servants.

They were definitely somewhere in the poorer quarters of Clarel. All Pip knew was that he definitely didn't want to go wherever the people were going.

At last the crowd emptied itself into a large square and the pressure around him lifted. Pip breathed out with relief and shook his arms, which were aching from being pummelled.

Now Pip could feel the mood of the crowd in his bones: excited and jubilant and defiant. It was contagious, and for a few moments he wanted just to be part of it, to go where everyone else was going. But the crowd was also tense, on the verge of explosion.

Every minute, more people were pouring into the

open space, and it was beginning to get tight again. People could suffocate and die in crowds like this. Pip started pushing between the hot, packed bodies, guiding himself by a clock tower that he could just see over the heads of the crowd. People swore and cuffed him, but there was still enough space to squirm away before anyone could start a proper fight. It was slow going, and every moment that passed he felt more frustrated.

I don't like this, said Clovis. *We're in the wrong place.*

You could have said before, answered Pip crossly. *When I was asking for directions. You plonked me somewhere I don't know. It's not my fault.*

It's not mine either, said Clovis petulantly. *I was just trying to help.*

Pip ignored him and kept pushing. At last he reached the edge of the square and started worming his way along the walls. Once he got out of the crowd, he thought, he could find a way to escape the city. He had no clear idea of what to do after that. Pip was used to surviving moment to moment, so he normally didn't worry too much about later until later turned up.

A roar started at the other end of the square, voices raised in anger or fear, and there was a violent surge. Pip scanned the walls desperately: there were doors, shuttered shopfronts, a broad flight of steps leading up to some

343

posh building... There had to be an alley somewhere...

And yes, at last, there was a gap, so narrow he could easily have missed it if he hadn't been looking so closely. He lunged inside, praying that it wasn't a dead end, or that if it was a dead end, that the walls might at least be climbable. It was dank and smelly, little more than a foot wide, but soon it opened up into an alley. Pip breathed out and continued onwards, diving down some damp steps through a crumbling archway. For some reason, this alley was completely empty. After the crowd, the emptiness felt a bit sinister, but Pip began to feel hopeful that maybe luck was on his side, after all.

He scuttled around a corner, and tripped over someone who was crouched against the wall, their face hidden in their arms. Pip swore and picked himself up, turning to abuse them.

He couldn't believe his eyes. It was Princess Georgette. She was dressed in breeches and a tunic, and her ringlets were mostly tangles, but it was definitely the same girl. He gaped in astonishment and then pulled himself together.

"What the hells are you doing here?"

Georgette scrambled to her feet, clenching her hands. "Who are you?"

"Pip," he said. "We met at Amina's."

Georgette blinked, and he saw that she didn't remember him. He felt a twinge of annoyance. "I expect you didn't really look at me, me being a commoner and everything."

"No, no, I remember you," said Georgette hastily. "It's just… I'm just…"

"Running away?'

She nodded warily.

"Us too," said Pip.

Georgette looked puzzled, and peered behind him. "Us?"

"Who are you running from?'

Georgette looked as if she were about to cry again. "I'm not sure," she said. "There was a horrible fight, and some of my— my companions were injured. And then I just ran…"

"Which way was that? Were you in the square?"

"What square?"

Pip pointed behind him, trying to curb his impatience. "That one back there."

Georgette shook her head. "I came from the other way," she said. "And then I got lost and I ended up here, and I don't know what to do…"

Pip reflected that the last thing he needed right now was a tearful princess, but he felt a stab of sympathy. "Well, then, maybe come with us. I mean, with me."

345

"Where are you going, though?"

"Somewhere safer," said Pip.

Georgette stood up. "I'd like to," she said. Pip realized with surprise that she wasn't only frightened; she was shy. "I don't really know my way around."

There isn't anywhere safer, said Clovis. *Not here. Not anywhere.*

"Well, that's really helpful, thanks," said Pip, speaking out loud. Georgette looked hurt, and he added, "No, not you. Clovis."

"Who?"

"Clovis," he repeated impatiently. "The Prince. Isn't he some kind of cousin of yours?"

We can't take her, she'll betray us. Clovis sounded panicked.

Don't be silly, said Pip. *We can't leave her on her own here.*

He can smell her, said Clovis. *Like a dog. Like dogs sniff people out. He'll track her down and then I won't be able to hide us.*

Pip hesitated. Georgette, puzzled and afraid, tried to drag together some of her dignity. "I understand if you can't help me. Of course."

"No time to explain," Pip said, taking her hand. "Let's go."

Chapter Fifty

"WHERE'S PIP?"

Oni was the only one who heard El's question. The witches were still discussing what to do next. El had given up trying to follow what the witches were saying, because she hardly understood any of it.

Oni had said nothing for ages, and was just sitting there, frowning and picking at her lip. Pip had disappeared to look for a privy but it had been a long time since he left the tent. Too long.

"Oni, maybe we should go look for Pip? Do you think he got lost?"

Oni quickly met El's eyes. *Be quiet*, the look said.

"Oni?" El felt her chest tightening. "Do you know where he is? Has something happened to him?"

Oni shook her head, and put her finger on her lips. But it was too late: they had attracted Amina's attention.

She glanced at the two girls sharply, and then her gaze swept to Pip's empty chair. Her lips set into a straight line and she settled back into her chair, staring at her daughter.

"Where is that boy?"

Oni shrugged. "How should I know?" she said.

"The Heart boy?" said Juin.

"He isn't back," said El. "He went to the privy ages ago and maybe someone's kidnapped him or he got lost and now..." She yelped because Oni kicked her under the table. "Oni! Why did you do that?"

Now everyone was looking at Oni. "I told you, I don't know," she said.

"I am willing to bet my last silver piece that you do know," said Amina. "And now is not the time for games, Oni. I'm serious."

Oni swept a fiery glance around the table. "He ran away because he thought you were going to kill him. And I don't blame him."

Helios looked appalled. "Why would he think that?"

"Oh, I don't know," said Oni. Her eyes were sparkling with anger. "Maybe it's because you wouldn't listen to him – or me. Maybe it's because all you can talk about is how to destroy Clovis. Maybe if you want to destroy Clovis you have to destroy Pip."

There was a shocked silence, and then everyone started talking at once.

Amina stood up, her voice carrying over the rest. "Are you saying he's run off?"

"You frightened him. And Clovis. Clovis was terrified."

El stared at Oni, her lower lip trembling. "They wanted to kill Pip?"

"Pip knows what Old Missus Pledge did to make the Heart, better than any of you. Of course he thought you wanted to kill him."

"You knew he'd run off and you said nothing?" Amina looked as angry as Oni. "Knowing everything you do, with the fate of the city in the balance?"

"None of you would *listen*."

Oni folded her arms mutinously and refused to say anything more. Juin leapt out of his chair and said he would search for Pip in the Undercroft, because he was sure that even a day person couldn't be so ignorant as to walk out into direct danger. Helios was suggesting a search party. El began to sob quietly, her face hidden in her hands.

Sibelius d'Artan emerged from the back of the tent in the middle of the chaos and stood with his mouth open, trying to make sense of the babble. Amiable glanced over at him and almost spat. "Day people!" she said. "We should never have let them in."

Sibelius bowed awkwardly. "My apologies," he said. "I was just wondering…"

"Go back to sleep. Back with your precious princess. At least none of you are any trouble when you're snoring."

"Princess Georgette?" said Sibelius, looking bewildered. "She's not asleep."

Amina whipped around to face him. "Georgette isn't in the bedchamber?"

"No," said Sibelius. "I thought perhaps … I thought she could show me where to get … to get breakfast…" He trailed off, looking from witch to witch. "Of course, if it's inconvenient…"

Oni snorted. "Georgie was probably frightened and ran away too," she said. "I bet you weren't very nice to her."

"Witches aren't *nice*," said Amiable. "That's not what witches are *for*."

"She was talking about wanting to lead the rebellion," Helios said, looking conscience-stricken. "But I was too busy…"

"See, I told you," said Amiable. "Never trust a royal."

Missus Clay slowly stood, lifting her hands for

350

silence. She suddenly seemed very weary. "We must search the Undercroft first," she said. "Juin, you do that. But it seems very likely, does it not, that the two people who most matter in our fight against the Spectres are now loose and unprotected in the streets of Clarel?"

"Yes," said Amina. "It does. And my own daughter had a part in it."

Missus Clay drew a trembling hand across her forehead. "Then we must find them. If it's not too late."

"They're probably hiding from witches," said Oni. "But they both trust me. So maybe I should look for them."

"You dare move a step outside the Undercroft, young lady, and I will have your hide." Amina's voice was trembling with rage. "You've done enough harm already."

"It's not me who did the harm," said Oni. She was standing very straight, and her mouth was set in a stubborn line. "I bet some of you would be very happy to murder Pip, and Georgette too, if you thought it would save your scrawny necks. Well, I'm not happy about that. It's not their fault we're in such a mess."

"It will be their fault if the Spectres get hold of them," said Amiable. "And yours too, if you helped them betray us."

Oni gasped, as if she had been slapped. "I've betrayed

351

no one," she said hotly. "But maybe some of you should have a good hard look at yourselves and think about the Laws. Do you remember those Laws? Maybe you're just like Spectres and think they don't matter."

"I think everybody should calm down," said Missus Orphint. Like Oni, she had been sitting quietly apart, not participating in the argument. "Yes, it might be too late. But Oni has a point. Nobody listened to her, or to young Pip. Or, it seems, to Princess Georgette. It could be that Old Missus Pledge was wrong about the spell. Maybe there's another way."

Bottomly popped into sight on the table. "With all due respect, Missus Orphint, we've been trying to come up with another way for hours and there isn't one."

"Well, I don't care what any of you think," said Oni. "Everybody says that we have to find Pip and Georgette, and that it's my fault for letting Pip go, so I'll go find them. No, Ma, you can't stop me. I'm not a child any more. I'm pretty sure I know how to find Pip. So I'll start there."

El looked up at Oni, blinking tears out of her eyes, and took her hand. "Will you really, Oni? You'll find Pip and bring him back to me?"

Oni's face softened. She bent down and kissed El's hair. "I will find him, my dearest El," she whispered.

"It'll be easy, I'll use a spell." She strode to the exit, and then turned around, her eyes flashing with rage. "You all look after El. She's worth more than the rest of you put together. At least she has a heart."

After Oni stormed out, there was a long, awkward silence. It was broken by a loud gurgle from Sibelius's stomach. He flushed and apologized. "I haven't eaten, you see, since..."

Amiable studied him thoughtfully, her expression inscrutable, high spots of colour flying on her cheeks. Sibelius, already familiar with Amiable's sharp tongue, braced himself for abuse.

"If you like, I'll take you to the bakery tent," she said. "They've brought in new supplies from Armand's. I'm hungry, too."

Chapter Fifty-one

"WHICH WAY DO WE GO?" PRINCESS GEORGETTE pushed a sweaty lock of hair out of her eyes. They had hit another dead end. She had had no idea that Clarel was so full of streets that went nowhere.

"Just wait here," said Pip, and disappeared back the way they had come.

For an hour she and Pip had been scurrying through the outer suburbs of Clarel, heading, so Pip told her, for the city walls. Pip had said he was planning to hide in the countryside until the trouble passed. He was a bit vague about where they would go, or who would hide them, though he said he had relatives who would be happy to see a long-lost cousin and would help them.

They had had a short argument when Georgette suggested they return to the Undercroft. Pip was adamant that they shouldn't, and Georgette, unsure that she would be permitted back after running away, didn't feel confident enough to push it.

Making their way through the dusty streets of Clarel on Midsummer Day was thirsty work, especially the way Pip did it. Sometimes they ran down narrow lanes, sometimes they crept along walls, sometimes they doubled back the way they had come, sometimes she stood for ages in a doorway while Pip peered around corners. When she had complained of thirst, Pip had bought a mug of sour ale with some coins, and shared with her. It was Georgette's turn next, he said. But Georgette didn't have any money in her pockets. Princesses never had coins. They didn't need them.

Pip returned and tapped her shoulder. "Left," he said. "I think."

"Do you really know where we're going?"

"Sort of." Pip suddenly grinned. "More than you do, anyway."

"It doesn't look like it to me."

"I can find ways," said Pip. "And I know how not to be followed. Trust me."

Georgette, reflecting that she had no choice, sighed and followed him. She was too tired to argue anyway.

For a while, she had thought things were about to work out in the way she had always imagined they would, and that she would be queen after all. It had been exhilarating, being borne aloft among a crowd of cheering followers, all headed to the palace to overthrow the King. Georgette could see herself taking the throne as the people celebrated, sending her father with a lordly gesture to the dungeons – with which he had so often threatened her – and making everything in the city of Clarel right and just. But it was a naïve lie that she had told herself.

When they had charged into the square in front of Clarel Palace, they had run right into a line of soldiers, whose silver armour gleamed in the sun. Nobody had been frightened, at least at first. Everyone had shouted defiantly and waved their weapons and kept marching. They had expected the army, after all. But Georgette wasn't prepared for what happened next.

The horsemen lowered their spears and charged. Georgette had fallen to the ground. She still didn't know how she hadn't been trampled to death. And then there was the fighting, the smell of blood, the feel of it beneath her shoes.

And Georgette, brave Princess Georgette, had run away.

She didn't know if the soldiers had killed everybody or if the people had fought their way through and taken the palace. She had scrambled desperately through the fighting, dodging the clashing weapons. And then she had run until she was so exhausted that she had collapsed in a heap. And she had stayed there until Pip tripped over her. She wasn't brave at all, like she had imagined she was. She was a coward.

With every step she took, she felt more ashamed of herself.

Georgette was so wrapped up in her own miserable thoughts that she wasn't taking any notice of what was going on around her. When Pip halted suddenly, she cannoned straight into his back. He cursed, and that was when she saw the fear in his face. It was so stark that she went cold all the way through her body.

At first she didn't know why. There was nobody near by. They stood in a narrow, empty street lined with shuttered windows and locked doors, the afternoon sun shining on the cobbles. A street like hundreds of others in Clarel.

And then a shadow swept over them, and she wasn't in the street at all. She and Pip were in another place. She could hear someone crying as if their heart would break. She knew at once that it was the same boy she always heard in her dream, the dream where her mother sat on the throne in front of the stained-glass window. A little boy, weeping and afraid.

Everything around them was shadowy and insub-stantial, as if it weren't quite real. It was like the street where they had been, only drained of life, as if they were surrounded by the ghosts of buildings. Pip alone seemed solid. Instinctively, Georgette grabbed his hand. He didn't pull away. She could feel his pulse hammering under her fingers. Pip's hand was the only warm thing in the whole world.

"Did you really think that you could escape me?"

The voice came from behind them. It was a beautiful voice, low and rich, rippling with amusement. Pip and Georgette whipped around, still clutching each other's hands, but there was no one there.

"I'm afraid that you underestimate me. Princess, you should have known better. You did know better." A low laugh. "Yes, I saw how you cowered when you saw me. I know how afraid you are."

Clovis hiccupped and stopped crying, and for the first time Georgette could see him: a small boy, his shoulder-length hair the same colour as hers, crouched in a ball against Pip's legs, like a small animal that was too afraid to move.

As if the darkness coalesced, a form took shape in front of them. Georgette gripped Pip's hand even more tightly. It was King Oswald, as she had last seen him, in the sober but expensive dress that he favoured.

"Come, Princess," he said. "Your pointless rebellion is now over."

Georgette stirred. "I won't," she said thickly.

"Leave her alone," said Pip.

Oswald cast Pip a look of contempt. Pip felt a pressure on his throat, as if someone were resting their hands around his neck, wondering whether to strangle him. He gulped and steadied himself. "I told you, leave her be."

"I'll be dealing with you in a moment," said Oswald. He turned his attention back to Georgette. "Dear me. A girl of your lineage hobnobbing with a common thief. How low can a princess go? Imagine the scandal if anyone knew. In this one instance, I will overlook it, and allow you to retain your honour." He smiled and reached out a white, ringless hand.

Georgette recoiled in horror. "I'd rather die!"

Oswald's smile snapped out. "How disappointing you are," he said. "You could make this so much easier for yourself. But I assure you that, although you will be severely punished for your disobedience, I will not permit you to die."

"I don't care what you permit," said Georgette, although even she could hear how hollow her defiance was. The assurance in Oswald's voice was absolute: he knew she had no way of escaping him. He was just playing with them, a predator teasing his prey. She could see in his eyes what her future was going to be. It was worse than anything she had imagined back in the palace.

Clovis scrambled to his feet.

"You are the dishonourable ones," said Clovis. The arrogant young prince was back. "You, and my father, and all of you. I condemn you all."

"And yet I prevail." Oswald's form was flickering now, unstable like the shadows around him. "And I shall prevail for ever."

A green shimmer began to lighten the darkness. Oswald laughed. "I'm very sorry, Your Highness," he said. "But your magic is weak here. Just as you are weak."

"You will not hurt my friends. I won't let you."

The glimmering grew in strength, throwing a livid light. Pip, battling a growing horror, suddenly felt a gleam of hope. Clovis had pulled them out of Oswald's clutches before. Maybe he would do it again...

But then Oswald snapped his fingers, and the green glimmer vanished as suddenly as a candle being snuffed. Clovis stumbled forward and cried out. Pip instinctively reached out and pulled him up with his free hand, putting his arm around Clovis's shoulder.

"I'm sorry," whispered Clovis. "He's very strong."

"Never mind," said Pip. "At least you tried."

"But not enough."

"Friends can only do their best…"

Chapter Fifty-two

IT SEEMED MUCH DARKER THAN BEFORE, AS IF THE shadows had thickened. The only light, a lifeless blue-ish illumination, came from Oswald. He was now in his Spectre form, and towered over them, the edges of the rippling cold flame drifting towards their faces.

"Enough," he said. "You try my patience." He lifted his skeletal arms.

Pip's breast swelled with anger and grief. It wasn't fair; he wasn't ready to die. And he knew, deep inside, that what would happen to the Prince and Princess would be much worse than death.

He let go of Georgette and Clovis and lunged at Oswald, his fists flying, and hailed him with punches. He didn't really expect that it would have any effect. He just didn't want to be killed without some kind of resistance. But Oswald, who hadn't expected any such attack, fell backwards onto the ground.

Pip had time to kick Oswald once more in his bony ribs. He could feel Georgette and Clovis behind him, coming up to join in. And then unseen hands closed about his throat again, squeezing tighter and tighter until he couldn't breathe and a red mist rose in front of his eyes. Georgette shouted his name as he fell over and the thought crossed his mind that this was the last thing he would ever hear.

"No!" It was Clovis.

Pip wasn't quite certain what happened next. It felt as if the whole world tilted and turned over. There was a brilliant flash of green lightning, which struck Oswald full in the face. For an instant it lit up the eye sockets in his skull. Looking into them, Pip felt dizzy, as if he were teetering over a cliff; there was no end to the depths inside them.

The pressure lifted from his throat and he rolled over, gasping. Georgette grabbed his arm and hauled him to his feet.

Clovis stood in front of them, his arms upraised. He looked very tiny before the Spectre, whose form was shifting, swelling into a boiling black cloud shot through with red fires. Pip watched, his heart in his mouth, as the cloud expanded, pluming up before them until, with a terrifying rapidity, it had covered the entire sky. In the centre, just above their heads, it was pitch-black; no, it was darker than that, as dark as the void in the Spectre's eyes.

Out of that centre, a whirling funnel of cloud began to descend, twisting and bending like an evil whiplash, and strike out viciously at Clovis.

Clovis staggered, but he was still standing. "I don't care if you destroy me," he said. His voice was very clear. He didn't sound angry, just determined. "But you're not going to hurt my friends."

The cloud laughed. It was the worst sound Pip had ever heard. It seemed to come from everywhere at once: inside his head and outside his head. The whole sky was laughing at them.

"You think you have the power to defeat me?"

"No," said Clovis. "But I'm going to try anyway."

Pip's heart suddenly lifted. The little Prince's defiance made him feel reckless. He had nothing to lose.

"Me too," he said, and stepped up next to Clovis.

Georgette drew in a sharp breath and put her arm around Clovis's shoulder. "You'll have to kill us all," she said. "And then there won't be any Spectre babies for your foul kingdom."

To Pip's surprise, that seemed to give Oswald pause.

The cloud boiled ominously, without doing anything. Perhaps Oswald was trying to figure out how to defeat Clovis without actually destroying him or Georgette.

Georgette staggered and fell against Pip, who automatically clutched her and held her upright. Between them, where Clovis had been, there was now an empty space. Clovis had vanished.

"Clovis!" Pip spun around wildly on his heel. "Clovis, where are you?"

There was no answer. The strange, shadowy buildings that lined the street stared back at him with their blank windows. They were glowing dimly now, each brick and stone faintly outlined in silvery blue against the boiling sky. He thought the stone was rippling, like the walls in Clovis's royal bedroom in the Rupture.

Everything was absolutely silent. That was the most frightening thing of all.

"It was too much for him," Georgette whispered, taking Pip's hand again. He could feel her trembling. "He's only a little boy."

"It's too much for me, too," said Pip heavily. The rage and defiance that had briefly filled him was ebbing away.

Despite everything, he had thought that Clovis might pull something out of the hat. He had thought that maybe they could outface the Spectre. He should have known better. His whole life had taught him to expect the worst.

"I can't blame him for running away," he said. He felt his eyes prickle hot with tears of hopelessness.

The sky was growing redder and redder, like a giant pit of embers. Pip was sure that Oswald was brewing some terrible new spell. He was absolutely sure that he was going to die. And he was equally sure that he didn't want to. He wasn't ready. Georgette started pulling him towards the buildings, instinctively looking for shelter.

They had only gone a few feet when Pip dug in his heels and pointed. Georgette looked up and gasped. A white thread of light was zigzagging through the middle of the cloud, tiny but incredibly bright. As they watched, it swelled, forcing aside the red embers, and a golden cloud spilled out of the gap.

And suddenly the sound was back. A huge roll of thunder made the ground vibrate beneath them.

"It has to be Clovis," said Georgette breathlessly.

Pip didn't feel any more hopeful about their prospects, but the fact that Clovis hadn't abandoned them made him feel like cheering. Now there were two clouds, and a strange and terrible battle was taking place above their heads. The thunder was so loud Pip thought his eardrums would burst.

It seemed at first that the golden cloud was dominant,

perhaps because Clovis had taken Oswald by surprise. But gradually, inexorably, the black and red cloud began to swallow the other. Clovis wasn't giving in without a fight, but there was less and less gold.

All they could do was watch helplessly as the golden light grew smaller and smaller. As it shrank, it intensified, until it was so bright that Pip could barely look at it, and he allowed himself to feel a little hope: perhaps, even though the black cloud was swamping it, Clovis was becoming stronger?

But just as he thought that, the golden light snapped out, plunging them into total darkness.

Beside him, he heard Georgette moan with despair and Pip automatically reached out for her hand. It was all over. Maybe, he thought, this was what dying was like...

Another flash of green lightning, much brighter than the first, threw everything into grotesque relief. It was so dazzling that he was blinded: all he could sense was a throbbing reddish-green afterimage, and warm tears running down his cheeks.

"Pip." Georgette was tugging his hand. "Pip!"

He blinked several times, trying to clear his vision, panicking for a few moments that he had gone blind. But gradually his sight returned. The sky was empty, starless and dark, but the dim silvery light that seemed to come from the buildings showed they were still in the strange cobbled street.

Clovis lay on the ground before them. He was horribly still, his face white as paper.

Pip forgot everything else and ran to kneel beside him, his heart in his mouth, and put his arms around him. In this place, he could embrace him: here, he wasn't merely a presence in his head. For the first time, he realized how very small Clovis was.

Poor Clovis. He had tried so hard, and after all, he couldn't help being a snotty prince. It wasn't fair. He had suffered more than any child should. Yes, in his short life he never went hungry and always had somewhere to live, but then he was murdered and locked inside a tiny box all by himself for fifty years, with only a dreaming princess to hear his sobbing. Pip couldn't imagine anything more lonely or more terrible.

"He sacrificed himself for us," said Georgette in a whisper. She was stroking his pale face, a tear rolling down her cheek.

Pip sniffed. "He just wanted a friend. That's all he wanted."

Georgette met his eyes. "I think he found one, in the end," she said. "Maybe that makes up for the rest."

"Nothing makes up for it," said Pip. He didn't want to

cry in front of the Princess, even in this terrible moment, but he could feel that his eyes were hot and damp.

And then the little body stirred in his arms.

"I did it," Clovis whispered in his ear. His voice was very faint. "I undid the spell. You made me brave."

"Pip," said Georgette. "Look."

Pip started. He had forgotten all about Oswald.

He too was back in human form, writhing in front of them a little distance away, clutching at his face. He was an old man, a man Pip didn't recognize. As Pip watched, he realized that the old man was becoming younger: his hair darkened, his body filled out, his wrinkles vanished. And then he began to shrink, until he was a child of about five years of age. At that point he convulsed, and he was old again, but a different old man, winding back to childhood. The process repeated over and over again. The Spectre's mouth was open as if he were screaming, but no sound came out.

It was horrible, and it seemed to continue for ever. Georgette made a sound as if she was going to be sick, but her eyes were fixed on Oswald in fascinated revulsion.

"What did you do?"

"It's all the people he's been," said Clovis quietly. "All the souls he ate."

"There are so many of them…"

Pip looked at Clovis. "Did you know you could do that?"

Clovis shook his head. He looked exhausted, as if there was nothing left inside him. "Not until I did," he said. "It was like something went click inside me and I just knew what to do."

"How did you know?" asked Georgette.

"The spell is me. The old witch made it out of *me*. I was like ... like a spring inside a watch, all wound up the wrong way. And all I had to do was unwind it. It was quite simple in the end. So I made everything run backwards."

"Can he do anything about it?"

"Not now. None of the Spectres can." Clovis was watching without any visible emotion. "He kind of wanted to do the opposite thing. He wanted to wind it all up so hard that it could never be undone."

He glanced across at Georgette, who was looking baffled. "It's hard to explain. It's because of what the witch did. If you push the spell the other way, the opposite happens. Instead of winding back to the beginning, until he was just a mortal man, like he was at the start, he could use me to multiply himself endlessly, into every body in the world... And it would all happen at once. Like in alchemy ... when you add just one more tiny bit to a solution, and then, all of a sudden, it turns into crystals."

370

Georgette nodded. "I kind of see," she said.

"I don't," said Pip helplessly. Unlike Georgette and Clovis, Pip had never had alchemy lessons.

"It means that he would instantly have power over everything. Even over the other Spectres. There would only ever be him. No one else. For ever."

"What's the point of that?" asked Pip.

"He's the loneliest person there ever was. I thought I was. But he's even more lonely than that. Because he never understood that other people were real."

Georgette shuddered. "I don't feel sorry for him," she said.

"I don't either," said Clovis.

They watched until the end, until the final old man wound back through middle age and youth and childhood to babyhood, and then dwindled until there was nothing there at all.

It took a long time.

"What happened to all those souls, I wonder," said Georgette.

"They died," said Clovis. "Like I will one day. I hope."

Pip wiped his brow with his sleeve. "I thought that was going to happen right now. But we didn't die." He looked down at Clovis and grinned. "You saved my life. That's being a real friend."

Clovis blushed bright red. Pip looked away to save him embarrassment.

"What now?" said Georgette, looking around at the shadows.

"We go back to Clarel," said Clovis. "That part is easy." He took both of their hands in his, and then hesitated. "I won't be there, though. Not like this, anyway."

"Does that mean you'll be back in my head? It's better being able to see you, like a proper person."

"Do you mind very much?" Clovis looked down at his feet, and his hands were twisting nervously. "It's just that I've got nowhere else to go."

Pip looked doubtful. "What if I want to be on my own once in a while?" If there was always someone inside his head, it might be embarrassing.

"I can go somewhere private, I promise. And I won't argue too much. And I'm not a Spectre, I promise. Not a real Spectre. I won't try to eat your soul or anything."

Pip thought about it. It was true that Clovis had nowhere to go, and Pip knew all too well what that felt like. It was weird, for sure, having another person inside his brain, but on the whole it was better than being dead. And Clovis had saved all their lives.

"All right then," he said. "Though we shouldn't tell the witches. They won't like it."

"Oni will know," said Clovis.

"I always trusted Oni," said Georgette.

"Of course we can trust Oni." Pip smiled at Clovis. Maybe it would be all right. And if it wasn't, maybe they could work it out. "That's settled, then. Though if you ever call me a commoner again, I'll throw you out."

Clovis laughed. "I promise I won't," he said.

In the next moment, although Clovis didn't appear to do anything, they were back in the daylit street that they had been walking down – when? Minutes ago? Hours ago?

Pip and Georgette blinked as a dazzling shaft of late-afternoon sunlight hit their eyes. Pip wasn't sure if it was the sunshine or the sheer relief of being back in Clarel, but he could feel a tear creeping down his cheek.

Thank you, Clovis, he said.

Oni's coming, said Clovis. *She looks all kinds of cross.*

Pip looked up and saw Oni walking towards them, very fast. She did look cross.

Chapter Fifty-three

GEORGETTE DIDN'T EVER BECOME QUEEN. TO HER
surprise, she didn't mind at all.

The battle in front of Clarel Palace that she had run
away from had been nasty, but short. There were other
struggles that day, all over the city, and in the end the
people did win. Not even the King's soldiers could
withstand the entire city rising up against the palace.

Arresting everyone in the Weavers' Quarter on the
day of the Midsummer Festival had been, it turned out,
a very bad idea indeed. Everyone was already sick of the
nobles and the Cardinal's assassins, and the arrests were
the final straw.

After a few days of chaos, Missus Clay, as chief of the
Witches' Council, announced a new Republic of Clarel.
There was to be a People's Parliament, and witchcraft
was to be taught properly to anybody who wanted to

know it. King Axel was put in the tower instead of being decapitated, in deference to Princess Georgette, who had decided to take her mother's name and was now just plain Georgette Livnel.

Georgette thought on balance that it was better that her father didn't have his head cut off, but she also thought, in a secret part of her, that she wouldn't have especially minded. The King had never shown her a moment's kindness in her whole life, and she wouldn't have spared him a single tear.

A lot of nobles fled the country in that first week, taking as much gold as they could carry. Queen Theoroda asked to return to her own kingdom, and most of her ladies-in-waiting wanted to go with her. Others, like Sibelius, stayed and gave up their titles. Sibelius was, to his surprise, appointed to the committee that was going to organize the new elections. The Witches' Council suggested that he should be nominated as a minister in the new People's Parliament. So was Harpin Shtum, who was even more surprised.

But people had to vote for them first, and organizing an election was a lot of work. Everything took much longer now, because there wasn't a king to give orders. Sometimes, despite everything, Georgette missed that. There had been far fewer arguments back then.

The only person the witches thought should be executed was the Cardinal, but obviously King Oswald had taken care of him. His chief assassin was nowhere to be found. In the end, they decided that Ariosto must be dead, by unknown means. Perhaps it was something to do with the breaking of the Spectres.

Amina felt a bit sad about Ariosto: she had always thought that there was something that could be redeemed in the chief assassin. She made a blessing for his soul, and busied herself with the Cardinal's orphanages. Heironomo Blaise became one of her chief helpers, so El had been right that he wasn't all bad. What Amina saw in the orphanages made her sorry that they couldn't try the Cardinal and sentence him to some long and horrible punishment.

Making a new republic was a lot of work, most of it quite dull. There were people to feed and laws to be made and rubbish to be collected and questions of public hygiene to be determined, and almost every public building had to be repaired, because King Axel II had spent most of the taxes on his palace and his private wardrobe. Getting everything in order was going to take ages. And not everyone was happy about it, and already some people were plotting to bring back another king.

Children didn't starve in the streets any more, and there was more and nicer food for everyone, but that didn't stop anybody complaining, especially the former nobles. Life is never perfect, after all. But most people felt as if a huge weight had lifted off the City of Clarel. No one more than witches, who no longer had to hide who they were in case they were burned at the stake.

Pip and El got their apartment back, and Oni returned to work at the Crosseyes. Georgette moved in with Amina because she didn't want to live in the palace, and she used her princessing skills to help the new ambassadors, who were having to deal with a lot of upset monarchs in other parts of Continentia. So far no one had threatened to invade them, mostly because they didn't know what the Clarel witches might do if they did. Georgette counted that as a victory.

A few weeks after the Storming of the Palace, Pip, El, Oni and Georgette met up at the Crosseyes to have an evening meal. Pip and Oni still annoyed each other, but now they were also the best of friends, so they didn't quarrel quite as much as they had before.

It was a while since they had all seen each other, because everyone was busy, and in the end El had personally visited each of them and insisted.

"I love you all," she'd said. "And that's that."

And so they met up. El was wearing a pretty dress that Georgette had given her – pale blue with fichu lace at her throat – and Georgette was wearing trousers and a cloak, because she thought those clothes were much more comfortable. She had caused a scandal when she first wore trousers, but now the most daring young ladies were copying her. Oni had never been one for fine clothes, but tonight she was wearing a pale pink dress and had ribbons threaded through her hair.

Next to Oni, Pip was looking a little self-conscious in a new green velvet jacket that he had bought with his own money. Amina had found him a job in a bookshop near the Weavers' Quarter. He still didn't know how to read, but he did know his numbers, which was really all that mattered in selling things. Secretly, in his spare time, Pip was learning his letters. Oni could read, and was sometimes a little superior about it.

They ordered roast goose and buttered peas for dinner, and the yellow parsley wine that was the Crosseyes speciality. El smiled at Pip and lifted her cup, and suddenly Pip remembered his old daydream: that he would take El out for a slap-up dinner in a new dress. And there she was, sparkling with happiness.

He lifted his cup. "Here's to everything!" he said.

Oni laughed, and lifted hers. "That's pretty general, Pip," she said. "How about just us?"

"All right, us too. We're part of everything, after all." He was feeling light-headed: the parsley wine was quite strong.

El put down her cup. "Remember when you found the Heart, Pip, and I was so frightened?" she said. "I thought it was the most horrible thing that ever happened to us. I would never have believed it would turn out like this. I thought I had lost everything. Even you."

"I knew it was going to be our fortune," said Pip. "I just didn't know how."

Oni smiled. "It was all of our fortunes," she said. "Because we all remembered how much we like each other. We always did, you know, even when we fought like cats in a bag. Even Georgie. She'd forgotten about me, but then she remembered."

"I never forgot you, Oni," said Georgette indignantly. "I just wasn't allowed to see you."

"Whatever you say, Princess," said Oni, grinning mischievously.

"Anyway, we're friends now."

"Of course. It's better than being a queen, isn't it?"

Georgette blushed, because she was still a little embarrassed about her old ambition. For a moment she wished she hadn't told Oni about it.

Oni poked her in the ribs. "I'm only teasing, Georgie. You shouldn't take it amiss."

Georgie met her eyes and smiled. "Well, you're right. It is better than being a queen. For one thing, I can wear whatever I like, and for another, I get to talk to whoever I like, and I don't have to speak to Duchess Albria ever again in my whole life."

"Who's Duchess Albria?" asked El.

"She was my senior lady-in-waiting. She hated me, and I hated her. She went to Awemt, of all places. I hope she's happy there."

"Meaning that you hope she isn't," said Pip.

Georgette thought it over. "No, I don't mean that," she said. "I don't want people to be unhappy. I just don't want them to make me unhappy."

"It's time for pudding," said El. "Do you want to ask the landlord, Pip? As the only gentleman here..."

"Not the *only* gentleman," Pip said. "What will we get?"

"It's plum season," said Georgette. "Let's order stewed plums. With custard."

Yes, please, said Clovis. *I love plums.*

ALISON CROGGON is the acclaimed author of the high fantasy series The Books of Pellinor. She is also the author of *Black Spring*, a fantasy reworking of *Wuthering Heights*, which was shortlisted for the NSW Premier's Literary Awards; and *The River and the Book*, which was endorsed by Amnesty International and was shortlisted for the YA prize in the WA Premier's Book Awards. Alison is an award-winning poet whose work has been published extensively, and she has written widely for theatre, with her plays and opera libretti having been produced all around Australia. Alison is also an editor and critic. She lives in Melbourne, Australia.